I0694310

BREAKING FREE

LARISSA GAULT

Larissa Gault

This book is a work of fiction. Names, characters, places, and incidents either are products of the author's imagination or are used fictitiously. Any resemblance to actual events or locales or persons, living or dead, is entirely coincidental.

First Larissa Gault paperback edition May 28, 2022.

Manufactured in the United States of America

Gault, Larissa
Breaking Free

Cover artist: Paige Coffer
Cover designer: Whimsy Book Cover Graphics
Line editor & formatter: Ariana Tosado

Paperback ISBN: 979-8-9858553-0-2

FOR CAMERON BOYCE.

You were a light to this world, and an inspiration from the beginning. I cannot thank you enough. Though I never got to meet you, I hope I will be able to run up to you in heaven and thank you for the impact you had on my life. You were the one who inspired a character in my head, the character I needed at the time, and you got me through this novel.

I wanted to give up more times than I can count, but I never did. I never stopped, because I knew someone would need to read about that character just as much as I needed him. You've made an incredible difference in my life and countless others.

Your fate brings tears to my eyes, as does finishing this book, but I am forever grateful to you. This is for Jesse Price, who is always in my heart, and this is for you.

This book contains discussions and descriptions of violence, death, murder, depression, anxiety, kidnapping of children, harmful scientific experimentation, weapons such as handguns and knives, PTSD and its symptoms, ADHD and other neurological developmental disorders, and sensitivity disorders.

This book contains extremely brief mentions of suicide and fleeting suicidal thoughts, forced sterilization, self-harm via burning, suggestive material, sexual assault, and alcohol and drug use. Some moderate language in appropriate situations is used.
This book is not recommended to readers under fifteen or sixteen years of age unless their parent or legal guardian feels the individual is emotionally mature enough to handle its content. Discretion is advised. Please read reviews to ensure the content is not exceeding the level of comfort for any reader.

PREFACE

Breaking Free is a novel I started four years ago, in the wake of my mental health's decline. Since then, I've vastly improved…depends on who you ask. I remember writing the first draft (the one I'd rather forget) on the mattress that dwelled in my sister's room at the time—our basement was being renovated, and I was staying in her room. Thankfully, my laptop fit in a lovely place beside the mattress, and the internet connection to Wattpad was strong.

But I suppose if I tell you all this used to be inspired by another published work, I should probably tell you what it was. After you read this, you'll probably know, though. In that time of crippling doubt and a need to start a new hobby, I was watching more Marvel movies than I could count. Once I had an idea for some characters and a plot line inspired by *X-Men*, *Breaking Free* was born.

It soon spiraled into the deepest obsession I've ever had, and eventually, I knew the universe of Ivankov better than I knew myself. Thankfully, that has proven to benefit me, as three years later, I began an Instagram account and also started watching *Agents of Shield*. I've now attracted a concerning amount of people who want to read my work, and I'm not sure whether to be grateful or worried for all of your sanities.

In a lovely twist of irony, this book has supported me through worse times than its origins and all the way to present day—which I am happy to report is on the upside. Once the second draft was reached, the unoriginal plot lines were removed and I scrapped half the scenes. I wrote many of Lavesse's best moments while in the midst of a mental breakdown, and you'll probably realize that along the way. Many of these characters served as vessels for the myriad of complicated emotional roller coasters I've been through in the four years of writing it. Persephone and Liam mainly represent the childish sides of me that never got the chance to bloom (woohoo, trauma), while Grace and Sarvesh represent the maturity I wish I didn't have. Anastasia is a mom friend I wish I did have (I am the mom friend), mostly just because she'd threaten anyone who hurts me.

And for Lavinia and Jesse…where do I even start? The parts of me that died with the two breakups I went through in this four-year journey are facets of Lavinia and Jesse that sometimes I forget are there. They're complicated characters, perhaps more complicated than anyone I've met in real life, but I think that adds to the story.

Life is always going to be a mess, no matter who you are or where you're going. Problems will come at you, and these characters are no exemption to life's troubles. Lavinia and Jesse are a huge part of this story because they showcase how love is such a vital factor in surviving all of life's pain. Love is a beautiful thing, a sacred thing, and if it weren't for love, I never would have finished this book.

TABLE OF CONTENTS

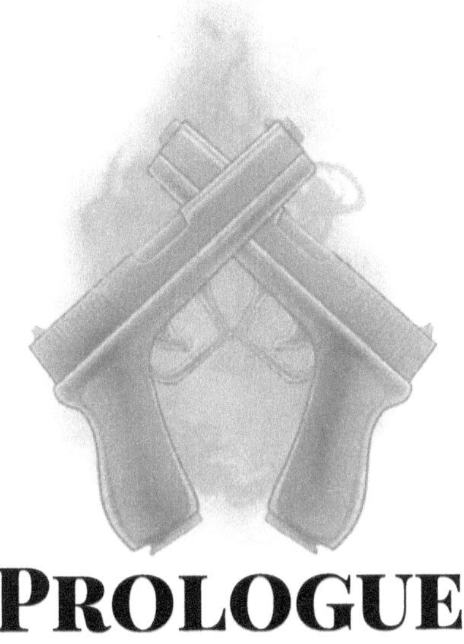

PROLOGUE

The dreams were getting darker, and the little girl grew afraid of falling asleep.

Each morning, her younger siblings would wake up to her crying in her sleep. In the next room, her father lay, unknowingly dreaming the very same thing. His daughter was being tortured by his dreams—exact replicas—as if they were her own.

The dreams were forgotten each morning and never mentioned again. But then, other things started happening when the children would go exploring the ruined remains of the factory behind their house. A few weeks before, the family was woken in the dead of night by a rumbling beneath them. Seconds later, an explosion sounded.

Chaos erupted, but the children remained safely inside with their mother huddled around them in protection. A few hours later, the father returned to his family. They were safe. The energy plant inside the factory had an accidental explosion, but the entire building was leveled.

Volunteers had shown up to help shift through the remains, but there were no survivors. Since that night, the children had begged their mother to explore the now empty field. Until the metal cooled and the crew wiped the ash and any reminder of the building away forever, she held them off with a stern shake of her head.

But early one morning when breakfast had been finished and the dishes had been cleaned, with her permission, the children ran to the field as fast as their small legs could carry them. The oldest, at six years old, whispered warnings to her siblings with every unfamiliar sound or crack in the nearby woods. The little girl would be lying if she said the ruins didn't make her uneasy.

But in their excursions throughout the summer, the girl's memories of the dreams receded, and the shouts in a fire, cries over bodies, and charred faces soon were replaced by laughter and the children's findings.

Until one day, the little boy cried out, "Look!" He promptly pointed past his twin sister's shoulder at a piece of rubble that was waving in the wind.

"What is it, Parker?" the oldest girl asked, her back turned to her siblings while she knelt over in search of sticks for their pretend fire in the makeshift camp.

Upon hearing squeals of delight from her brother and sister, the oldest girl turned around and swept her brown hair out of her face. She thought of how pretty she would be when she was older, when her mother would finally let her dye it a beautiful auburn. For now, she frowned in confusion at the sight before her and forgot all about her hair troubles.

A piece of the old factory, what could best be described as a clear, rubber trashcan lid, was suspended in mid-air. The girl rushed forward and pushed her siblings back so they wouldn't touch the strange object.

"Lavinia! Stop pushing me!" her little sister whined.

"Don't touch it, Persephone," Lavinia whispered, but she had an undeniable urge to reach out. She wanted to touch it. Her curiosity grew. She wanted to move it herself.

Could I do that? What if...?

Lavinia reached out, but without touching it, she moved her hand in a gesture toward the sky. *Move it higher.* She jumped when it moved; twisted in the air; and, as if it were connected to her, shot up so far that she could no longer see it.

Her younger sister squealed a small shriek of surprise, and the piece came crashing down on the ground again. This time, it landed right where it had begun moving just moments ago. The children looked at each other in disbelief, then confusion; then, they all burst out into laughter.

"I can't believe it!" Parker shouted as his blond hair bounced up and down.

"You moved it!" Persephone squealed in delight, a twinkle shining in her blue eyes.

"I…I did, didn't I?" Lavinia looked pleased with herself, but unlike her siblings, she wondered how that was possible.

How could someone do that, and why did it work? Why just her?

The next morning, her brother ran off farther into the field to find a new piece for their decorations. Before her eyes, he disappeared into the woods and rushed back to the field immediately, sobbing. Before she could cry for help or yell to Persephone to go back to the house, Parker regained his composure. Lavinia ran to his side and comforted his shaking body. He sniffled once and shook his head, pushing his sister off.

He seemed to be feeling every person who was in the same emotional state as him a thousand times over. Lavinia tried teaching him how to block it out, to ignore the emotions crying out to be found. At Lavinia's confusion, Parker would grow panicked and confused too. Even Lavinia didn't feel everything he did. She soon realized that he was hypersensitive to people's emotional states, including his own.

Her little sister had the same glow of Lavinia's hands when she used her newfound skills, but Lavinia discovered that Persephone couldn't control as many things as she could. Lavinia accidentally played a memory right in front of her wide eyes and read her mother's mind. For a six-year-old, it was strange to see her memories in front of her in a muddle of smoke, glowing and changing like it were from a movie.

In the grocery store, hiding behind her mother, she even flew a can of beans off the shelf toward a strange man—going unnoticed by both her distracted mother and the man.

It was only her ability to move items with her mind that she shared with Persephone. While that made little sense to the girls, it seldom mattered. They were having fun.

Every afternoon when the children would return home, a word of their fun was never spoken to their parents. They were afraid they wouldn't understand or that they would never let them return to the field again.

But their silence would be far worse of a punishment. Far, far worse.

GRUMPY BEGINNINGS

{ *Lavinia* }

"**E**rnest Labzina! Just what do you think you're doing?" I shouted, my eyes flashing.

The tall, burly, and dark-haired man sparked anger within me. *Never liked him.* Now, he had confirmed everything I knew to be true—he was a lying and sniveling man, a high-ranking agent and handler who had used Ivankov's occasional carelessness to his advantage; that meant continuing tests that had long since been proven to be harmful.

I stood inches away from Agent Labzina and bristled in anger as I proudly stared up at him from my short stature. Anastasia stepped out from behind me and hurried to Persephone. My younger sister was huddled in the chair, and her naturally red hair was limp, blue eyes dull.

I clenched my jaw after recognizing the needles, the labels of the bottles attached to the tubes, and nodded to Anastasia to help Perse up from the tragedy in front of me.

"Doing my job, child, what do *you* think you're doing?" Our handler's face was red.

He knew he couldn't harm any of us no matter how much he wanted to. So he had resorted to the worst forms of torture.

In Ivankov, our autonomy had disappeared. Wishes of home and normalcy were beaten out of us, and through training, we learned to defend ourselves and attack anyone who stood in our way.

Ivankov's way of progress and world domination, more like it.

"I'm saving her like I do every other day in this cursed place," I retorted. "And *don't* call me a child. You made sure I grew up a long time ago."

I spun away from him and reached Persephone, leading her out. Anastasia lingered behind me, and Ernest's voice reached my ears as he spoke to her in passing.

"Frankly, Agent Rabinova, I'm disappointed. Out of all the gifted agents here, I would think you would not be one to defend that girl."

Either she didn't respond or I didn't hear her answer, but I soon detected her footsteps following Persephone and me to the office where I'd left Parker. I swung the door open, helped Persephone through, sat her down, and slid next to Parker.

He blinked open his bright blue eyes in confusion, so I passed a hand over his wavy hair and activated my well-trained powers to clear up his memory of the last few minutes.

Anastasia and I had been training, and when we had returned to our room, we were startled to find that Parker and Persephone weren't in theirs. I hadn't seen either Ernest or Margaret, his wife, in a few hours. Anya had become suspicious, and upon visiting the basement floors, we found Parker in a room with Margaret and Persephone with Ernest.

I huffed in frustration and looked up to meet Anastasia's deep green eyes. The two of us knew exactly what the Labzinas were trying to accomplish. My siblings and I had been taken into Ivankov when the M3 experiments were still being developed, and during the testing phase, I had been a subject. At the time, I was clueless to its true purpose. Now, I wasn't sure I wanted to figure it out.

"What were they doing anyway?" Parker mumbled, though his Russian accent was still noticeable.

"Something new," Anastasia amended, but the two of us knew the truth.

While we were all native Russian speakers, our parents began teaching us English from a young age. But Persephone and I didn't understand English very well until tutors in Ivankov introduced it and many other languages.

After moving to America when the twins were so young, Parker was the only one to struggle with Russian. Anastasia taught him while Persephone and I got by. Through their lessons, he had since surpassed even me with his Russian skills. I'd even catch him muttering under his breath in Russian or struggling to find an English word. With Anastasia's accent to influence him, he had kept his accent from long before we left home.

Left, I thought wryly. *More like were stolen from.*

I jumped in. "It was very risky, and you could've been—"

"We can take care of ourselves, Nia," Persephone insisted.

If only that were true.

Anastasia sat down on the bench next to her and nodded. "Even I won't be able to stop him if he tries again. He'll make sure of it."

"How?" Parker breathed. "You're our in-team. You have more authority than individual handlers do, right?"

Anastasia frowned. "I have to pick up your training schedule, which usually means something big is happening. We're probably splitting up the team and moving, but they won't tell me for sure,"—she glanced at me—"but I've heard there's talk that the Assassin himself will be there."

"You're leaving us?" Persephone exclaimed.

Parker swallowed. "Both of you? They're treating us more like lab rats and less like agents, and if they've done it once, they'll do it again."

I took a deep breath. "We can't stop them, but we can help you two. Anya convinced Higgins to change your handlers to another couple when we leave. And you'll join us for training from here on out instead of later with your usual group."

"Training!" Anastasia gasped in realization. "We have to go, Nia!"

She leapt up, sending her long hair swinging, and bolted out of the room.

I jumped in surprise, grabbed both Persephone's and Parker's hands, and followed her out the door. We caught up soon, and Anya pushed us through the equipment room door. While the twins stood, unsure of what to do in our training rooms, Anastasia and I hurriedly slid on sneakers and wrapped our hands.

I tossed sneakers to the twins. "Put these on."

Once Anya had fastened her mess of dark red hair into a braid, she helped wrap their hands. If they were sparring today, we needed them prepared.

I led us back out into the hallway until we reached the familiar, large, metal doors. I held up my finger to the sensor, and once it let out a small beep, the left door swung open.

I stepped back to let Anastasia lead us into the vast, metal room. As our in-team supervisor of six years, she was responsible for each member to be at their allotted locations on time and to make sure they followed every rule. And there were a lot of rules.

Thankfully, Anastasia, who was ten years older than me, hated Ivankov as much as we did. She frequently bent rules and snuck around with our team, and if we could be trusted, she gave us more freedom than we deserved.

In a year, I'd be moved to another team separate from my family and without an in-team, but until that—or our possible move—I happily spent every second with Persephone, Parker, and Anastasia.

The familiar room was cold but brightly lit. Our team's corner was filled with everyone except us.

I hated being late. It meant everyone staring when I walked in, and this was a day where I needed to be fitting in. I pushed my turning stomach into stillness and nodded for the twins to follow Anya ahead of me.

The three of us lined up next to the rest of the team, and I ignored the glowers. *It's not like you're any better.*

Anastasia walked confidently to our trainer, Higgins. He was a short man, but he was much tougher than he looked. His voice was loud and sharp, but as Anya offered her annoyed excuses and blamed us, he whispered fervently in response.

The man standing next to him, whom I had never seen before, looked bored at the contents of their conversation. But there was no mistaking who he was. The man towered over Higgins and must have weighed twice as much.

He was dressed in black mission gear—boots, pants, shirt, vest, jacket—and the gloves he wore were unlike anything I'd seen. They were meticulously crafted from genuine leather, but they seemed to be thinner to allow freer movement.

The dark hair was pulled away from his face. His eyes, a dark brown, mirrored his mouth set in a firm line. His gloved hands were crossed in front of him, but his arms flexing underneath his grim sleeves told me exactly who he was.

Both of his arms and legs were made entirely of metal and other synthetic materials. It was the finest prosthetic in the modern world, and while I suspected Ivankov did not make it honestly or humanely—or without Masters—it made the Assassin the strongest, fastest, and best killer Ivankov possessed.

At the thought of Masters' torture within Ivankov, I recalled Anya's news that she shared just yesterday: a team of young Masters was receiving a new in-team, who was one of Anastasia's old friends, and he had requested an older Master to instruct his team more about who they were.

Masters were those who controlled the world around them by what many thought was magic. I knew it to be circumstances. And though we were powerful, Masters had a long history of being used by different governments. The facts remained the same: we could end the world as we knew it if we only had a leader.

I sighed internally and dreaded the job already.

Why bother teaching these kids, who can't be more than twelve or thirteen, about what a privilege it is to be a Master serving Ivankov when I don't even enjoy it myself?

Until we were assigned a Master of our Order, my family was stuck with teammates who would never receive a Master mentor, people called Routines. For now, we had to settle for handlers and an in-team—the Labzinas and Anastasia.

The Assassin was only the best Routine killer, however. There were Masters, both famous ones of history and those still of Unknown Rank, far more advanced. Once I rose to my Destined Order, I would be much more powerful than he is.

At least, I hope so. I couldn't wait to get revenge on the man who had ordered and organized missions to abduct young Masters.

The Assassin surveyed us in a hard stare, and his brown-eyed gaze came to rest on me for a moment that jolted me out of a trance. He passed on without a second thought, but I couldn't deny the terror he had invoked that made my blood run cold.

Higgins began to pace and barked out, startling me. "Each of you will be witnessing the Assassin's strength, and after today, training will increase. In four weeks' time, those who best him even for ten seconds will be transferring to our full training compound. Today, the three most advanced members of this team will be sparring with the Assassin while the rest of you will observe."

I took a deep breath. Parker glanced at me with his eyes narrowed, but I just nodded at him and exhaled.

Higgins kept going. "Agent Moren…Agent Everton…"

I held my breath again.

"…and Agent Markov."

Damn it.

I looked around at my siblings, Anastasia, and Higgins, and then at Agent Moren and Everton. Upon their satisfied faces turning my way in challenge, I frowned at them. Viktoriya and Alek were inseparable, though we all had a sense it was more of a begrudging alliance and less of a friendship. People like them didn't make friends.

I sighed in resignation and turned my head to face Higgins. He wore a proud smile on his stupid face and waved a hand to beckon the rest of the team to the bench, which left the three of us standing in a line.

Alek stepped forward first, and at the Assassin's provocation, the two came to the mat and took their stances. I studied the taller man and his remarkable speed, but I noted his off-set, staggered walk as a result of the weight of his arms. He might have had the strength, but I was much shorter—and I could outsmart him.

PREPARED FOR NOTHING

Oh, come on, just—

Alek flipped the Assassin over and won the fight, much to my chagrin. If the Assassin hadn't held back, the irritating, dirty blond would be dead.

Viktoriya stepped up next, and though she didn't have Alek's lankiness, she had his height. She grinned cockily and took a fighting stance. Their combat was more graceful than Alek's attempts—thanks to Viktoriya—and she used the skilled, agile moves to best the Assassin in record time.

This sounds like so much fun.

But I ignored Viktoriya's pained face when she sat down hard on the floor, meeting the Assassin on the mat. He was a lot taller than I'd expected him to be. I took a deep breath and paused, waiting for him to begin.

Once he threw the first punch, I defended myself by blocking his movements. He ruthlessly swung and lunged at me; he used brute strength instead of his brains. I almost laughed at him until moments later, when I miscalculated a step, and he had me pinned.

I was pressed up against the floor, his metal hand growing tighter and tighter around my neck, when Alek's final move finally made perfect sense. The Assassin gave one final squeeze before I kneed him in the stomach and flipped us over.

He was pinned underneath me, my legs pushing against his throat so far that I thought his face might turn blue. But his brown eyes remained focused on me, cold and empty, until he calmly hit the mat beside us with one hand.

I stood rather regretfully and stalked off the mat, letting him scramble to his feet. Alek raised a prideful eyebrow at me when I met him and Viktoriya.

"Shut it," I threatened, beginning to unwrap my hands.

"You used my move!" He wore a grin.

Higgins silenced us all with a bark of dismissal. Upon turning to leave, I noticed that Anya had already led the twins out. I hurried to catch up, the door slamming shut behind me, and breathed a heavy sigh of relief at leaving that terrible room.

Or, you know, because he's not choking you anymore.

I caught the door of the equipment room before it swung closed and stepped inside to see my family standing there. I tossed the wraps down and let my hair out of its braid, the bright auburn pieces sticking to the sweat on my forehead.

The adrenaline was beginning to wear off. Anastasia glanced at me in concern as I collapsed onto the floor and winced at the aching muscles in my legs.

But the pain was hardly worth the heart-wrenching moment I knew would come when I moved. At least the physical aches would soon dissipate. Thanks to the energy that had given us our powers, the three of us healed exponentially fast.

The twins started to ramble excitedly, but it turned into questioning and anxious mutterings. While none of us wanted to move, protecting our place here was more important. If our protests were perceived wrongly…

We all knew the dangers of defecting or even having the appearance of doing so. Several of our past friends would break a sacred rule or ask a grave question, and the next day, we discovered they had been moved to the Reconditioning Center. Never to be seen again.

I had my own suspicions about what that place held and why we always seemed to have new recruits—new Masters—a few days after someone would disappear into it. And why the General would always seem to be in a good mood, giving more free time or rewards to all of us kids.

Anya cut off my thoughts, rising to her full height. "Guys, cut it out, okay? We don't like this any more than you do! You know the dangers of defecting. Besides, like Lavinia said, you'll both be able to handle yourselves. You have four weeks with us and Higgins, you...you'll be fine." She softened her voice with a gentle smile.

With his clear blue eyes trained on her face, Parker retorted, "Anya, you two are the only family we have. Even if we'll be able to take care of ourselves, which we *can*, you'll still be gone. We only have each other."

"Then be thankful they won't separate you," Anastasia snapped.

Parker blew out an exasperated breath and looked ready to throw a punch, but he decided better of it and stood up to follow her out of the door. Persephone and I exchanged an amused glance, and she rolled her blue eyes as we trailed after them.

Our team's living quarters were at the other end of the base, and it took passing through the double doors in the lobby, the main entrance, the general gym, and the cafeteria to get to our elevator. Anya stepped into line at the food counter, and we loaded our food onto our trays. We sat down at the usual table before the rest of the team arrived.

Parker hated hearing people eat, and our team wasn't brought food in our rooms like higher-ranking agents, so we made do with just the four of us eating at a time. Our rooms fit two agents each and ten to a group bathroom.

Just when we finished our dinner, the rest of our team entered the cafeteria and flocked to our tables. Viktoriya and Alek had an Indian boy trailing behind them, Sarvesh Kuhn, as they stalked toward us. I turned to Anastasia and rolled my eyes, but when they approached, I smiled through my teeth.

While it was Viktoriya's humble opinion that everything revolved around her and Alek never stopped smiling and making dirty jokes, Sarvesh was more reserved and, unlike anyone but myself, actually quite funny.

Sarvesh sat next to Parker and nodded before turning his attention to the food. Viktoriya raised one of her bleach blonde eyebrows in an irritated gesture, but she sat down beside me and Anastasia.

Sarvesh glanced at the blonde but muttered something under his breath to Parker. Alek opened his mouth to make a smart remark until Higgins came up behind him and cleared his throat. His jaw snapped shut.

"Anastasia," Higgins said shortly with a nod to his left.

She took a few steps away from the table. I took the last sip of my coffee, brushed my hand under the table, and twitched my fingers to manipulate the sound waves in my direction, allowing me to hear their conversation.

"The Board wishes everyone on the team to transfer to a school, North View High School, with lighter academics and shorter hours, which will allow them more time to train. The twins will remain on our training schedule as previously discussed."

We're moving schools? I grimaced slightly, and the twins exchanged a glance at my expression of displeasure. *It's not like I have friends at our school*, I tried to convince myself.

"I'll arrange it," Anastasia answered quietly.

"Good." Higgins clasped his hands behind his back and nodded once in dismissal.

Anya turned around to face me and crinkled her nose. Both of us knew that the likelihood of Sarvesh beating the Assassin was low, but it was little solace that in four weeks, he could be here with my siblings and I might not.

Who am I kidding? I thought bitterly to myself. *You beat him today, so you can beat him in a month, and if you lose on purpose, Higgins will just reassign you somewhere with a cover so deep that you'll never see them again.*

I stood up, gathered our trays, and waved my glowing hand to float them over to the bin. Viktoriya frowned in disapproval, as if she knew she could never be as cool as me, and Alek stared at the whizzing trays in mild interest. I spun on my heels to walk past Anastasia to the elevators.

Conversation resumed behind me, and while I pushed the button to wait, Anya stepped beside me and cast me a bemused glance. I was about to retort when the door dinged and opened, and Parker beat us inside.

"Not fair."

"What, like you could have walked those trays over yourself?" He grinned.

Persephone pushed her way past me to stand inside next to Parker and laughed. "You would have done it too, you big oaf."

"I am not a big oaf!" he protested with a frown, jabbing a finger in Persephone's face.

"Are too." Persephone rolled her eyes, yellow flashing in them as she used her telekinesis to slide the ring off his pointer finger and onto the floor.

I sighed and closed the elevator on them, leaving Anastasia and me outside. I'd be happy to wait for an empty one without their jabbering.

"Shut up, you—"

"I will not—" Persephone's voice faded out.

"Do you think they noticed?" Anya snickered.

"Probably not."

"They will when they get to their room and realize I took their key."

"Anya!" I gasped. "You did not!"

Her smirk was enough of an answer for me, but I laughed and shook my head. Their room, unlike ours, didn't have a bio keycard function like a fingerprint sensor or a retinal scan—it only needed their key.

Once they turned fifteen—in a few months—they would have a biometric lock installed. I'd be seventeen by then; their birthday was less than three months after mine.

They'd have to bicker until deciding on coming to mine and Anya's room to take their key back. We made the journey to our room in a comfortable silence. Upon stepping inside, I set an alarm on my phone, collapsed on the bed, and barely heard Anastasia leave before I fell asleep.

◆ ◆ ◆

A loud beeping startled me out of my position on the bed, and I breathed a sigh, pushing the stop button on the alarm. I roused myself fully and peered out the window to see the darkening sky. The room was empty, and the only light was the setting sun and the courtyard lamp shining through the window.

I crawled out of bed and slipped on a fresh pair of socks to walk down the hall to the twins' room. The two sat on one of their beds, playing cards, while Anastasia's tall frame was curled up on the small couch in the corner, reading a book. She looked up to meet my eyes and smiled in greeting before returning to the pages.

"You missed it—Persephone tried tackling me for the key after I told her you three were moving schools tomorrow morning," she said without looking up.

"And how'd that turn out for you?" I looked at my sister before sitting down next to Parker.

"Don't wanna talk about it," Perse grumbled under her breath. Then she picked up a card, studied it, and then discarded it.

Parker beamed and snatched the card before leaning toward me and whispering, "It did not turn out well."

I whispered back, "I imagine not."

Anastasia looked up from her book and spoke lightly. "Ballet is cancelled today. Something about Madame getting sick, and since she doesn't let anyone in the studio without her, we don't have to attend practice, either."

"Yes!" I hissed. "Now I can go back to sleep!"

Parker chuckled. "You're going to regret that decision."

I grunted and gave him a shove. "Then I'll play cards! Deal me in the next one."

Playing cards was one of our favorite indoor activities when we were little, even though none of us were good at it. Only shreds of my memories from home remained, but it was better than what the twins remembered—which was nothing.

But sometimes I envied them. They were too young when we were taken to remember what a normal life was, and I knew…I craved to grasp it once again. I sighed and wondered if a life like that would ever be close enough to reach.

Or would it forever remain a dream?

THE START OF SOMETHING TERRIFYING

{ *Lavinia* }

"**Y**ou three know the drill: no hints, keep up your covers, and above all—don't be suspicious."

"Yeah, yeah. Thanks, Ming. See you at 2:30," I replied in Russian to our driver, shutting the car door behind me.

Schools were nothing new; we had been to dozens, and I had seen plenty of people. Our covers would always change, and if I got lucky, they'd let me dye my hair for it.

Whoever 'they' are anyway. I had never been in contact with a Board member or someone with a higher rank than Higgins, Anastasia, and the Labzinas. *If I ever meet them, I'll need to be on a full stomach. That will lessen the chances of me stopping their breathing.*

"You could have asked her where the offices were, genius," Parker piped up as he breathlessly climbed the granite stairs.

"Well, there's only three entrances," Persephone huffed from behind me, "and it won't be the theater or the gym. It has to be this one."

"Fine. But if you're wrong, I'm not going to—"

"I'm not wrong!"

"Guys!" I exclaimed. "Just shut up for a second!"

I rolled my eyes, pushed past Parker with a glare, and waltzed into the building. I glanced around at the brick building's lobby, followed instinct, and headed down a hallway. The twins caught up before I turned a corner and was met with a door adorned with a plaque that read "PRINCIPAL FAAGU."

"See?" I said with a glance to Parker.

I politely knocked on the door with three raps. Upon hearing an enthusiastic, "Come!" I opened the door and walked inside. We were greeted by a woman whose smile glowed next to her warm-toned skin as she waved a hand to welcome us in.

"Good morning! You're the Markov children? From the city?"

I stood in front of her desk and beamed brightly. "Yes, Principal. That's us."

She stood up from her chair and extended a hand over the desk, so I took it and shook her hand. She quickly stepped around the desk and greeted the twins while we introduced ourselves.

With a nod, the tall woman pulled out some papers from a drawer and handed them to us. "These are your schedules. A few of my choice students should be arriving soon to show you around. You'll find that the school can be…" She paused and seemed to search for a word. Her low voice muttered under her breath in another language for a brief moment, perhaps Samoan from what I could tell. "—complicated! So you'll always have one of them in a class with you. Ask them any questions you'd like."

I nodded. "We'll just wait here for the other students?"

"Yes, please do." She gestured to the plastic chairs lined against the corner near the door and sat down behind her mahogany desk.

I nodded and turned to sit, Parker and Persephone following. I lifted the paper up to study its contents.

Geometry, economics, study hall, chemistry, lunch, literature…

I internally sneered at the classes. *I can't ever get away from science, can I?* But I resentfully committed the list to memory and folded it inside my bag.

Persephone showed me her list of classes, and when I glanced over my other side at Parker's, I noted that the papers had simply been duplicated. Principal Faagu kept filing her stack of papers as the minutes passed, but not long after Parker began to fidget, the door was pushed open as two students stepped through.

One was a blond boy of Parker's height, and the other was a girl, who stood a few inches taller than me. The boy was clearly younger, freckles scattered over his pale skin like a spilled container of paint. His green eyes pierced the air when he glanced at the three of us.

"I'm Liam." He smiled charmingly and extended a hand.

I shook his hand first and introduced myself. He and Parker then exchanged nods, and as he grasped Persephone's hand, I fought a smug look from creeping onto my face. The two paused shortly, and they met each other's eyes before grinning. Then, to my dismay, Liam pulled back his hand.

Oh my gosh—I heard from Persephone's mind.

Control yourself! I chided, but the flush spreading across her full cheeks told me she didn't think I was referring to her powers.

Liam turned to gesture to the taller girl and introduced her as his older sister, Grace.

"Nice to meet you, Lavinia." Grace's brown eyes crinkled. As she nodded, her dark hair bounced around her broad shoulders. "Parker, Persephone." She pushed out a tanned hand to greet them.

"Where's Jesse?" Principal Faagu asked from her desk. Her glasses teetered on the tip of her flat nose when she looked up at us through the growing stack of papers.

"Oh, he's late," Grace said with ill-concealed disdain.

"Ah," Principal Faagu remarked shortly before bowing her head to her work. "As usual."

"Who's Jesse?" I asked lightly.

"My twin." Grace scowled. "But *I'm* always on time. He'll be here before class, I'm sure—you have geometry first?"

I nodded in reply, and she turned to Liam, who spoke next. "You both have history first, right?"

Parker and Persephone responded positively, to which Liam waved goodbye and good morning to the principal and gestured to the twins to follow him out. Grace beamed warmly at me and turned to follow the group out, but not before she was stopped by Principal Faagu.

"Yes?"

The woman pulled off her glasses and neatly folded them next to her before speaking. "Tell your younger brother to meet me here during his lunch period, will you?"

"Of course," Grace replied with a prim nod that sent her hair flying from her shoulders with a single bounce.

I wish my hair could look like that.

Once she led me out of the grand door and back through the foyer, Grace rolled her eyes and scoffed. "You know brothers."

I laughed airily. "They never listen to you."

"Never talk to you unless there's a girl they like and they have to text her back, or they need you to smell-check their socks," she snorted.

"One time, Grace! It was one time!" another voice barked from behind us.

We were at the second-floor landing, about to tour the right hallway of classrooms, when a boy came sprinting up the stairs to plant himself in front of us. His chest heaved, and a tendril of his curly, dark hair clung to the shine on his forehead.

"Run all the way here?" Grace spun to stare up at her twin brother. Though only an inch or two taller than her, the boy held himself confidently even against Grace's hard gaze.

"I had to get the thing for the project! With Nijaz!" He jumped defensively and swung his bag onto his shoulders. Dark freckles stood out against his pale cheeks.

Without giving him time to acknowledge me, Grace stalked down the hall with me in tow.

"And that's him. Jesse. The worst way you'll ever—"

"Oh, shut *up*," Jesse groaned. "Let the nice girl form her own opinion of me."

Now it was my turn to glance behind to peer at Jesse. "Who said I was nice?"

Jesse bared a toothy grin, showing the sparkle in his brown eyes that matched Grace's perfectly. He tossed a piece of hair out of his face. "She speaks!"

I turned around to face forward, and Grace smiled at me. "When she's not being stopped by arguing, that is," she said. "And her name is Lavinia."

Jesse rolled his eyes. "It wasn't arguing, it was—"

"Bantering?" I offered.

"You're not helping," Grace scoffed.

I grinned. The two were easy going, and as the tour continued, we were comfortable together. They asked few questions about my personal life, and for that, I was grateful.

I had gotten used to lying. I had been trained for it, done it every day, even to my family. But there was something about Jesse and Grace that made it difficult to stomach every half-truth and every small lie about my cover story. I wondered if Persephone and Parker were feeling the same way about Liam.

Ming told us to be careful a thousand times; every morning, every new school, she'd remind us in her smooth Russian—though she cursed in Mandarin at "American drivers"—that above all else, we were never to let our guard down.

But Jesse, with his smooth smile and charming jokes, and Grace were questioning my ability to protect myself and keep myself locked in my own little cage, as Anastasia called it. She joked with me late one night about how I was a bird: I could fly free if I just let myself out, but I was too stubborn and too scared to pull the latch open.

But when Grace turned the final corner and completed the second floor, my attention failed to focus on the stairs in time. My foot missed a step, and before I could cling to the railing, my face fell toward the twins in front of me. I collided into Jesse with an embarrassed grunt, but he held himself upright with a hand on the railing.

I reflexively wrapped my hand around his arm to stop myself from knocking him down. Uncomfortably, his muscles twinged under my hand, and my face flushed a pale pink.

I wonder what sport he plays…

Jeez, Lavinia.

Our eyes met. Though he grinned at my awkwardness, he politely reached over with his other arm and helped me stand up straight. I cleared my throat and mumbled an apology, internally sending a surge of my powers through my face to return it to its pale self.

Grace chuckled from a distance, and when I stared down the stairs, I pressed my lips together in irritation. She seemed amused at the situation and didn't bother to hide the smile playing on her wide lips.

"Oh, shut up, Grace," Jesse put in, "you're embarrassing Lavinia!"

"I didn't say anything!" She grinned.

"You shut up! Who said *I* was embarrassed?" I shot back at Jesse with a challenging stare. I sauntered down the stairs.

Grace started walking again, and I followed her. She sent me a playful glance and chuckled.

"The look on your face said you were embarrassed. That, and where you put your—"

"Do stop talking." I glared at her but broke quickly with a smile.

Now I really need to find out what sport he plays. Or what gym he goes to. Maybe I can convince Anastasia to excuse me from training one day to…

I sighed at myself in exasperation and shook Jesse out of my head.

That was the last word we exchanged before Grace pushed open the gymnasium doors and held it for Jesse and me to step through. I spotted Liam and the twins walking through the door on the other side of the huge room and waved to them.

Grace led us over to them and called out, "Hope you're all having fun!"

"We are! None of them have extracurriculars, though, so I didn't show them everything," Liam responded, gesturing to the high ceiling and the folded bleachers across from us. "The gym was the last stop."

"We're all right here." Persephone laughed.

The freckles on his pale skin flushed momentarily as he apologized. "It's just curious why you aren't taking any extracurriculars."

I didn't miss the absence of Parker or myself in his statement, or his chastised glance at my sister. The younger set of twins looked to me to answer Liam, and when his head swiveled in my direction, a piece of his light hair landed gracefully on the side of his face.

"We don't know how long we'll be staying. We're never in one place for long, with our dad moving job locations every month or so."

Grace's face creased with a dimple. "It'll be nice to have you around however long you'll be staying! But it's almost time for class." She waved to Liam. "See you later.”

I gave Parker and Persephone a quick hug and sent my sister a wink before following Grace and Jesse back through the door from where we'd come. Grace glanced behind her to make sure I hadn't fallen behind as she ascended the stairs, Jesse right behind.

At the top, Grace paused and waited for me, but Jesse turned to the right. I glanced between the two taller members of our small group and took note of the way Jesse's lips pulled into a tight line.

Whatever he had been doing this morning—whether he had really been getting something for a project, I would never know—had made him nervous now as Grace arched a thick eyebrow and opened her mouth to speak to him.

“Have fun with that project.”

“I will.” Jesse rolled his eyes. He glanced at me and bit the inside corner of his mouth, seeming to shake an image out of his head before he swung around.

“Jess, wait—” Grace started. She waited for him to turn. “Faagu wants you to come to the office during your lunch period.”

Jesse ran a hand through his tousled hair and sighed. I sucked in a momentary breath at his open mouth and creased eyebrows, barely hearing his reply to Grace.

Snap out of it, Markov. He's just another pretty face—

No. I was not going to let him beguile me.

“Did she say why?”

“No.” She pursed her thick lips together. “But I think it might have something to do with you being late. Again. For the third time this week.”

“It's only Thursday,” Jesse pointed out. “Besides, we had to get here earlier.”

“And that's her point. You need to figure it out and get here on time, or else you'll—”

“Yeah, yeah, thanks, Grace.” He rolled his dark eyes. “See you in study hall.”

“Don't be late for economics!” Grace called after his disappearing figure before she turned to me and walked in the opposite direction.

Grace expertly weaved her way between the growing crowd, and I hurried behind her, mumbling excuses at the occasional shoulder collision. She reached the classroom and pushed open its door, leading us to two empty seats.

“Why isn't he in our geometry class?” I asked curiously. Grace sat down, set her bag on the floor, and plopped her book down on the desk with an audible thump.

"He's still in Algebra 2."

I mulled over the information and mimicked her movements, though my book landed on the desk gently. I tilted my head toward her, and my bright hair fell onto my shoulder.

"And the reason he's late all the time?"

Grace returned my glance with a twitch of her wide mouth. "Ask him yourself."

UNKNOWNS

{ *Lavinia* }

That afternoon after training and dinner, we had a break before ballet.

If only Madame had stayed sick longer.

The four of us and Sarvesh settled in the twins' room discussing today's events—it was mostly Persephone reporting in. Sarvesh and Parker listened to every word, no matter how boring the detail was.

Anastasia and I were on the small couch side by side, and when the three gathered on the bed burst into excited chatter, she tilted her head toward me.

"Did you enjoy your day?"

"Well enough." I shrugged.

She turned her attention to the rest of the group in silent response, her brown eyebrows twitching in acknowledgment. They mismatched with her dark red hair, though I supposed it was a wise decision not to dye them to match. She had beautiful green eyes, and I, for one, would have hated to see them ruined by faulty dye.

Sarvesh turned to face us. "Meet anyone special today, Nia?"

"Wouldn't you like to know."

"Yes, he would!" Persephone chuckled. "We all know Jesse's your type!"

You have no idea how right you are, Perse. It was times like this where I was immensely grateful she couldn't read my thoughts unless I let her.

"Jesse?" Anastasia raised a brow and looked at me.

I'd be gravely embarrassed if Persephone or Parker knew just how many times I had looked him over when his back was turned—and that was today alone. I cursed myself when I realized how many more days I'd have to spend with him.

"She brought him up!" I said defensively. "Ask her what she thought of Liam!"

"Liam?" Sarvesh echoed.

"Oh, come *on*, you guys!" Parker interrupted. He pushed his blond hair out of his face and gestured with everyone to stop. The room's overhead lights caught the glint of his rings. "The Price family showed us around the school today at Principal Faagu's request. Grace and her twin, Jesse, the one who flirted with Lavinia the whole day, showed her around, while Liam, the cute blond with a taste for redheads, showed Perse and me around."

Why do you have to be so smart and annoying at the same time?

The brat had the nerve to grin at me.

"Flirted? The whole day?" Anastasia's eyes widened. "And how did you feel about this, Lavinia?"

"I think everyone should stop asking us so many questions and wait until we've had a chance to know these people—"

"You mean—" Sarvesh grinned.

"I'd take her hint if I were you."

Alek stood in the doorway of the room, and as our heads swung to look at the new voice, he leaned against the side of the frame.

"Lavinia doesn't take kindly to people prying into her love life." He lifted a corner of his mouth into a smirk.

"Like you would know," Persephone scoffed.

If only he didn't.

And as soon as he arrived, he was gone. I got off the couch, turning to leave. I could almost see Anastasia's smile.

"See you in the studio." I waved to the younger three and then led myself and Anastasia back to our room.

Once the door was closed behind us, Anastasia spun on me. "What did you really think of Jesse? What did he look like?"

"Damnably handsome." I sat heavily on my bed. "He has the most gorgeous, curly, dark hair I have ever seen—"

"Prettier than Viktoriya's blonde?"

"Much. And when I tripped on the stairs, I accidentally grabbed his arm to stop me from falling, and—" I paused as she lifted a chin in ill-concealed interest.

"Go on."

"His muscles." My eyes grew large.

Anastasia laughed for a moment and shook her head. She walked over and sat on her bed across from me, smiling. "Why didn't you say anything in there?"

I frowned. "I can't give Persephone the wrong idea. You should have seen Liam."

She nodded in understanding but hesitated to speak. "Do you think you'll let it happen?"

I met her eyes and let out a breath. "I can't. Even if I wanted to."

"Sounds like you want to."

"Want *him*? Of course. But I doubt I'll ever feel for him."

She grinned. "I wouldn't be so sure about that."

5

PILLOW FORT

{ *Lavinia* }

"I think I'd make a good stand-in for Tom Cruise," Grace mused, her gaze on the movie.

I titled my head. That didn't seem like something Grace would say, but I could have been wrong. "Yeah?"

"Internet stalking has prepared me for anything." She smirked at me.

I shrugged, knowing these movies weren't really accurate to an actual spy's life. Every moment I was out in the field renewed my spark of excitement for life, but once I got to be Anastasia's age, I knew it would grow old and dull.

Especially if you have to kill as many people as she has.

We resumed our work, only paying attention to the movie occasionally. Homework didn't thrill me, especially not this math assignment, but at least it wasn't chemistry. Currently, Jesse was at Nijaz's house working on a project, and Liam was still at school with Persephone and Parker. Grace's and my last class got canceled because there was no substitute available; instead of sitting at school with nothing to do—we had both left more important assignments at home—I came over

41

to work on the math assignment due tomorrow. Not that I didn't want to be in bed right now, but I didn't have many options.

Ming would be on time, as usual, to take Parker and Persephone home; Liam would catch the bus; and Anastasia would come pick me up in time for training tonight.

Wish I could sleep my way through that one too.

Grace and I had talked often enough, but without Jesse or someone else there, we sat in silence most of the time. It was how both of us preferred it, without someone more outgoing to help make us laugh—or help me go unnoticed.

I guess Jesse did serve a purpose.

Time passed to the last few scenes of the movie when the kitchen door opened, and I turned my head to see Jesse stepping through from the garage. Our eyes met, and he smiled in greeting. I returned it and faced forward, completing the last math problem and closing the folder.

"Finish the project?" Grace called out to him, her focus still on her work as the pencil scratched along the page.

"We made some headway," Jesse replied lightly. "We'll finish in time."

Grace picked up her head and glanced over her shoulder at Jesse. "I'm surprised." He had begun to walk across the kitchen to the living room, sliding in his socks across the dark oak floor.

I tilted my head when I looked at Jesse. "Why? Do you usually submit things late?"

Grace let out a small chuckle. Jesse, now at the back of the couch, flicked the back of her head and rolled his eyes.

"Listen," he began in defense, "*I* might be late, but—"

"So is your homework!" Grace laughed again.

I chuckled at them and drew my knees to my chin, tucking in my feet. Jesse kept grumbling as he settled into the armchair next to the couch, picking something off the floor.

A flannel.

Jesse shrugged it over his shoulders and seemed to just notice the movie, but he averted his gaze from the screen and returned it to Grace and me.

"What?" Grace asked. Jesse was staring behind us.

He blinked once, focusing his brown eyes on me. "Wanna build a fort?" He looked at Grace. "We can get that massive beanbag from up in the garage."

Grace shot up off the couch without an answer and darted to the garage, leaving Jesse and me smiling.

"I guess that's a yes. Here…" He stood and walked to the foot of the stairs, near the kitchen. "Come help me gather all the blankets. Grace can start pillows when she finds that beanbag."

"Will she need help?" I followed him up the stairs and into Grace's room to the left, pulling the throws from the floor into my arms.

"Oh, she'll be fine. There's a little ladder she can use."

◆ ◆ ◆

"Where did the Doritos go?" I called after Jesse had pulled the blankets apart so I could peek my head out.

"I'm coming!" Grace shouted from the kitchen or the dining room next to it; I wasn't sure. The house was open on the ground floor, though I hadn't gone into the rooms at the back—connecting to the dining room.

"Don't forget the brownies Mom made last night!" Jesse put in.

We retreated back inside the fort, our heads inevitably brushing against each other. Jesse sat back to give me space, but his eyes remained on my face.

"Your hair smells nice. Like coconut. Maybe flowers."

I blinked. "Thanks."

"You're welcome." His face creased as his lips tightened into a sheepish smile.

Grace thrust the blankets open and broke our concentration, revealing her full arms. "I bring snacks and good tidings."

Jesse reached for one of the bowls, and I took the bag of Doritos so Grace could travel to the back of the fort and sprawl out. Jesse and I laughed when she clumsily flopped onto the pile of pillows.

"Shut up, you two," she grumbled.

BANDAGE THE PAST

{ *Lavinia* }

"**W**hat is that?" Jesse's gaze left Grace's departing figure to rest on me.

"Oh, this?" I reached an arm across my body to hover a finger over the marks on my outside upper arm. "It's just—"

He shook his head, brown eyes focused on the red spot. The blood had dried into a scab across the knife wounds littering my pale skin, and underneath, the beginnings of a bruise began to form.

Since this morning, I had been wearing a sweatshirt, but now that I had taken it off in Grace's warm room, the rest of my arms were visible. And it seemed Jesse was paying attention to that instead of the homework strewn on the bed.

"That's not just an accident, Lavinia, who—no, you're—" Jesse stood and took a hold of my uninjured arm's hand, forcing me to get up.

He stalked with purpose from Grace's room across the hall to the bathroom, let go of my hand, and nodded to the sink.

I raised an eyebrow. "Do you want me to—?"

"Sit down."

I could heal it myself, but—

"Fine," I muttered, hoisting myself up to sit on the counter of the double vanity. "But what are you—?"

"Shush," Jesse chastised, "and be patient." He opened the cabinet next to the door to reveal bandages, tubes of antiseptic cream, and bottles of over-the-counter pain reliever.

I shut my mouth and waited, watching him turn on the faucet and unfold a small piece of linen. He turned to me and reached out the wet cloth, about to place it on my skin, before hesitating and pulling back.

"Go ahead." I nodded and rolled up my short sleeve so that it wasn't in the way.

Jesse continued, placing the cloth on top of the wound to slowly separate some of the blood from my skin. Once he was satisfied, he rinsed the cloth and set it down on the counter. Then he turned his back to me, facing the cabinet.

His hair fell forward as he leaned down to a lower shelf, and I noticed a small scar behind his left ear. I stared for a moment, curious; it didn't look like a wound.

He faced me again, this time holding a small tube and a large bandage. His gaze focused upon the materials he held while he put the bandage on the counter. Opening the tube, he gently applied the cream to my arm. I hissed in a breath as the scratches lit themselves on fire in the name of healing.

This is why I should have done it myself.

"You okay?" Jesse asked in a quiet voice. He was still close to me, screwing the lid onto the tube in my peripheral vision.

"I will be." I exhaled through my teeth.

"Just take a deep breath," he cautioned.

"What do you think I'm doing?" I winced and squeezed my eyes shut as he spread the cream farther across the wound.

I hate this.

Jesse chuckled lightly, a sound I welcomed. Pain was not my strong suit. I let my lips curl and he drew back, done with that step. A comfortable silence enveloped us once more, and my eyes stayed shut.

His feet quietly shuffled across the bathroom tile to stand almost in front of me. I could feel his arm close to my front as he lifted a hand to adjust the bandage onto my arm. I opened my eyes, and deep brown ones stared back at me.

"You wanna tell me where you got this?" He lowered his eyes after a moment, focusing on the bandage.

I swallowed and glowered at the wall behind him. "Not really."

He paused momentarily and let his hands stop. "Fine, then. I'll guess."

Bad idea.

Jesse resumed his work. "Gang fight. You're a secret mafia boss."

"What the—?"

"That's a no, then." He grinned and glanced at my baffled expression. "You *really* angered Parker. By stealing his cheese."

"Not this time." I paused. "But in what universe would I steal his cheese?"

"What if you didn't have your own? That's quite a pressing matter, after all. It's cheese we're talking about."

I sighed at his terrible attempt at bandaging my arm. "Jesse, where do you even get—?"

"Moving on!" he declared, removing some of the bandage. He rummaged in the cabinet for a moment and pulled out an Ace bandage. "This will work better," he murmured to himself.

"I'm still here."

"I know." He began to wrap my arm, keeping one end of it still with his fingers. "Was it your dad?"

I froze. His hands were cold, and he was even closer than before. My mouth went dry.

"No," I lied.

But Ernest isn't even your real dad. So technically it's not a lie. Even if he's the closest dad you'll ever have.

How would I explain to Jesse that I was close-weapons training, my opponent had decided it was the perfect day to forget their practice weapons, and I was too distracted to properly defend myself the way I knew how?

I knew Ernest didn't forget. I was thankful, though, that Jesse couldn't see the multiple other wounds I bore from this morning's early training session. I'd heal those later before Anastasia noticed.

Jesse thought for a second. "Then—"

"Why are you two—what—?" Grace interrupted, peering into the bathroom.

Jesse jumped away from me, having finished wrapping my arm. I lowered my eyes and smoothed the bandage before flipping down the sleeve of my shirt.

Grace brushed past her brother and stared at my arm, a bag of chips and dip in hand. "What is that?"

"She's fine now," Jesse interjected quickly and hastily put away the supplies while Grace glanced between us, baffled.

Jesse shut the cabinet and motioned to the Ace bandage wrapped around my wound. "You can keep that."

I nodded in thanks and jumped off the counter, ignoring his outstretched hand. I strode out of the bathroom and occupied myself with looking at my arm until I sat down on Grace's bed, picking up some of the homework.

If the twins were saying something as they followed me, I didn't listen. It was enough that Jesse had seen my wound, let alone helped me. I was supposed to do that. He shouldn't have a clue as to how to treat a knife wound…

Well, it looked more like a burn or scraped skin from falling on the pavement. They all probably got those a lot as kids.

Jesse and Grace sat down on either side of me, forming a small circle, and startled me out of my thoughts.

"So where were we?" Grace asked. She placed the bag of chips and the container of dip into the center of our huddle, balancing them on a pillow, and picked up a pen.

Jesse sighed regretfully. "French history. Which, I'll have you know,"—he grabbed a chip and pointed at his sister—"is nowhere near as entertaining as cleaning up blood."

I kept my chuckle under my breath, giving Jesse a sideways glance to discover his eyes already on me and mouth curved.

"We haven't gotten to the Revolution yet," Grace pointed out.

Jesse and I broke eye contact when he picked up the right folder and opened it. "Where's my—?"

"Here." I handed him a pen, and he nodded in thanks.

"Honey?" Mrs. Price's voice called from downstairs before we could resume our work.

Grace shot up from the bed and opened the door, calling out, "Yeah?"

Footsteps echoed on the staircase, and when Mrs. Price reached the door, they exchanged a few more words. Grace turned around and waved for us to continue without her. "I'll be back."

But the mischievous smile on her face didn't quite convince me it was because of something her mother had asked her to do. When she left the door open, Jesse put down the sheet he had been staring at and slid his pen behind his ear.

"What is it?"

I stared back at him, toying with the edge of my notebook. "What is what?"

"Don't play dumb. Where did you get that—thing?"

When I didn't reply and cast my eyes downwards, he sighed. "You can trust me."

"Everyone says that."

"We've known each other for a little while now. We're friends, aren't we?" His light tone relieved me in a sense.

But still...

"Of course we are," I said, looking up at him. "And I do trust you."

He raised his dark eyebrows. "So...?"

"Just not with this. Not this time."

He fell into silence again, studying my face. I kept our grey and brown eyes locked, and we blinked in sync like waves pulsing against the sand. Jesse wasn't usually this serious, but I understood why he was freaked out at my wounds.

I was supposed to be a normal high school girl. I just moved from out of town, and I'll be moving again eventually as far as he knows. I wondered how terrified he would be if he knew the real truth about where that blood came from and the power running through it. If he knew what I had lived through.

I supposed that the surprise he might show to the truth was nothing in comparison to the terror I felt every day, the terror I had become accustomed to.

Grace sauntered back through the open door, breaking our spell. She took her seat again with a look of disappointment that she wasn't interrupting anything this time. Jesse and I both glared at her, though I suspected for different reasons.

What did she think was going to happen? We'd be in each other's faces?

NEVER ALONE

{ *Lavinia* }

"You don't keep secrets from everyone, do you?" Jesse asked curiously.

"Excuse me?" I froze from my spot on their couch.

"You have to have a best friend or something. Someone who knows where you got that from." He gestured lamely to my bandaged arm from yesterday and looked at me instead of our economics project.

I relaxed slightly, glancing down at it. "Yeah. I do."

Anastasia, I thought. *And Persephone and Parker. They're all I have.*

"And do they know what it is?"

"Yeah. She does," I said quietly.

I chuckled to myself. *She's no happier about it than you are.* I deliberated on even telling him Anya's name.

"And—" he started again.

"Why do you care so much? I'll be fine," I said curtly, letting my pen fall out from my grip and onto my lap with a thud.

"It's not making you seem very normal," he pointed out, raising an eyebrow.

"What sixteen-year-old girl gets that kind of injury?"

"Apparently someone who could have stolen her brother's cheese."

I frantically ran over situations I had conditioned myself to do if someone ever came close to—or actually—finding out the truth about me.

Divert their attention. Make them laugh. Bring something else up; change the topic. Leave altogether. No, that's too much work. *If I can just distract him from—*

"Don't change the subject."

Never mind.

Jesse's eyes affixed to my face. "I understand if you don't want anyone to know because then it could get worse for you. But at least let me call someone who could—"

"What are you talking about?"

Jesse's expression turned blank, and I stared right back. *Just play dumb.*

He thought better of the abusive dad angle and said simply, "Nothing."

He must have assumed that, had I been a victim, I would know what he was referring to. Seeing as how I appeared to not have a clue to his intentions, I must not be in danger of that.

Silence filled the room again. I picked up my pen, ready to resume the project.

"One of my best friends died from that kind of thing," Jesse said.

My head shot up, and I met his wide-eyed stare. "Your—"

"We were little. I don't remember it much." He broke our gaze.

"Yeah, but still—"

"Just know that…I know how it feels. Even just a little bit." Jesse studied the floor.

A few moments of silence passed, and my eyes remained on him. Then, he gathered himself and looked at me with those deep brown eyes.

"Whoever's doing that to you—even if it's you—just know you're not alone. You're never alone."

LATE NIGHTS

{ Lavinia }

*B*zz. *Bzz.*

My eyes pried open from my temporary mid-study nap.

Bzz. Bzz.

The phone was sitting on my bed stand, shining to the ceiling with a single photo of Jesse as the caller ID.

"What is he—?" I muttered to myself.

I unplugged the phone and picked it up, staring at it in contemplation. Anastasia was already asleep, but it was still after 11:00 at night. I decided to flick the dim light off next to my bed and swing my legs off to the side. My tired legs stood up and carried me to the door.

I knew the phone would go to voicemail if I left it ringing for much longer; I hurriedly unlocked our door with a stream of powers from my hands and answered the call, closing the door softly behind me.

"Hey," I said quietly, padding along the hallway.

"Hi. Sorry it's so late, I, uh—" Jesse answered quickly, "—didn't know if you'd be up or—"

"It's okay. I couldn't sleep anyway."

Though I was almost at the end of the hall, I glanced behind me just in case. Our rooms had alerts for when they opened at certain hours of the night, so it was a regular routine for me to trip the sensor with my powers when I left to do anything but use the bathroom.

Safe so far.

I opened the hall door in the same fashion, quickening my pace down to the main corridor, where I began my descent down the stairs.

"What's up? Besides not being able to sleep."

Jesse chuckled lightly from the other end. "That's pretty much it. I wanted to talk to someone."

"So you decided on calling me?" I had reached the ground floor. When I opened the right door at the bottom of the stairs, the familiar, cold air enveloped my shoulders.

"Well, yeah," he responded plainly, as if it were the most obvious answer.

"Grace goes to bed early, doesn't she?"

I twisted a few fingers in the air by my side to determine if anyone was in the courtyard or could see me.

"Yeah." He snickered. "Grandma."

I let out a distracted laugh, and once it was safe, I took another few steps onto the stone. Fallen leaves of the maple tree across from me crunched under my feet.

"Are you outside?" he asked.

"Yeah," I said lightly. "It's quieter out here. Don't want to wake anyone up."

"Your parents are light sleepers?"

"Parker is." I purposefully neglected to answer about "my parents." The less he knew, the better.

But...

"Really? He seems like the type to sleep so deeply that he snores."

The corner of my mouth lifted. "That's Perse. You'd be surprised how hard it is to wake her up."

Jesse snorted in amusement. "What about you?"

I exhaled lightly as I sat on the stone retaining wall built around the maple tree.

It was a little cold through my sweatpants, but not uncomfortably so. "Depends, really. If I'm tired, I sleep deeper. But I wake up easily most mornings."

"You don't strike me as a morning person," he mused.

I let out a dry laugh. "I'm not."

"Me neither."

"Hence why we're calling this late: we're night owls."

"Exactly, and, even after we hang up, it'll be a few hours."

"Yeah." I smiled despite knowing he couldn't see me. "This isn't good for our sleep schedules, you know."

"Oh, I know,"—his tone dripped with sarcasm—"but at least we're not alone."

Jesse's words hit me like a punch to the gut after saying almost the same thing yesterday. Of course, he knew the effect it would have on me, and he still said it.

He really cares, doesn't he?

"Do you wish you didn't have your own room? So you wouldn't have to be alone?" I asked to keep the focus off of me.

"Good question. I, uh…" He paused. "…don't think so. I can always just go downstairs for company. Or call someone."

We shared a chuckle.

"How was your day?" Jesse asked.

I furrowed my brows. "You were with me all day. At school."

"I know. But we both have lives outside of school. So how was your day after school?"

"Fine, I guess," I said lightly, running through the day in my head. *Homework. Training. Dinner. Showered.*

"That's it? Fine?" He scoffed. "There has to be more than that."

"Homework was boring, as usual. Got through it but not without complaining. Parker threatened to steal my earbuds, though, so I finished it."

Jesse laughed.

"And we had chicken and rice for dinner."

"That's a good dinner. Basic, but good."

"Yeah. Now, how was your day?" I sassed, hoping he would give more detail than I did.

"Oh, not much, just—"

"Don't you start that with me, Jesse Price!"

Jesse laughed again, and he tried to quiet himself. But he couldn't.

Sounds like sunshine.

♦ ♦ ♦

"Are you still awake?" I whispered.

No answer came from Jesse's end of the call. Nothing but the quiet rhythm of his breathing, softly filling my ear, a smile flitting across my lips. I leaned against the wall next to my door and closed my eyes, debating on whether to go back in.

A creak sounded from behind our door.

Anya?

I took my hand out of my sweater's pocket and took hold of the door handle, using my powers to trip the lock, and then opened it. I stepped inside and shut it quickly so the light wouldn't wake Anastasia.

Too late.

"What are you doing up?" she mumbled from across the dark room.

I muted our call and pushed the screen of my phone up against my chest. "Just to the bathroom. Go back to sleep."

Anya let out a groan and shifted in her pile of pillows and blankets.

I will never understand that woman.

Once her breathing had slowed into sleep again, I lifted my phone and stared at the ticking call clock underneath Jesse's contact name.

Almost two hours.

But he was asleep now, and that was the deal we'd made. So I nestled myself deep into the blanket and put my phone on the nightstand, only clicking the red button at the last moment.

See you tomorrow, Jesse.

9
NEVER DOING THIS AGAIN

{ *Parker* }

A dull voice sounded in my ears, muffled as if underwater. *Sarvesh.*

I opened my eyes and squinted in the blinding light while the world swam. I blinked, now clearly seeing all five feet and four inches of him standing in front of me.

"What are you doing here?" He looked impatient, but his voice was gentle.

I scowled at my sleep's interruption.

But...

I owed him an explanation. I sat up from my spot horizontal on his couch and scratched my head.

I met his dark eyes, and they snapped back to my face.

Was he looking at my hair?

I self-consciously reached up and tried to fix it, but he chuckled and sat next to me.

"Why are you sleeping in here?" Sarvesh questioned again.

"Perse and I fought," I grumbled. *Only a little lie. Technically, a half-truth.*

"About what?" he pressed.

"Something stupid."

Though it was a mumble, Sarvesh understood and raised a neat brow. His brown skin glowed with sweat from his late work out, but he didn't look tired. He was hard to read sometimes.

I think he does it on purpose.

"Clearly you did something stupid to be found asleep on my couch."

I thought there was something more to his words, but when I turned, he wore a brash grin upon his lips.

I sighed. "Stop it."

"Why?" Sarvesh tilted his head, which flew a piece of hair in his face.

"You're distracting me."

"From what?"

"Being angry," I retorted.

"And you want to be angry?"

"It's better than paying attention to reality. Hearing too many things. Touching things."

"And that's why you were asleep?"

I nodded once in response and stood.

He doesn't need to know all of this. He's smart enough as it is. Why am I even telling him this?

I thought about leaving, but he'd just yank me back into the room and tell me to sit. So I walked over to the window and crossed my arms to stare outside. There wasn't much of a view except for the small courtyard of stone and plants, which was better than nothing. But it was a lot to me, so I shut my eyes. I tried to ignore the sounds threatening to snap my nerves in front of Sarvesh and shook off the touch of my sleeves and socks.

Not here. Not in front of him.

It pounded against my head. The hum of the pipes behind the walls. The rattling of the radiator. The low footsteps on the floor above me, the clanging of distant dishes, the ticking of the clock in the hallway: it all made me want to scream. I shook my head rapidly to push the feeling away, the noise.

Too much, too much, too much, too much—

"Parker?"

I whirled to face Sarvesh, but my vision was clouding. His voice was distant again, pleading.

"You're shaking—bouncing, really. What's wrong?"

I can't move.

"Parker?"

I can't touch him.

Sarvesh reached out to grab my hand, and a monster inside me screamed, terrified—I jumped back. I hit the window with a crash, but I panted and studied the floor, cradling my hand as if he had burnt it with his touch.

A dread clung to my temples and pushed till the pain grew larger and larger. I clenched my jaw, locking it, and suddenly realized Sarvesh had backed up away from me. He stood by the door, and as I looked up, he smiled in comfort.

I could barely see him through the tears burning my eyes, but his soft brown ones twinkled, and he spoke just loud enough for me to hear him.

"I'm not going to touch you or be near you. I won't make any noise. You're gonna be okay."

I hesitated but swallowed my pride and cleared my throat to speak. "C-Could y-could you—uh…" I cursed in my head in frustration.

I hate this. I can't even get words out of my mouth.

"Could I what?"

I tried again. This time, I raised my voice to sound more confident. I wasn't sure if I did that for my own benefit or to pretend that none of this was happening in front of him.

"Could you turn on some music?"

There. I said it. He knows. I have to listen to music to distract me. I can't bear too much noise? Too much to touch? I sound like a toddler.

He hastened to the side of his bed and pulled out his phone. A second later, loud music pushed through the speakers of the radio. I gasped for a steady breath while the air in my lungs pressed out.

Sarvesh grabbed a ring of mine I had left on the side table and tossed it on the end of the bed so I could reach it. I let go of my hand and flexed it to regain some feeling. I had been pulling my fingers so hard that they had gone numb. Now, I reached out to grab the ring to slide it on my finger.

It was cold. Cold, comforting, and safe. Familiar. I extended one shaking hand to the speaker and slowly turned the dial up.

Just a tad.

Everything else was silent now. I paid attention to the music. I focused, listening to the beat and creating a rhythm for my breathing, and whispered the words to myself under my breath. I felt reality returning and my senses lowering as moments passed.

Relief flooded up to my face at the calm, the feeling of my feet on the floor, the silence surrounding me.

Peace. Finally.

I tried to ignore Sarvesh, but I turned around to face him. The music turned down, and he set his phone back on his bed. He stared at me, waiting for my answer.

Great.

10

THE UNSPOKEN THING

{ *Jesse* }

I let out a heavy sigh and pushed myself off the ground.

The shadows of the brick wall behind me did little to cool my raging temper and shield me from the glaring afternoon sun. It was steaming for a mid-October day, one of the hottest we'd had since the summer heat had rested its grip.

But it was a safe place to come to; the back corner of the school was unbothered by the teachers milling about with only their books and coffee for company. Even the teenagers there wouldn't spare you a second glance, and even if they wanted to, I doubted the groups on either side of me were sober enough to notice my dilemmas.

They were used to me, of course, but it was to my surprise that not a single one of them recognized me after coming here for so long.

Our spot.

I stood awkwardly and thought to myself in silence before realizing how stupid I looked.

I went back to my spot against the wall instead of sitting on the sparse grass. I pulled out my phone but didn't turn it on. Still, it was better to look like a loner on their phone than someone staring off into the distance, surrounded by smoking teenagers.

Trying not to think of the past memories of this spot, I took deep breaths to calm myself, smoke filling my lungs with each one. A small cough forced itself out, and upon setting myself upright again—this time, with a clear head—I let myself lose a bit of focus.

Now that it had free reign, my mind filled with thoughts of two girls. *Not just girls*, I corrected. I hated their brothers as much as I loved them.

Loved. Past tense. And—I caught myself—*I don't love Lavinia. Not like I did her.*

I swallowed the somber thoughts of the first two siblings, knowing I would never see them again, and instead focused on the ones I had just seen a few minutes ago.

I don't hate Parker, actually, I amended. He was kinder than both his sisters, at least to me. *Who knows what he's like at home?*

But that didn't erase Lavinia's gentle moments from my mind. If anything, it strengthened them. The few memories I had of them together, which were only slightly more than those with Persephone, were the purest form of love I'd seen on this earth.

Our families had the same dynamics with twins and another sibling with only a small difference of ages between us, but I had a hard time figuring out why my siblings and I weren't anything like the Markovs. Maybe it was because they moved so often—they had to rely more on each other than friends. With my family, we were closer with friends than each other because, let's face it, we were vastly different.

And I like to be alone.

Grace, being the social butterfly she was, was most like Persephone. Liam and Parker made wonderful friends from what I'd heard—they both let Persephone do the talking. I was pretty sure they wouldn't be able to get a word in edgewise anyway.

Lavinia and I were a different story. With the unspoken thing between the two of us, Grace had to constantly mediate between utter destruction of insults or complete silence. The third option, which I would much prefer to take, didn't involve Grace—or anyone else, for that matter—and would make the unspoken thing the *spoken* thing.

At least, if not spoken, we could do something about it…"something" being a little more than just staring at each other when we thought the other person wasn't looking—when we clearly knew. It had only been a week of knowing her, and already, it was torture.

Not quite torture. Torture would be what I had already gone through, and I would rather not remember all of that again. *Again.* I almost laughed at myself—as if I didn't think of it every day I walked into school. I thought of it every time I did the homework of a friend. Like she would do mine.

Every time I saw someone dark-skinned with their hair dyed blonde or a girl passing me on the street with blue eyes, I remembered. There was no forgetting the storm constantly raging inside me. Because every time I'd walk downstairs in my house and Liam was watching one of his medical shows, my lungs were sucked dry of air.

Any given moment I saw a hospital, I would panic. Any given moment that I thought I saw something, someone—her—I knew it would be what felt like hours until I could hold a conversation again, until I remembered what day it was.

Until I remembered I was late for something.

Class—Lavinia! Our lunch period was over by now, but because none of the teenagers around me had left, I hadn't realized I was late.

Again.

{ Lavinia }

"Where'd you go for lunch?" I asked incredulously. I had been waiting for the past few minutes on the granite steps waiting for a particular person who never seemed to look at the time.

Jesse huffed up the steps, and when he reached me, he looked me over and shrugged.

"That's it?" I shot back. "You're going to make us late for literature."

I turned on my heels and went inside without him, but his footsteps fell in behind me while I ran up the stairs and turned down the hallway.

"What's the rush? We only have an hour before classes are done."

"I want to go home," I lied, glancing at him as he fell into step next to me and matched my pace.

No, it's because I want to be away from your pretty face because it makes me want to do things I should never want to do.

I was prepared for the weekend without him as a distraction—I intended it to be productive by way of training myself and the twins—without a single thought of the freckles on his cheeks.

He gaped in disbelief, and for a moment, he looked ready to challenge my determined stare ahead. But after looking at me a second longer, he simply turned his eyes away. I knew I hadn't mistaken the hollowness behind his usually lively eyes.

"So? What was it this time?" I questioned.

"Huh?"

"Why weren't you here on time? Again?"

Before he could answer, we reached the classroom door. Jesse's face morphed into a blank expression as he opened it for me. I sighed internally and forced myself to pay attention for the duration of class, but every time he moved out of the corner of my eye, my thoughts yanked back to him.

I've known him for how long? No wonder he doesn't want to tell me.

♦ ♦ ♦

"Stop looking at me like that." We began the descent of the main stairs.

"Like what?" Jesse kept his eyes on mine, a bright smile on his lips. He tilted his head slightly, and his hair moved with it. A piece off to the side now hovered in the air between his eye and ear.

I playfully rolled my eyes. "You know how."

"I do?" He nonchalantly raised an eyebrow as we reached the bottom step.

{ Jesse }

"See you Monday," I continued, cutting her off before she could reply.

Her lips drew themselves together in a small pout, but I was glad she didn't get the chance to continue. I, for one, was not confident in my self-control. So I turned away from her and kept walking to the car.

"You better not be late, Price!" she shouted from behind me.

No promises, sweetheart.

"And miss seeing your face for another few minutes?" I turned around and gave her a wink as I walked backward, calling out, "Never!"

11

FATE IS CALLING

{ *Lavinia* }

The dark room was crushing me from the inside out. I tried to breathe, but my lungs faded and faded until I was lifeless. Boundless black stretched all around me, but I could see something.

Huh?

As pressure was relieved from my chest, I woke up, gasping. Now sitting up, the single source of light came into vision. The red digits on the clock were glaring. I blinked my fitful sleep away, focused on the time.

2:07 a.m. Great.

It was clear. My lungs were free, and the sweat started to disappear from my face and limbs. I could think somewhat plainly, had it not been for the overwhelming fog of busyness looming over my mind.

Why can't I shut it off?

I was always an expert at keeping my thoughts in control, and this moment should have been no different. But I couldn't stop it. It was so noisy. Unbelievably noisy. I couldn't focus; everything was starting to swim.

How could anyone live like this?

I knew I must have been feeling someone else's emotions. It's happened before on accident, but as soon as I realized it, I could stop.

But I can't stop it. I—I can't.

Persephone and I had accidentally created a connection like this in our sleep once. That out-of-control spiraling we went through was far from this. I was thankful that we had moved our rooms farther apart.

Proximity strengthened the connection, and this—this chaos—was too strong, too powerful, and too disruptive to be anyone not on this floor. I'd felt enough emotions and read enough minds to know that the severity of turmoil I was unwillingly feeling had to be coming from someone's nightmare.

Using my powers, I closed my eyes and blanketed the turbulent feelings with silence. I read my sleeping teammates' minds and didn't pay attention to the content, just the emotions. That was all I needed.

No luck. No one is feeling what I feel. Except…what if…?

Startled, I opened my eyes. At that moment, a courtyard light turned on, casting a dim-enough glow through the curtains for me to pick out Anastasia's sleeping figure in her bed.

I quietly got out of bed and crossed the short distance between our mattresses. She was peacefully sleeping and perfectly content. I didn't need to read her mind to know that her sleep was dreamless.

For once.

I thought about waking her, but I left her side and returned to my bed, shuffling my socked feet against the carpet. The pain, fear, and shame I was experiencing were replaced by mild irritation. I almost chuckled to myself, but it didn't last long. As if a single hated word had been spoken, the feelings flipped on a switch.

Emotions came flooding back, and tears pricked my eyes at their intensity. Raging anger, sadness, love—but the strongest was fear. Fear rushed into my heart so strongly that I panicked. My heart raced while I muttered in confusion, and a pain so glaring pounded bells upon bells in my head.

It was overwhelmingly pain and fear. But every time a pang of fear rushed into me, so did a wave of love. I didn't know which one was worse, more powerful, or put me in the most amount of agony.

Whoever this is, I hope you stop. Please, let me sleep. It hurts. I can't take it all at once.

I didn't know if I had even reached them or, if I did, they had heard me. But after long, painful minutes, it finally stopped. I didn't care how or why, but it stopped.

I hadn't realized my soft sobs were shaking my shoulders until my mind fell silent. I went cold as a shudder ran through me. Slowly but carefully, I lay down fully in bed. I had stopped shaking, but the cries kept going. I didn't want them to stop. It felt freeing to cry in the utter darkness in silence, completely alone.

Well, not completely—

"Nia, what is it?" Anya's soft voice grabbed my attention. She sat next to me, and her gentle hands soon came to rest on my hair.

Wordlessly and without waiting for a response, she plodded to the other side of my bed and curled up next to me. As I sniffled and moved closer to her, she cradled my head in one arm and drew me close with the other. Her fingers stroked a few of my stray hairs.

"What is it?" she murmured softly.

I let out a sigh of relief and tried to loosen the muscles I was tensing. My legs hurt, and my arms had gone numb.

I whispered, "I don't know what it was, Anya, I just—I couldn't stop it…"

"Couldn't stop what?" Her fingers settled on my head.

"The—The feelings. I was feeling someone's nightmare, and I couldn't figure out who it was. I couldn't"—a hiccup escaped my lips—"stop feeling it."

"Was it on accident? You didn't mean to connect to them?"

"I woke up like I was waking from a nightmare." I paused. "I didn't connect us."

"Then how else would it work?"

I frowned slightly and let another hiccup out, followed by a sniffle. "Maybe we have a connection already. An emotional one. Maybe it doesn't have anything to do with my powers."

"A connection like what you and your siblings have, you mean?"

"Yeah," was my soft response. She didn't speak for a few long moments but instead drew small circles on my back with her hand that wasn't on my head. Her touch was light and soothing.

I miss this. We hardly ever spend time like this anymore.

"You don't have to answer this, Nia, but…is it possible you've fallen in love with someone? And they love you? What if that's the connection?"

Her questions were like a shot to my face. I was dumbfounded.

It makes perfect sense, but…

I had tried to ignore everything I had been feeling lately toward Jesse. No matter how much he irritated me and how everything he said seemed to be sarcastic or annoying, there was an unmistakable bond between us. Whether that bond was simply finding him attractive—which I definitely couldn't lie to myself about—or if it was a real connection that would last, I couldn't say. I was trying desperately to ignore all his positive traits…

He was funny, of course, and his smile was so contagious that you could sit there and listen for hours upon hours. Whenever he walked into the room, he brightened someone's day, and no matter his own mood, he cheered you up.

But even when he was down or seemed off, he tried his hardest to hide it. It was only effective to a certain degree since I could sense his feelings if I wanted. Not that he'd ever open up to me, but…I couldn't help wondering what he'd gone through.

I was curious as to why he acted so passive sometimes toward me. What if he'd been hurt so badly by another girl that he didn't want to let me in? He didn't want to open up? And even if he did, was he stopped because he didn't believe I would ever open up to him?

I've got my fair share of problems, that's for sure. But…what about him?

12

PATH OF SILENCE

{ *Jesse* }

The air was cold. So cold. And it was dark. Very dark.

I tightened my sweater around me and crept toward the fireplace. My socks plodded across the wood floor and scratched the stone in front of the logs.

After flipping the switch on the electric fireplace, I sat down and stuck my hands out in front of the flames, just close enough to heat them. I was thankful we had installed one that warmed up so fast. Tonight was colder than usual.

Now it was quiet. And I didn't like the quiet. It made me think, and I didn't like that, either. The thinking was intolerable, and my mind was too loud. It would have been more bearable if my thoughts made any sense. But it was all senseless noise and feelings. Just raging feelings.

I had gotten used to this—how I would get after…one of those. After I could breathe again, I was always cold, and it was always quiet. Nothing could make it stop. Nothing except—

"Jesse?" Grace's voice called out softly.

I didn't turn around, but I knew where she was: at the bottom of the stairs. After flipping the dimmer switch for the pendant lights above the kitchen island, she called my name again. It matched the light shining through the lower level of the house. She knew now what had happened.

Her voice was just above a whisper. "Do you need me?"

I was thankful she couldn't see my face, because then she would have come over immediately. But I didn't trust my voice, either, so I shook my head no.

I knew myself, and I knew that even just someone speaking could stop the endless tirade of pointless ramblings in my head. But I didn't need her to see me like this. Again. For the countless time. I couldn't stand it.

For all the times I'd been through this, Grace hadn't seen me for more than half of it. I couldn't bring myself to tell her until months after it had been happening. But she knew about it now, and she tried to help.

She was getting better at it. She knew what worked and what didn't, what helped, and what made me worse. But bad days made nights like this extra miserable for me. And nights like this didn't ever get better, even with her help. They only got better when I pushed everything down. When I got rid of the thoughts, when I got rid of the feelings, then everything was okay. But I couldn't bear it otherwise.

Grace was still standing there; she hadn't made a sound, but she would have turned off the light if she had left. And I would have been able to hear her footsteps creaking up the stairs and opening her door.

I waited patiently for the light to flicker off and for her to walk away, but the sound never came. It never got dark again. Moments crawled by, feeling like hours until Grace flicked the light off. But instead of the stairs creaking, she was walking toward me.

I resisted the urge to panic. There were no tears dried on my cheeks, but the tense lines of my face and the colors under my eyes were enough clues for her, even in the darkness. I tried to will the flames' light to dim, and I stayed still until I saw her feet beside me. I glanced over.

Her whole figure came into view as she sat beside me. But she didn't look at me. Her dark hair clouded my vision from her face, but she wasn't looking at me. I turned to stare at the flames again.

Why is she here? I told her to go away. I don't want her help. I don't need her help.

"What was it this time?" she asked, interrupting my thoughts.

"I don't know."

She swept her hair out of her face and stared at me. "Yes, you do."

I steeled my jaw. Grace knew how stubborn I was. She knew I wouldn't tell her.

"I'm not telling you. I can't."

"Was it me?" She was less sharp this time. Did I detect a note of fear in her voice, though?

She isn't really scared...right? I...I'm her twin. She wouldn't—

I spoke rougher this time. "No, it wasn't you. But I can't tell you."

"Why?"

She's just curious. I relaxed an inch. *She just wants to help.*

"Because I can't."

"Then tell Lavinia. She understands. If you won't let me help you, at least let her."

The name she had uttered startled me. Jolting my thoughts silent and sending warmth, unbearable warmth, through my body was the name of that girl. That...

...girl you love. Just admit it, Jesse. You love her. And she doesn't love you. You know that.

I had tried so hard not to let Lavinia remind me of *her*. I had distracted myself every time she'd look at me or touch me accidentally because even just a brush of her shoulder or a smile playing on her pretty lips would send my thoughts racing.

Racing to her. I wanted my attraction to Lavinia to stay just that—physical attraction.

I didn't want to fall in love with her.

But I kept my face calm at the thoughts plaguing me. I kept my eyebrows level and my jaw locked. Grace wasn't looking at my eyes, but I kept those still, too. I kept them trained on the flickering flames.

And Grace knew all that, despite me not showing her, and I knew that she knew. Of course, she knew. Grace knew everything. She watched everything. She knew things were wrong with me months before I told her, and she knew how I looked at Lavinia. She knew how much I thought about her and dreamed about her.

But what she didn't know—and what I was determined never to let her know—

was that I didn't just dream about her.

Tonight was the first nightmare that I had killed someone I knew. Tonight was the first nightmare that I had watched someone die by my hands. Tonight was the first nightmare I had been helpless about the outcome.

Every other nightmare had been the feelings. All the thoughts and feelings about the trauma of the past and the present were in my nightmares. It was the concept of the pain but never the actual thing.

In a way, I was thankful I never had to relive her dying, but that had changed tonight. I had to watch someone else die. And that someone was Lavinia.

I had to watch someone that I knew. Someone that I trusted. Someone that I looked in the eye every morning and said goodbye to with a laugh every afternoon. Someone, just like last time, that I loved. I couldn't bring myself to think about it anymore. She—

Her name rang over and over again in my head. Her coarse, dyed, blonde hair; her wide, blue eyes; and her sweet face were stuck in my mind, but this time, it wasn't her hair matted with blood and her eyes glossed over. It wasn't her dark, soft hands going cold in mine.

It wasn't the chaos of the hospital. It wasn't the nurses covering her as I retreated to the corner, sobbing, collapsing, only a few years ago.

No. It wasn't. This time, it was the face of someone still alive.

The auburn hair that still glowed. The grey eyes that still shone. It was the rough hands that still held life and warmth, despite me never feeling it for myself. It was the silence of the dark room held only by her body, mine, and my shadow behind her. It was the numbness I felt even now, sitting beside Grace.

I had to watch my figure in the shadows loom over us, drawing the gun on her before her body fell away from me. I had to watch, and I couldn't do anything. I couldn't reach her. I couldn't catch her. I couldn't stop her breath from fading into a cold, lifeless silence.

I had to watch *her* die. I had to watch Lavinia die. And the worst part wasn't even that. The worst part was that I knew I would never get her back. It wasn't a dream or a nightmare. It was real. It was terribly real. And I had lived it. I had felt it.

I would never hold her hands again or see the spark in her eyes. But that wasn't what crushed me. I didn't love her anymore. I don't wish she were here.

The worst part was that the love I felt for her, the longing I felt for her touch, and the dreaming so fervent that it hurt were all the same now as it was then. I felt so much for Lavinia.

And I was scared. I was scared that a shadow really would destroy her. Or worse, that I would destroy her. I was scared that no matter how much I loved her, no matter how much I pleaded for her, she would die anyway. But I knew that Lavinia would die. Sometime in the future, whether it was by her hand, someone else's, or the hand of fate—even if she was a stranger to me then—I would have to watch her die.

I got up silently, muttered a goodnight to Grace, and made my way up the two flights of steps to my room. It was warmer up here, so I comfortably crawled into my bed. I curled up as close as I could to myself.

But the only thing I could think of was Lavinia's face. Her auburn hair, her hands, her grey eyes, and her smile. I hadn't touched her. I hadn't brushed her hand or swept her hair out of her face or even stroked her back to comfort her.

I wondered how much time we had. I wondered how much time I had to do those things I'd dreamt of. The feelings and sweat I craved. And then I realized something, just before the darkness swallowed me into a fitful sleep filled with blood and pain:

You'll have less time if you never tell her. And then who will really die first inside?

13

I SHOULD'VE STAYED IN BED

{ *Lavinia* }

Waking up the next morning proved itself difficult as I struggled to crawl out of bed.

I slammed the alarm clock on my bed stand and shouted at Anastasia, who was still fast asleep. I called out again, and while she groaned to turn around so her back was to me, she threw a pillow at my face. I threw it back at her.

She spoke groggily. "After twenty-six years it never ceases to amaze me how hard it is to get out of bed..."

I shook my head and laughed at her through my dry throat. I grabbed my water and chugged a few sips before making a trip to the bathroom with my toothbrush. Upon my return, Anastasia sat up in bed to avoid a reprimand. I gave her a warning glare and opened my dresser, pulling out jeans and a sweater.

I changed quickly and ran a brush through my straight hair as I walked back to the nightstand to hurriedly massage the lotion onto my face. Anastasia's soft hum floated behind me, and when I glanced around, she was rummaging through the bottom of our closet in an attempt to steal one of my leotards.

I chuckled under my breath and sat down on the edge of the bed. I pulled out my phone, checking messages from Sarvesh, Jesse, and a few from Grace. Mostly about homework. It seemed Jesse forgot his assignment for Monday, and since he already asked to copy Grace's unsuccessfully, he was now petitioning me.

I replied to him before unplugging my phone and sliding it into my back pocket. I waved goodbye to Anya and met a few other members of our team outside the hall. Saturdays were an outsource training day, where we would meet with our team and train or work in the "real world" for the day.

I hoped today would be a real mission, not something stupid. I itched to do something, to go somewhere. I hated staying home.

Home. I hated that too.

I managed to weasel my way into the first group down the elevator. Thankfully, Alek wasn't here. We had a terrible habit of using the elevator at the same time, which made for several awkward conversations.

Persephone and Parker had gotten up earlier than I did, and when I walked into the cafeteria, I spotted them at a table with three trays.

"Thanks, you guys," I breathed in relief, sitting down next to Parker.

"Of course," Persephone mumbled through a mouthful of food.

I glanced down at her near-empty tray and concluded from the half-eaten waffle and the cream cheese-covered knife that she had just finished scarfing down her bagel.

I widened my eyes at her food choices, to which she claimed defensively, "It's protein *and* dairy!"

"Yeah, Nia," Parker put in and gestured to my tray with toast, sausage, and a small bowl of fruit.

"You're not much better," I pointed out. "Eating cereal without milk."

He rolled his eyes, grumbled, and turned back to his large bowl of cereal. It was a curious mix of Lucky Charms and Cocoa Puffs.

Not like he needs more sugar, but whatever. It helps him focus.

I noted the two rings on one of his fingers; he normally only had one on each.

Parker sulked for a moment, and Persephone started chattering again before he joined in. I let them ramble, and while I tried to pay attention to them, my mind had other plans that involved a certain dark-haired, sarcastic friend and what he'd think if I told him who I really was.

If I told him, he'd know the truth and I'd never have to worry about it again, but if he got mad…And there would be nothing stopping Ivankov from getting rid of him. I wouldn't be able to do anything about it. Jesse might want nothing to do with me.

A sudden snap brought me out of my thoughts. I swallowed and realized that Parker was talking to me…again. Persephone giggled under her breath and shook her head. She grabbed the trays and stood up to put them away near the door.

Parker cleared his throat and waited for me to respond.

"I'm sorry, Parker," I said, trying to sound apologetic. "My mind drifted…What were you saying?"

"I was discussing the differences between Jesse and Liam, but you clearly don't want to know that I think Jesse has the nicer hair," he sassed with his sharp accent.

"Oh, *do* you, now? I don't know, the blond hair is growing on me…"

He stuck his tongue out at me. "Dark hair is better. Brings out the face!"

Parker got up from the table, so I snickered and lagged after him. Persephone stood by the door, arms crossed but smiling, and waited for me to pass her before she snatched my hand and swung by my side.

Parker led us to the parking garage, but before we stepped into the door, Persephone leaned closer to me.

"Are you gonna tell him?" she whispered.

Jesse. I wish.

Parker spun around and walked backward, yelling, "I can hear you!"

"So can we!" I stuck my tongue out. He rolled his eyes, turned around, and shoved open the heavy door.

I haven't decided yet, Perse. That's what I was thinking about instead of listening to Parker, I said telepathically.

She opened her mind in return, and as if on cue, Parker sighed. We knew that he didn't like not being able to do this with us, but I suspected the real reason was along the lines of him not knowing what went on.

Why not tell him? I think he'll understand, besides the whole "I was kidnapped as a kid by a secret organization that trains children into assassins and I got superpowers from a power plant explosion" thing.

My younger sister's sarcasm had never driven me crazier than at this moment. She was in the same situation I was whether she liked it or not, but I knew how terrible the consequences would really be.

When you say it like that, it's worse.

Oh, just tell him, Nia! What's the worst that could happen? He won't talk to you for the rest of the month and you'll never see him again?

She had no idea how bad that would be. I hated the truth—that I'd be gone forever, never seeing him again, never hearing him laugh again. I hated the thought. It scared me, really.

I chuckled inwardly at how pathetic I sounded. I barely knew the kid, and what I did know—well, I liked. But I didn't like him that much. Why was I so scared of leaving him behind?

I'm not that far gone, am I?

14

MASTERS

{ *Lavinia* }

"**A**gent Markov."

"Agent Pamuk." I rolled my eyes and faced the team members gathered in front of us in the common area.

"Everyone, meet Agent Lavinia Markov. She's a Master Manipulator, which I'm sure you've heard, and she's here today to teach you all a bit more about Masters. Lavinia?"

The ten young children in front of us stared with wide eyes. This was their first time on a team, and they were scared. I was too at their age. Several of them, I was sure, were Masters. But Ivankov didn't trust them until a later age to cultivate their powers, so I doubted they knew much about it. I was here to fix that.

"Well, like Agent Pamuk said, I'm a Master Manipulator. Manipulators are an Order that can manipulate different elements of the world to their will. Most often, as long as it has matter, it can be manipulated. Who here can think of an example of something I could manipulate?"

A girl raised her hand, and I nodded at her to speak. "The floor, but not the air.

Or wind or fire."

"Correct. But," I paused and took a step toward them. "I can manipulate what's in the air, such as sound or light waves, or even gas."

"Gas? Like—"

Before the boys in the group could laugh, I held up a finger. "Gas like butane. Not farts."

Too late. A few kids laughed softly, but I continued.

"Other Orders of Masters exist, obviously. There are new Orders being discovered every day, but common ones are Empathors, who can locate and sense someone based on their emotions. They're sensitive to emotions that Routines don't even realize."

"What about the rare kinds? Like Seers and Sensors?" a boy piped up.

"They aren't discovered very often. The process of Master creation is random and can't be predicted. Most often, Masters are found as children, and their powers were created by a surge of energy like a power plant exploding. That's how I got mine at six years old."

"Can you manipulate other things, outside of matter?" another girl asked. "The better a Manipulator is, the more they can control, right?"

"First off," I started, "Manipulators don't control. Every Manipulator has a limit to their powers. They can only use their powers to manipulate things around them, and the more power they have, the more they can manipulate."

"Oh," a few girls chorused.

"But to answer your question, yes. I can manipulate matter, memories, and thoughts. It's the highest Order of Manipulator there is."

Pamuk raised a dark eyebrow in fascination. I had a feeling that he didn't know I was of the Highest Order—or, at least, I would be because, until I turned eighteen, I wasn't considered a part of any Order, let alone my Destined Order. As I completed the training program and became a fully operating Master Agent within Ivankov, I would be given my Destined Order.

To some, including me, it was obvious what Order they would become. For others, it didn't come until much later when their powers were properly trained and used.

"Wait, so—" a short girl frowned. "The process is random? So there's no logic involved when two people go through, let's say, a gas fire explosion thing, and one dies while the other becomes a Master? There's no reason?"

"There is a reason, but it can't be predicted," I amended. "The very first Masters that were created are the ancestors of all Masters today. It's in our genetic code, but it's a recessive gene, and it can't be detected. Until someone interacts with something to trigger the gene, their Master powers and Order lie dormant. Some Master genes—and they're all different—can lie dormant for thousands of years, even when someone encounters a triggering event."

"So that's why there are still Routines? Because they don't carry the right stuff in their DNA?"

"Correct. That's also why different siblings can go through the same event and either have different Orders or not survive at all. Like my brother and sister. She's a Manipulator, but she doesn't carry the same genes I do; she can only manipulate matter and, if another Thought Manipulator begins the connection, read minds. My brother is an Empathor."

"But aren't they twins?" Pamuk prompted for the kids.

I smiled. "Unless it's a pair of identical twins, any relatives' Orders are going to be different. Many Masters are created by a triggering event and not by birth, since many Masters don't continue their line. But when a Master or two Masters have a child, they will have an Order from birth. They won't need a triggering event since their powers are already active."

"But if a Master and a Routine have a child, what happens then?" a boy asked.

"It depends on the child because of the recessive gene. Some will have powers from birth, and some won't. Any other questions?"

One of the boys closest to the front raised his hand politely, and I called on him. "What about the Unknown Masters?"

"Unknown Masters are the ones unapproved or undocumented by Ivankov. Next question."

"*Are* there Masters outside of Ivankov?"

"Very few. It's almost unheard of for one to escape once they're a part of Ivankov. If they leave and they're caught, they're shown no mercy for defecting."

Think you'll be the one to break that tradition? I thought bitterly to myself. I had been vowing since I was seven years old to escape Ivankov's clutches.

"Has the world ever come close to running out of Masters?" a girl asked.

"No. If there's a new Master to be found, Ivankov will find them. There's always more."

After a few silly questions, I was glad when I was asked, "What happens when a new Master is found as an adult? That's rarer, right?"

"Usually, because people encounter their trigger events at a young age. It's easier for their bodies to adapt and live through it. But it's not unprecedented that an adult Master is found and recruited by Ivankov. When agents turn eighteen, the ones that became Masters as children are assigned an Order and a Master of that Order to learn from. Until then, agents will have their in-team and handlers."

"Like how some of you," Pamuk jumped in, turning to the group, "will have a Master Mentor and some will only have handlers when you turn eighteen. I'll keep an eye out for you all before you turn the big eighteen."

I bit back a remark of how Routines are almost never as high of a rank as a Master is, but I remembered the Assassin. He was the best Routine killer Ivankov possessed; although there were Masters far more advanced than he was, both famous ones from history and those still of Unknown Rank, I knew I could be far more powerful than him.

I would just have to wait.

15

Maybe This Wasn't a Bad Idea

{ *Lavinia* }

I sat in geometry, restraining myself from screaming in frustration at proofing equations and angles.

I bit my lip, pondering over Persephone's echoing thoughts and then glancing over at Grace. She was tapping her pencil on the desk with her left hand and resting her chin in her right.

I had no idea how she would react to me telling the whole Ivankov ordeal to Jesse, so I thought it would be better for her not to know at all.

But what if I told her? She could give me advice on whether or not to tell Jesse, couldn't she?

While class labored on, I decided on telling her during study hall. That was after economics, which was after geometry. Hopefully, she wouldn't freak out and I could tell her without Jesse being too nearby. I sneaked out my phone and clicked on my messages with Persephone.

what do you have 11-11:30? i'm planning on telling grace during study hall that time but jesse also has that time for study hall. you wouldn't want to distract him, would you?

Within a few minutes, I felt the phone vibrate softly in my hand. Looking down at her message, I read it twice just to make sure I'd read it correctly.

me and parker both have biology. try to tell her before you get to study hall in that 10 minutes we have in between classes. me and parker can find him, and if he tries to get to you, we'll make an excuse and distract him in the halls before the bell rings. sound good?

good as it's gonna get, i guess… it'll be a close call

no closer than missions you've been on before lol remember that one time where you and anya had to go to a charity ball in las vegas and take down that sponsor? and you almost fell down those stairs bc you were distracting that one guy while wearing that red dress with the slit? that was entertaining

can we get back to the topic at hand? this is important to me, perse

sry about that. why are you telling grace anyway? why not just tell jesse and get it over with?

well if i tell her, maybe she could give me advice on how to tell jesse—if she thinks i should even tell him in the first place. who knows maybe she'll think that him and liam shouldn't know

yeahhhhhh abt liam not knowing…

you did not tell him persephone you better not have told him perse?

i'm not even that upset i just wish you would have told me!! well with you so worried abt telling jesse i just figured i would wait till you told him to tell you that i was telling liam, ya know?

sry about not saying anything

> *it's ok, perse. i don't mind*

okay

> *hey, now i actually gotta pay attention to geometry, so ttyl.*
>
> *love you!*

kay bye, love you! good luck

With that, I cleared the messaging app and shut off my phone, looking up at Mr. Woods. After he made an apparently humorless dad joke, Grace sighed. I turned my head to look at her and noticed she was looking at her phone and not the teacher.

I looked forward again as to not invade her privacy. "Who you textin'?" I whispered.

Her head snapped up, and she pushed her phone against her stomach while I heard the click of her power button. Still facing forward but leaning toward my desk, I slipped my phone into the pocket of my faded jeans. Grace copied my motions and resumed her fiddling with the end of her pastel yellow sweater.

She shrugged in response. "Nobody important, but I could ask you the same thing."

"Oh, that was just Persephone. She forgot something," I explained. *Which was true.*

Grace nodded and turned for a second to look at the clock in the back of the room. The rest of class was uneventful.

During economics, though, I began chewing my pencil in an effort to distract myself from Jesse in his desk beside me. He peered at me through the lovely hair that had fallen in his face.

He leaned sideways toward me. "You okay?" he whispered.

"Fine." I nodded and put the pencil down.

"You're sure?" His brown eyes were fixated on my face.

I wonder what he's thinking about me right now.

I resisted the urge to find out with my powers, but I swallowed hard and hoped he didn't notice my glance at his lips before I spoke again. "I'm fine, Jesse, just stressed out. Family stuff." *That's technically not a lie.*

"Okay."

{ *Jesse* }

"You're sure?" I asked her.

Lavinia didn't look fine, no matter what she told me. I kept my eyes on her clear grey ones for fear of them wandering. They had a mind of their own that I did not appreciate.

But the sharp line of her jaw and the arc of her neck tempted to distract me from her slightly upturned nose and the lines creasing her tense eyes. I gave myself an internal shake of reasoning and blinked.

Though it was only a small movement, I could have sworn her eyes looked somewhere farther down my face.

Wishful thinking, Jesse. Get over it.

"I'm fine, Jesse, just stressed out. Family stuff," she finally said. I could see her lie, but it wasn't worth pressing her.

She'll tell me when she's ready. At least, I hope she will.

I tried to divert my attention away from the curvy lines of her lips and the shine of her hair to the rest of the ongoing lecture.

At the end of class, Lavinia disappeared into the hallway before I could stop her. I made my way to the library, picked up a few books, and dropped some others off. I turned the corner and strode to the tables lined up along the wall.

Lavinia and Grace sat at the end of one of the tables with Lavinia's back to me. They were engrossed in deep conversation, and neither noticed as I approached. I caught only the last sentence, spoken by Lavinia.

"I just don't know how to tell Jesse, which is why I told you first."

I tensed at the mention of my name. *What isn't she telling me?*

"Tell me what?" I stopped walking when I reached the end of the table and glanced between the two girls. I set my bag on the table and swiped a piece of hair out of my face.

"Nothing, why do you ask?" Lavinia asked all too innocently.

I scoffed and met her eyes, furrowing my eyebrows. "Tell me *what*, Nia?"

It was one of the rarer times I used her nickname, although I wished I had the opportunity to do so more often without appearing…well, like I liked her.

I totally didn't.

"I don't know what you're talking about! I have nothing to say!" she exclaimed indignantly.

Wow. She's good.

Grace turned her eyes from me to Lavinia, giving her a harsh glance. "Yes, you do. He deserves to know as much as I do."

"I—" she started, but Grace had already gotten up from her chair, picked up her bag, and was shoving me into the seat.

I sat down with a thud and let my eyes meet Lavinia's. She was clearly angry, but the anxious pull of her eyebrows deepened when she gave her lips a single swipe with her tongue and pressed them together so tightly, they went pale.

While her reaction worried me, I couldn't deny the spark that her simple motion sent through me. I pondered for only a moment what she would do if I stood up and pulled her close to me.

Please kill me now.

"What is it, Lavinia? What do you have to tell me?"

I almost didn't want to know which secret she was about to disclose. How many of them would I never have the chance to know?

She opened her mouth to answer, paused, then shut it again. But she had a certain tenderness in her eyes, something I hoped I wasn't imagining.

I could stare at her for hours.

But I didn't have hours. And by her next statement, I wasn't sure I even had minutes.

"We're moving, Jesse. Moving away."

"I—" My brain slowed to a puddle. I shook my head rapidly, back and forth, trying to clear it.

She's moving away. She's leaving. She's leaving me. Lavinia is leaving me.

"It won't be for another three weeks."

"You just got here! You've been here, what, seven school days?" I snapped.

Lavinia's face was stunned at the outburst, and though it was nowhere near to how angry I could have gotten, that was the worst she'd seen me. I'd never been angry at her before, and I didn't want to start now. I was just…

"I'm sorry," I whispered, letting my eyes fall to the table.

"It's okay."

"No, it's not."

"Jesse—" Lavinia interrupted.

I put a hand up to stop her and met her eyes that had filled with tears. "It's not your fault, and I'm acting like it is. I'm sorry. I don't want you to leave."

"You—" She looked surprised, though I wasn't sure how much of that was a pleasant surprise or yet another lie she was telling me.

Lavinia cleared her throat. "Why, you'll miss me?"

Her eyes were playful now, and I wondered how she was able to hide her true emotions like that. I didn't imagine her near tears seconds ago.

Without a second thought, I nodded confidently. "Yes."

I disarmed her guard with that. I was glad. Lavinia's eyes fell again, and as she readjusted herself in her chair, a piece of hair dropped in her face. Before she could fix it, I reached across and tucked it behind her ear.

My hand hovered for a moment when our eyes nervously met. *If I wasn't obvious before, I am now.* I blinked once, withdrew my hand, and sat back in my chair.

"So…where are you moving to? Why?"

16

UNDER LOCK AND KEY

I sneaked around the large pillars and tried to be as quiet as possible.

I glanced around the marble and gold-interlaced column I was behind and spotted a familiar head of black hair. He was tip-toeing around and looking for me in particular.

I had snuck off just ten minutes ago from the movie night and found my one friend, the nurse—Taras Vackorev—in the library. He always spent his nights there when he wasn't in class in the hospital ward.

When I had arrived in the library, he spotted me and chased me out as fast as he could, abandoning his book. I squealed the whole way, leading him down the massive, curving staircase and into the large foyer at the back end of the building.

Throughout the foyer, connected to the intricately painted ceiling by thick arches, the marble pillars reached high with carvings along the full height of them. The floors were tiled white and dotted with black, and on the sides of some pillars sat red, cushioned armchairs and tall, potted plants—trees. At the opposite end that I ran through was a large archway, guarded by heavy, red velvet curtains draped *to the floor.*

Inside the archway through a step up was a room half the size of the foyer, lined with grey marley. Along the sides of the room were floor-to-ceiling mirrors and wooden barres that extended a foot or two away from the mirror. Across the entrance, lining the plain wall, were three large, open-glass windows. A big, black grand piano stood between two of the windows, closed.

I didn't need the curtains to be open to know what lay in that room. I had been in it often enough. I didn't know that this was where I'd led my friend.

I had run where my feet had taken me. I never got to have fun because I almost never had time outside of training. It was so enjoyable to let my thoughts run free and dream about what I could do when I finally escaped Madame.

Glancing once again around my pillar, I was met with a dark-skinned face full of joy with twinkling, green eyes and lips pulled into a smile.

"You found me!" I gasped.

He swept me up into his arms and plopped unceremoniously onto the velvet chair next to us.

His voice was soft, like always, and his accent was thick. "Of course I did, my dear. I always do." He winked.

We sat in silence for a while and enjoyed the dark. I stared up at the several glistening crystal chandeliers hanging from the dome ceiling. I opened my mouth but decided against words.

"What were you about to say, child?"

"Oh..." I whispered. "I was just wondering if you'd sing me a lullaby or a song."

"Of course, darling! Hm, let me think. Oh, I know just the one," he finished, bopping my nose with his strong finger. I giggled and snuggled farther into his arms to close my eyes.

His quiet voice sang out, "'The water is wide, I cannot get o'er, and neither have I wings to fly. Oh, go and get me some little boat. And both shall row, my love and I...'"

As the lullaby came to a close, I drifted off into a dreamless sleep. I woke up when I heard a buzzing sound and a voice yelling, "Anastasia! Get your butt out of bed!"

But I'm not in bed...?

I snapped my head up to meet the cold air of the reality that it was just a dream: a faint memory in 1989, when I was only seven. I promptly pelted a pillow at Lavinia's head and buried my face back in my pillow.

When she shouted again, I rolled over. "After twenty-six years, it never ceases to amaze me how hard it is to get out of bed…"

I heard her chuckling as she made her way out of the room, so I fell back on the bed and sighed. I ran my hands through my messy head of dark red hair. I had been having that dream every night for the past two weeks, and I hadn't told anyone. It was a nice dream, I supposed, but it made me reminisce about the fact that Taras probably didn't make it out of the Black Box. I was lucky enough to survive, and even now, I couldn't wait to just pick up the Markov siblings and get out of here.

As soon as Lavinia was done getting dressed, I got up out of bed and made my way to her closet. I searched for that one leotard with the cool straps that Madame let me wear.

Involuntarily, I started humming that song. I knew Lavinia glanced over at me, but I decided to ignore her. I could always make a run for it if she decided to chase after me and the leotard, which was now in my hand.

But I ignored her while she got ready. I caught a glimpse of her outfit when she ran out the door while saying goodbye, looking behind her shoulder. I spotted my reflection in the mirror across from our beds.

My hair was messy, and my eyes were sunken in from the few hours of sleep I managed to get. I turned to my own closet and pulled out my tights, leggings, and dance bag. I slipped off my pajamas and slid on the clothes before my white sneakers to make my way down to the ballet studio. The studio here was far less glamorous than the one I grew up in, but I strode over to the barre after ridding my feet of my sneakers.

I thought back to my dream as my mind wandered, beginning to stretch my legs.

17

FULL OF SURPRISES

"They could kill you if they wanted to. And…" I took a deep breath. "I'm not supposed to tell you any of these things. If they find out I did…" I waved my hand around aimlessly.

"What could they possibly want with a guy like me?"

"You'd be surprised," I chuckled wryly.

Jesse tilted his head and fiddled with the hair on the back of his neck. *I just want to—*

"What's that supposed to mean?"

"We got taken when I was six. *Six*. The twins were four. A factory had exploded behind our house, and when we'd play in the ruins, it…it gave us those powers. They wanted to *experiment* on us, Jesse."

His face grew still, and his leg stopped bouncing under the table as he blinked at me. His freckled nose had twitched at every terrible mention of what I'd gone through, and now—I could tell that he was fighting an uphill battle to control his anger.

But I needed to use that anger. He needed to know just how much danger he was in.

"They were willing to take kids and beat them into submission and torture them with needles to get what they wanted. You really think they'd stop at a family like yours?"

"But they can't hurt me here. They can hurt you," he chided, leaning forward. "None of this is normal! Like, at all. You're *living there*, in case you didn't realize."

He paused. "Who's Anastasia?"

"She's…well, she's another agent—our group's in-team. It's her job to supervise and mentor the younger agents to maintain Ivankov's ideals and standards. When she was my age, she went through the same thing. She's me. She had it worse, sure, but she's…she's been there for me when no one else has. And I've been there for her."

"I'm sure I'd love her."

"Why's that?"

"You said she was just like you." Jesse met my eyes. His gentle smile was lined with concern and some level of nervousness, but he held my gaze.

I stared at him, my mouth going dry. "Really?"

"Really, Lavinia."

My heart pounded inside my chest, and I willed it to still. My stomach dropped and filled with dread even though this was *exactly* what I wanted.

I looked up at Jesse, almost afraid of what I was about to do.

"Jesse…I know how much this means to you—to us—but—"

"Lavinia, I've waited forever for this. To feel this way. And I'm not going to let you doubt us. I'm not going to let you doubt yourself!"

I shook my head. "I can't. Please understand! I can't hurt you like this." I hated the desperation in my voice.

I moved to stand up, but Jesse grabbed my arms firmly to hold me in place as he rose to his full height. He glanced down to meet my eyes.

"Nia, I can't let you do this. I don't care if it leaves my heart broken in the end, we have to make this the best few weeks of our lives. You'll leave happy, at least! All your memories will be fond of us, but if you don't try, you'll just live with regret. I know you will. *Please…*"

Hardening my resolve, I tried to tear myself out of his hands. But his grip on my arms remained strong, and though I could've stormed away, exhaustion crept in.

I'm tired of fighting.

I shook my head, and my voice cracked. "You don't want to do this."

I wished I could wipe away the tears I felt coming, to be held by Anya as I pointlessly tried to erase my own memories, to go to bed and wake up tomorrow to all this being a dream. But it wasn't a dream. I knew that. I knew life wasn't fair and the hurt in Jesse's eyes was all too real. I tried using my powers to break free of his arms, but my emotions were already so drained. All that happened was a weak shimmer from my trembling hands.

In my final attempt to break away from him, he leaned closer until our noses were separated by only a thin stretch of air.

He spoke firmly with tears flowing. "I can't let *you* go too!"

I tightened my throat as the turning in my stomach increased. Hoping my way out of this would be helpless, but I fought myself. The ache to run away and hide was too strong. I didn't want to know whom else he had lost, whom he had "let go," and what mistake he had made that he didn't want to repeat with me.

Jesse's face gave away his struggle to let me go, and when our noses momentarily brushed against each other, a tear of his fell on my cheek.

I bit my lip and took a shaky breath. "Why not? I'm not worth that much to you, am I?" *I can't cry in front of him, I can't!*

Jesse pushed our noses together and whispered so quietly, I almost couldn't hear. "Because I love you. You *are* worth that much to me, promise."

A single tear escaped my eye.

"Prove it."

He smiled back at me and grazed our lips together, whispering, "Gladly."

He pressed his lips to mine with a hunger I didn't yet understand and slid his hands farther up my arms, almost at my shoulders, and I copied his motions. My lips parted, and Jesse pushed further as he tilted his head.

The angle was awkward with the table separating the space between us, and when he pulled away a second later, we both laughed at the distance. Jesse kept his eyes on me and dropped his arms to walk around the table to stand in front of me.

But it was a sweet kiss. A good kiss, as both of us apparently knew what we were doing.

"Does *that* convince you? Or do I need to do it again?" he teased.

My smile beamed, and I shrugged. Jesse scoffed and stepped closer to me.

Though he was trying hard not to laugh, he kissed me with a wide grin on his handsome face. This kiss was shorter and sweeter than the first, and when he pulled away, he held onto my waist.

"That one was convincing," I assured him, gazing up.

He shook his head and wrapped his arms around my back to give me a hug, so I snuggled into his chest. In sync, we both sighed deeply. Sharing a laugh, I pulled away enough to glance up at him.

I put my head back on his shoulder and mumbled my next words under my breath, hoping he'd still hear. "What happened to not letting me do this?"

"What was that?"

I looked back up at him. "Even *if* it can't last, we should still be happy. Good enough for you?"

"You just admitted I'm right! Of course it's good for me!"

I rolled my eyes and whispered, "Maybe we should get to studying?"

"Shy all of a sudden?" Jesse asked.

When I didn't respond, he squeezed me a little tighter, and his voice lowered. "Of course we can, baby."

"Say that again…"

"I can say it as many times as you'd like." He winked and leaned down to kiss me again, hard.

Damn, this boy is full of surprises.

18

SOMETHING GOOD, FOR ONCE

{ *Lavinia* }

All day after school, Persephone had been pestering me with whispers or nudges. She thought she could get an answer from me. I ignored her and replied to every text of Jesse's as fast as I could. I already had ideas on when to sneak out.

I padded softly on the carpet and swung my bag from my shoulders while I walked tiredly to my room. Training had exhausted me, but it was nothing a good shower and a nap couldn't fix. My existential exhaustion could wait until later tonight. Anastasia had returned to our room earlier, and Persephone and Parker had left just before me, so I was alone to make the long trek back.

I hoped the new base had a separate wing for our teams so I wouldn't have to walk what felt like miles back from the training rooms. But when I turned out of the elevator, I collided into a tall person and was knocked to the ground.

I hate being short.

Muttered annoyances escaped my lips as I pushed myself up, shook my head to clear it, and saw Alek in front of me. He wore a chastising expression on his sharp face, which suited him, but I inwardly chuckled at his unusual clumsiness.

"Yes?" I asked.

He stood, unmoving, and kept his eyes cast downward on my face.

What is he—?

"Oh, sorry." He snapped out of a trance. "I didn't see you there."

I rolled my eyes. "Clearly."

"I'll just, uh…" Alek moved around me to step into the elevator.

I stepped out of the way and watched the doors close, but at the last moment, I put my hands between them to hold it open.

"Where are you going? Training is done, and it's late."

I didn't need to use my powers to find out. His face was obvious enough—that and his hesitancy to react when he knocked me over were all the clues I needed.

"You're going to see her, aren't you?"

Viktoriya was on this floor, so it couldn't be her; I knew he didn't like blondes anyway. But he didn't know that I didn't know who it was. Maybe I'd get it out of him now.

Alek's only answer was a curt nod. I stared at him hard while the doors closed once more, only slightly mad at myself for not pressing further. But I let it go.

I forgot about whom Alek might be visiting and spending the night with when I reached our door. It was slightly open, but before my suspicions could be raised, sounds of laughter floated toward me. I pushed the door open, swung my bag to the floor, and came upon the sight of my sister and brother attempting to tackle Anya.

A chuckle escaped my lips as I closed the door and joined them, immediately helping them push Anastasia onto the bed. Through his laughter, Parker yelped at my presence, grinned, and pulled me off Anya to tickle me.

I screamed in surprise and moved him out of the way with my powers to tickle him, but Persephone pulled me back to the bed with her own telekinesis. I fell with a heavy thud next to Anya, and Perse left a gasping Parker to sit in front of me.

Parker recovered quickly and sat next to Persephone, though he wasn't happy with stopping the fun.

"We were having so much fun, Perse!" he exclaimed. "And you're the one who started the tickle fight, so why would you stop it?"

Anastasia's chuckles waned off when she faced us in skepticism.

"I wanted to play a game," Persephone protested as she winked at me. "Truth or dare!"

We all groaned at her announcement, Anastasia rolling her eyes. She fell back on the bed rather dramatically. "We're family, though, we already know the answers!"

Parker shrugged. "It's better than failing to tackle you."

"My turn first, then!" Persephone shouted excitedly. "Lavinia. Truth or dare?"

I chose dare, and Perse's eyes hardened in concentration.

I know exactly what you want, Persephone. For me to tell them.

She smiled at me sweetly in thinly veiled sarcasm.

"I dare you to FaceTime Jesse right now and tell him we're moving tomorrow," she stated.

Anastasia let out an exasperated sigh. "Persephone-Willow…" she warned.

I bit my lip while Persephone continued. "Or you could tell him when we're *really* leaving."

Parker's lips drew into a frown, and Anastasia narrowed her eyes. I pulled out my phone and was about to dial him, but I stopped and made eye contact with Persephone.

"And what if I already have?" I said slowly.

Anastasia's head whipped around to face me, and Parker stayed silent.

"You told him?" she asked, incredulous. She lowered her voice in case anyone was in the halls. "What about Grace? Do you realize they could be *killed* if anyone here found out they knew? Apparently you don't even care about their safety. Why would you tell them?"

I grabbed her hand and tried to be as reassuring as possible. "Calm down, Anya. I know that they're in danger, but I already made that decision. I've told both of them, and they're both okay with it…"

Perse was about to burst with information, but I didn't think I wanted to know whether or not she had listened to our conversation.

"What about Liam, does he know?" Parker asked.

Now it was her turn to get flustered, and she glanced at me curiously. I shook my head.

She got herself into this mess.

"Well…he reacted the same way Jesse did," she explained with a smirk. Anya closed her eyes and muttered something under her breath.

"Which was how, exactly?" Parker deadpanned.

"With encouraging words and actions. Which involved mouths," I quipped.

Persephone's mouth dropped at my bluntness, but it soon turned into a giggle when Parker's and Anastasia's own mouths went agape. I burst out laughing with her and fell back on the bed.

Anya sat up in surprise. Parker sat with his fingers pressed to his temples, a sigh escaping his lips. I continued to smile at Persephone and jumped up off the bed. I snatched the items I'd need for my shower, fiddling with the ends of Jesse's sweatshirt I was wearing, and left them to their own devices.

My heart warmed in memory of Jesse's and my earlier moments and what we could be. What could happen. I had had enough doubt the past few weeks, and I was tired of thinking of the dangers ahead of us. I would enjoy the present for as long as I could.

Because I love you.

What's the worst that could come of us?

19

WORTH THE PAIN

I woke up to the sun shining brightly in my eyes.

I sighed and realized that I forgot to shut the blinds last night—and our windows faced the east. I closed my eyes and groaned to myself, moving to roll over, but I sensed someone next to me.

What the—?

Parker was fast asleep with his arm curled around my side, and his head was buried in the pillows near my neck. He mumbled in his sleep and shifted away from me, which left me free to get out of bed without disturbing him.

I smiled at what I could see of his peaceful, sleeping face. I remembered how, in the middle of the night, I'd woken up to the smell of something burning. I wasn't sure if I had imagined it, but in the dark, I could see Parker pacing back and forth. When he realized I was awake, he tugged down his sleeves and got back into bed.

"Didn't mean to wake you," he mumbled.

"No, it's okay." I beckoned him over to my bed. "C'mere."

Parker got up from his bed, crawled into mine, and settled next to me.

"What woke you?" I whispered.

"Nightmare."

I nodded and smoothed his wild hair until his breathing evened. Once he had fallen asleep, I'd turned over and did the same.

I finished in the bathroom, ignoring the few team members I saw in the hall, and returned to my side of the bed. Parker was now sitting up and blinking the sleep out of his eyes.

"Good morning," I greeted.

He hummed and rubbed his eyes. "How'd you sleep?"

"Well enough."

I didn't bother to ask him in return; he wouldn't answer me. So I got a change of clothes and my toothbrush and returned to the bathroom, forgetting all about last night.

♦ ♦ ♦

"Good morning, Markovs!" Liam greeted cheerfully outside the world history classroom.

Parker nodded in response and went inside, leaving the two of us standing alone. Liam raised a blond eyebrow and jutted a thumb in Parker's direction.

"What's up with him?"

"Ignore it." I shook my head. "He's never a morning person."

"Oh, that's fine," he smiled widely, "I like you better anyway."

I rolled my eyes. "Stop being so cheesy."

Liam let out a loud laugh and leaned closer to me. "But you like being cheesy!"

"No, Liam. I like you," I corrected. "Not being cheesy. There's a difference."

"There's no difference to me, sweetheart." He touched his forehead to mine.

We laughed at each other, and he reached out to squeeze my hand before pecking my lips. The bell rang at the exact moment he withdrew, and our eyes rolled in sync.

"After you." He reached for the door and waved me inside.

♦ Lavinia ♦

"If I fail the sparring on purpose, then…" I whispered, "they'll hurt me *and* my siblings. They don't deserve any of this. I can take it, but what—what if they never make it out of there?"

I curled my legs into a crisscross position on the library couch and nestled my head into Jesse's shoulder. He let his chin rest on me.

"They're a lot stronger than you realize, honey. You've taught them everything you know from being outside Ivankov. When they get sent on missions with your team, they'll do fine. You made sure of that, didn't you?"

I sighed and hesitated. "I just wish I could take it all for them."

"You already are, as much as you can," he pointed out.

I let out a heavy breath and closed my eyes, deeply breathing in the scent he carried. I remembered his confession three days ago, and I realized I had never told him in return that he was worth everything to me too—that I love him. I had known him for almost two weeks, and I had fallen in love with him.

I haven't even let myself believe it. How am I supposed to tell him that—?

"You know, we're having a Halloween party at my house next week," Jesse started. "It's a decade theme. Grace is very proud of the whole shebang; she's wearing a 1940's Army uniform. She has badges and everything."

"I'd love to come, but…I mean, I've gotten out a few times, but not for most of the night. It was only for an hour or two."

"The party won't last too long! It starts at 5:00, and Anastasia can tell you if people realize you're gone—you can leave whenever you want."

I waited for a moment before he smirked.

"We're having taco salad."

"Yes," I hissed under my breath. "I'll come up with a plan."

Jesse grinned in satisfaction and leaned down to reach my face, pressing his lips into mine for a brief kiss.

"Are you two ever going to *study* during study hall?" a new voice asked from in front of us. I turned my head to see Grace standing in front of the couch with her hands on her hips and bag slung on her shoulder.

"I finished my homework last night!" I defended.

Jesse laughed, his chest reverberating underneath me. Grace rolled her eyes and walked past us, but not before giving her brother a dirty look. Jesse turned back to face me, and I smiled up at him.

"You know something?" he asked.

"What?"

"It's impossible to find someone who won't hurt you." He paused. "But some people are worth it. Like you."

I stared at him, not in shock, but in surprise.

He thinks I'm worth all this pain? All of it?

"I want you to know that I won't regret what we've done here. I promise you I won't regret this. Remember that, Lavinia."

I set my resolve, reached for his hand, and intertwined my cold fingers with his. Despite the sweatshirt he was wearing, the one I had borrowed, he wasn't doing a very good job of warming me up.

A few moments passed before I spoke up. "When the twins got older—maybe seven or eight years old—they would ask me to promise them that everything would be okay. That we'd see our parents again. But I never promised them anything because even though I wanted to, I knew that fate didn't care about any of that."

"Who said anything about fate?" he asked with a questioning stare. "I've defied the odds before."

"But, Jesse, I—" I looked to the floor and closed my eyes.

Maybe it would hurt less to say if I didn't have to look at him. "Ivankov has far more power over me than fate does. I'll remember the promise, but you don't have to. You deserve to live your life as much as I do."

Jesse took a deep breath. "I don't want to deal with this until it actually comes."

"You've got a little over two weeks for that, sweetheart."

Jesse winked and began to lean down. "Good."

"Jesse!"

We both drew back from each other and turned, surprised, only to see Grace standing in front of the couch again.

"What?" he asked impatiently.

"Don't forget about the project due tomorrow," she warned.

"I won't! Nijaz is coming over this afternoon, I'll do it then."

"Good." Grace began to walk away.

"Ignore her," Jesse mumbled, close against my lips.

I smiled, which he took as further permission, and our lips met again. I pulled away after a moment, his brows furrowing in mild disappointment. But I conceded and slid one cold hand underneath his sweater, onto his torso.

I tilted my face upward to get a better view of his surprised and handsome features. "If I *can* come, what should I wear?"

"Well—" Jesse faltered and broke eye contact.

I struggled not to laugh at his blank face, so I moved my hand farther up his body until it reached his chest and stopped. When I looked back at him, his brown eyes were trained on my face with an expression I could not read.

Jesse swallowed once. "I'm wearing an old suit of my grandfather's with a thrifted hat and pocket watch. Grace told me it was Depression era fashion."

"Oh?"

"Yes, 'oh,'" he said. I grinned in return, to which Jesse tilted his head back and let his lips part. "Do you have a dress for that time period, dear?"

"I think I do, darling," I replied passively, starting to move my hand that was on his chest.

"You know…" Jesse paused and stood up.

"Excuse m—" I protested, my hand growing cold again. But he didn't let me finish and grasped both my hands to pull me off the couch, our faces now inches away from each other.

"The library really isn't the best place for this kind of thing," he mused.

"Oh? Where else do you propose we argue?" I replied sassily.

"I might know a place."

"Really?"

"Mm-hmm," Jesse hummed, "I do."

A second passed, and at that, he dropped one of my hands and walked us out of the library. I let my eyes stay on his face, studying his freckles. Jesse lifted an eyebrow.

"I still think you look better in this." He gestured to his sweatshirt with his free hand.

"I think so too," was my smiling reply.

Once we passed the door, he glanced at me. "And I remember practicing how to ask you out in the mirror."

"You did?" I asked before reaching a hand over to fix his hair.

"Yup. I did. Turns out I didn't have to—I couldn't let you doubt yourself and think you weren't enough. And I really wanted to hold your hand again."

ADMISSION

{ Parker }

I gently retreated from Persephone's arms and softened my gaze at the hair that fell in her eyes.

Earlier tonight, we had fallen asleep studying. Well, I say studying—more like a pen-throwing war that ended when she told me about the Prices' Halloween party. It was only 10:30—*Sarvesh will still be awake.*

I crept silently across the room and opened the door, sparing only a glance back toward my sister, who was still sound asleep on the bed. My socks padded quietly on the hall carpet, and when I came to a stop in front of the familiar door, I reached out and rapped a small knock with my right hand; it had no knuckle rings.

Footsteps sounded behind the door before it creaked open. A head of black hair peeped out from behind it, smiling.

"Back for another visit, huh? What'd you do to distract Persephone this time?" Sarvesh asked and opened the door farther, allowing me to step inside.

I laughed. "We fell asleep doing homework, and when I woke up, I remembered I had something to ask you."

"And what would that be?" he asked, facing me as he closed the door.

He was interrupted by a certain feline rubbing against my legs. I clicked my tongue at Tigger and reached down to pet him while he purred.

"It's kind of a big favor, actually."

He cocked his head, but the only sound made was an attention-seeking meow from Tigger. Sarvesh scooped him up and murmured to the young cat, petting him.

Sarvesh looked at me again. "What kind of a big favor?"

I shifted my feet and decided to tell the whole story. "Well…"

♦ ♦ ♦

"So, where exactly do I come in?"

"I need your help to distract whoever we need to get them out without being noticed Thursday night. They're planning to be there at 5:00, so right after training, they'll get ready and leave. Our job is to make sure no one sees them."

Sarvesh leaned to the side and scratched his chin. "You're not going?"

"Nope. You know how I hate parties." *They're too loud.*

"Hmm, yeah. What about Anastasia?" Sarvesh asked skeptically.

I could tell his wheels were turning; if Anastasia didn't agree, there was no hope of them sneaking out. If she wasn't completely opposed, how would she react? Could someone convince her?

I adjusted my legs to fold comfortably underneath me. "I think Lavinia's telling her right now—and convincing her it's not a bad idea. And convincing her to help them sneak out."

"That seems like an awful lot of convincing…" he mused.

"Yeah, but they're best friends. If anyone can convince Anya of anything, it's Lavinia."

"All right. So…what's the plan?"

♦ ♦ ♦

Persephone sat fully awake on the bed, pouring over her textbook. When I entered, her head snapped up to glare at me.

"Where were you?" Before I could get a word in, she spoke again. "Certainly not finishing your homework."

I sat down on the bed, and not one moment later, Anastasia and Lavinia burst through our door without so much as a knock.

"Perse! Why did I have to hear it from Lavinia that you were invited to Liam's party? Parker, why haven't you asked me about a plan for getting them out?"

Neither of my sisters responded to her grilling, so I chuckled at Anya, and Lavinia rolled her eyes in a typical fashion.

"Because Sarvesh and I came up with a plan of our own."

"What plan is that, exactly?" Anastasia's eyes narrowed, and her hands moved to rest on her slanted hips.

{ Lavinia }

I listened intently to Parker's plan and watched Anastasia's reaction. She seemed to like the idea so far, and so did I. Persephone was paying equal attention as we were, though it seemed something was arguing for her attention elsewhere.

An idea popped into my head, so I zoned out of the discussion and created a connection between Persephone and me.

What do you think of the plan?

I wasn't listening to much of it. I was thinking about them.

I knew exactly whom she was talking about and let my lips curl skyward. *I'm sure they'll be fine, Perse. Once they know we're coming, they'll probably both faint.*

Not them. Her clear blue eyes were now cast downward away from Parker and Anastasia's conversation. *What do you think happened to our parents after the agent took us? What do you think happened to the agent? Did the agent have to kill them…?*

I shifted uncomfortably in response. I was always supposed to be the big sister, the one with all the reliable advice. But right now, I didn't know the answers. At least, not the answers I wanted to know.

"Hello?" Anastasia's voice rang out. "Did either of you hear any of that plan?"

I nodded, though I was sure the two of them saw straight through me. Persephone mumbled an answer and got off the bed, stuffing items into her backpack. Anastasia gave me a questioning stare, but I had to shrug.

I'll talk to her later, I thought inside Anya's head. I said goodbye to the twins and walked out the door to my room. Anya followed in unusual but comfortable silence.

I heaved a sigh and planted facedown onto my bed, kicking off my shoes.

111

Anastasia chuckled, flopped down next to me, and propped her head up with her slender hand.

I didn't care that I had work to do and she didn't care that she had a meeting in a little while. All we cared about was this moment of comfort and love, and we gratefully welcomed life's reprieve in silence.

"How did he take it?" she whispered.

Though it had been a total of eight days since I told Jesse everything and eighteen days since I met him—not that anyone's counting, of course—she hadn't asked me about it since her initial reaction. I had inferred that she was either upset and didn't want to discuss it, or if she did, she would ask whenever she was ready. And now she was ready.

I took a deep breath into the thick comforter—*I wish I were under it and asleep right now*—and turned my head to face her. Her gentle, green eyes bore down into mine, and in the dim lighting of the room, her dark red hair cast shadows over her jawline and chiseled cheekbones.

"He didn't understand at first, but when he did, it was…"

Anastasia adjusted her position, motioning me to continue.

"He was mad. Very, very mad."

"At you?" was her surprised reaction.

"No, not exactly. Well—sort of. More like mad for me, on my behalf. Here I was, sitting in front of him, opening up about everything that's ever gone wrong in my life, and because he cares about me, he…he's angry."

Anastasia scanned my face and pursed her lips. "He doesn't want you to hurt."

"No, he doesn't."

"But what *was* he mad at you for?"

"Not me specifically, just mad that I had 'let' myself and the twins go through that…even though that's not exactly what he meant," I amended.

"He better not have."

Her feigned mad expression brought a chuckle out of me, which cracked her façade and allowed the sparkles in her eyes to dance.

"No, he didn't. But he needed a target for what he was feeling, and I was the victim. He got over it soon enough."

"And then?"

"He didn't think they'd want to get rid of him and his family now that they knew. He asked what they could possibly want with a guy like him."

"You told him, right?" She gave a wry chuckle.

"Of course." I turned on my back, sliding my hands underneath my head. "Then he realized how grave it was—how much danger he was in."

"How much did you tell him about that?"

I let a beat pass. "I told him that they stopped at nothing to get what they wanted from us," I started numbly. "It started with kidnapping, then torturing, beating, and experimenting on us. That Fridays were the worst."

"Nia," Anastasia started.

"No, Anya, it's okay. I love him, and I want him to know these things about me."

Her face was one of calm surprise, like she'd expected it to come—but not at this moment. I refused the urge to bite my lip and instead focused on drawing shapes on the ceiling with my eyes to keep focus.

"You love him."

"Yeah. I do."

"You haven't admitted it to yourself before now, have you?"

I don't think we need to answer that.

I took a deep breath. "No matter how painful it is, those things are a part of who I am. He needs to know that I'm not untouched, that I've survived because I've needed to."

"But why tell him *how* you've survived? Surely the details are—"

"Because I'm still ashamed of it." I faced her. "I'm still ashamed of how much I've hurt and how I've had to survive. I don't have to tell you that."

She gazed at me kindly and swept a piece of hair over her shoulder. My eyes were full of pain, but I knew she would see the love I was trying to let overcome me. I was used to hurting, and now that I was filled with this strong of a love…I wasn't about to let it go.

I wasn't going to let it break me.

"I've survived long enough, Anya, and just now—*just* now—does it feel worth it. Just now it feels like I'm really living. Even if it's a lie."

After realizing the burning behind my eyes was tears, I sniffled and attempted to swallow the lump in my throat. But Anastasia reached out a hand to cradle my face and gently turned it to face her. I met her eyes slowly, and the feelings swelled inside me once more.

"You don't have to worry, Nia. I'm going to be here as long as you need me."

Her voice was low and soothing, and I couldn't help but think what a wonderful mother she would make…if she could have children.

But that was yet another thing taken from us in Ivankov. It would only be two more years and all the girls my age on the team would be deprived of that temptation of distraction.

I choked out a sniffle and buried my face in her shoulder. "I can't get by with just you and the twins. I need someone to give my love to. God knows I have so much to give…"

21

GOOD PLAN

Rushing back into my room after training, I opened my closet door wide.

I pulled out my black heels and a pair of nylons, and once I took off my leggings, I put the tights and shoes on. Anastasia said she would leave the dress on the bed—sure enough, when I turned around, the pearled, purple flapper dress was on its hanger, draped over the sheets.

I flew the dress over me. My mind wandered back to yesterday, when I told Jesse of our plans to come to the party. Although, I had to admit to myself that he was more excited about what I told him I had planned to wear than of my presence.

Stop thinking about him, Lavinia, I chided. *Just think about getting ready so you can do Persephone's makeup.*

Anastasia and Persephone had gone back to the twins' room to complete my sister's hair while I got dressed. Once we were both finished, makeup work would commence.

I reached behind me and, with some level of difficulty, zipped the dress all the way. I reached into the closet and found the clothing and large, black hair bow for

Persephone's '50s costume.

I stood up at the sound of the lock mechanism whirring in the door. A small chirp sounded from the hall, and Anastasia entered, peering in to check on me. Upon catching a glimpse of my full costume, she smiled widely.

"You look lovely, Nia."

I smiled in return and self-consciously smoothed the fabric around my sides.

"You've seen far more extravagant gowns than this, Anya."

"Yes," she mused, meeting my eyes again. "But you wear the dress. Not the other way around with so many other agents."

I quietly thanked her, turned, and stepped to the dresser, pulling out jewelry. Anastasia walked to stand behind me and took her string of diamonds.

While I put in the earrings and slid the rings onto my fingers, she put the necklace around my neck. She delicately swept my hair out of the way to clasp the ends together. Once my hair swung down my back, I reached for a sparkling barrette and handed it to Anya. She wordlessly fixed my hair into the clip at the nape of my neck.

I noticed the red color painted on her trimmed fingernails. "Is that my nail polish?"

"Yes," she said unapologetically.

I shook my head. "I like it on you. You should wear that color more often."

"I would, but I like black better. Besides, red clashes with my hair," she stated matter-of-factly, giving me a shrug of sarcastic dismissal.

Before I could insist that she looked ravishing in any color, a rap sounded on the door. I accepted the unlock request on the indoor keypad and opened it to reveal Persephone, who waltzed past me.

She spun proudly and showed off her high ponytail—Anastasia had curled a piece of hair around the base. I complimented my sister and shooed her toward where her costume was lying, urging her to get changed. She did so, but not without sending me a fake pout.

Just as Anya and I finished the buttons on the back of Persephone's dress, a short knock sounded on the door. Once I opened it, Parker stepped inside.

"Almost ready?"

"Almost," I replied quickly before guiding Persephone to sit at the end of the bed.

Parker closed the door and crossed the room to sit on the small couch, trying to look bored with our feminine proceedings. He wasn't fooling anyone—no matter what we were doing, even if it involved face masks, he enjoyed being with us as much as he hated Alek.

Which was a lot.

Persephone's face was soon made up with blush and bright pink lipstick, and thankfully, I had picked a costume where not much makeup was required. I enjoyed applying makeup to Perse or Anya much more than I did to myself.

But mascara, eyebrow filler, two shades of eyeshadow, and a tinted moisturizer didn't take long to apply; once I was finished, I picked up my small bag and dropped the rest of my lipstick into it. Anastasia silently placed my phone inside the purse.

"Let's get ready to rock and roll," I announced to my family.

Parker rolled his eyes. "Wrong decade," he muttered under his breath when he strode by.

The rest of us smiled, and Persephone and I left the room after Anastasia. After unlocking it two different times to avoid detection, our group passed through our common room and into the outdoor hall that overlooked the indoor courtyard. Parker and Anastasia went one way, and Persephone and I went the other.

After we hadn't paid attention to the first explanation of the plan, both they and Sarvesh had refused to give us more details. We were only instructed to make contact at certain points when exiting and entering the property.

I held my head high as normal and glanced at a nervous Persephone.

"If you act like you're supposed to be here, you probably won't get caught. Confidence is key," I reminded her in a whisper.

"But the costumes—"

They think we're going to a dress rehearsal for the Halloween school show, I sent her.

Persephone nodded in reply and straightened her posture, clasping her hands on top of her wide and fluffy skirt. She had never been on a mission without Higgins before, and although this wasn't a mission, our goal was to *not* get caught.

Despite only knowing our part of the plan, I was calm when we traveled down the elevator and made our way to the parking garage. I trusted the other three to do their job, and since the halls were eerily empty, I knew they had succeeded. Before we could push the garage door open, two agents turned the corner in the hall.

I flicked a hand and used the air around us to conceal our presence as they passed us. Persephone and I pressed each other against the wall and held our breaths until they were out of sight. I let our camouflage fall with a sigh of relief and glanced at a nearby camera.

I turned, satisfied, having not heard a beep from the camera that would have signaled me to erase its recent record. I trusted Sarvesh to expunge it without my help and creaked open the garage doors. We treaded down the steps and found the car I had decided to steal.

Technically, it's borrowing. I'm returning it.

I reached out a hand and let my powers glow into the lock mechanism. Once the door popped open, I reached inside and unlocked the passenger one for Persephone. We both climbed in, careful to not rumple our costumes, and I reached my powers into the ignition as far as it would go with a finger.

"Good job," Persephone said proudly when the car started.

I smirked in response, well aware I had done worse with my gifts, and put the car into drive. We veered out of the parking garage and through the automatic gate, to which I thanked Sarvesh silently.

It only took us twenty minutes to reach the driveway. Though I had been here before, I marveled at the grandness of the Prices' house. The long stretch of pavement connecting to their garage allowed for a closer view of the side.

I stopped the car and mimicked the motion of putting keys in my purse in case anyone was watching when we both stepped out. The Victorian-style house was painted a crème color, complete with dark blue trim and shutters.

The main two floors were of equal proportion to each other, but the third and final floor was the size of a single room. That room was the only one with the curtains open, and peering through it, I discovered a familiar freckled face waving back down to me. *Jesse.*

Persephone skipped to the white steps in front of the large front door, and as I walked up behind her, I let the smile linger on my face. The setting sun was casting a warm and welcoming glow on this side of the house.

A shout sounded somewhere inside, and not a moment later, Grace's voice rang out to one—or both—of her brothers.

"Just open the door, you idiot! You look fine!"

I reached past my sister and opened the door myself, speaking loudly to the siblings inside, "I heard that!"

Jesse opened the door completely to allow both of us to step inside. We all greeted each other, exchanging hugs. I surveyed the inside of the house out of habit, though I was familiar with the floor plan already.

But Persephone took in the space, smiling at the house—to her left was the kitchen and dining area, and next to the fridge on the far side of the room lay the entrance to the stairway. Inside the dining room at the far side of the house, through an arched opening, lay a dark oak table, and atop it sat trays of food, dip, and drinks for the party.

"Let me take those, girls." Grace gestured to our purses.

We handed them to her, and she turned to place them on a shelf next to the door.

The walls were decorated tastefully with pieces of artwork, mostly sketches of people. The frames reminded me to ask who the artist was, but Persephone spoke before I could.

"Nice artwork," she commented, gazing around.

"Thank Jesse," Liam said. His arm was slung around my sister's shoulders in a casual gesture, but it meant much more than that to Persephone. Her wide eyes and parted lips focused on Liam while he talked.

"You draw?" I turned to the dark-haired boy standing next to Grace, only a few feet away from me. I was playing it cool, but really, I wanted to run over and hug him again.

"A little," was his shy reply, but a smile crept onto his face. I looked at him through my lashes and sent him a look that said, *I will find out later.*

Grace rolled her eyes, stalked back to the kitchen, and motioned us all to follow. Her heels sounded quietly on the carpet, then clicked on the wood floor before she reached the tile of the kitchen. Her curves were fitted into a vintage, olive green Army uniform; a white blouse and black tie rested under the jacket; and a small hairpiece sat atop her bun of unruly hair.

She began resuming her work at the large island. After Jesse stepped beside me and slid an arm across my waist, we lingered behind Persephone and Liam while they followed Grace.

"You look nice," Jesse whispered into my hair before pressing a kiss to the top of my head.

I gazed up at him and said softly, "Thank you."

"Welcome." Jesse's brown eyes flickered over my figure. I was thankful for the high neckline for once in my life. Only for his further torture, though.

Told you he was more excited about the outfit.

But when I leaned forward to press a kiss to his soft lips, I only had to reach a couple of inches.

I love heels…

Jesse's hand around my waist tightened momentarily while he returned the kiss before releasing me back to my normal height. I patted his suit-coated chest once, stepping around the counter and sliding up to Grace. Jesse took a seat next to my sister and Liam at the island counter stools.

"Can I help?"

"Oh, sure! Here." Grace handed me a few containers of cheese blocks and a knife. I took it, opened the first block, put it on the cutting board, and began to slice it.

I ignored what I knew to be Jesse's stare on me and kept my attention on Grace. Her jacket had several shiny badges pinned to its lapel.

"Cheese is cheaper to buy like that, but the downside is that you have to cut it yourself," she said as she turned to the stove momentarily.

I nodded along and listened to Persephone and Liam's growing conversation about cheese, not failing to realize Jesse's silence. I chuckled softly to myself at his apparent focus targeting me.

"Where did you get your badges?" I asked Grace, a short strand of her brown hair falling to her face as she came to stand beside me again.

"Our dad was in the service; he gave them to me," she noted with a glance in my direction.

"Thank him for me." I smiled, and Grace nodded.

"What does he do now?" Persephone interjected.

"Oh, he still works for them," Liam said. "We don't know exactly what it is he does."

"Ah," I remarked, moving on to the next block of cheese. *Cheddar. My favorite.* I sneaked a small slice into my mouth, and out of habit, my gaze found its way back to Jesse.

Though he wasn't surprised to catch me sneaking cheese, he sent me a scolding look before pausing. Then, when the conversation resumed with the rest of the group, he wiggled a finger to gesture what he was asking.

I sliced another piece—thicker this time—and tossed it in a smooth arc across the island counter, landing it accurately in the palm of his outstretched hand.

We shared a small chuckle and grew quiet, now attempting to pay attention to Persephone's chattering. Neither of us were very successful. I finished chopping the cheese, and Grace slid a plate for me to arrange it on. The vegetables looked neat on her tray, so I copied the pattern as best I could.

Just as I placed the last piece of cheese on the plate, Jesse rose from his stool and took a step forward to stand beside me. He bounced on his heels impatiently, and I looked up at him with an eyebrow cocked in confusion.

"I want to show you something," he said, softly enough for only me to hear.

"And?" I huffed before handing the tray to Grace's side of the counter.

"It's upstairs."

"Do I hear a question in that, dear?"

"Can I show you something upstairs?" He sighed and rolled his eyes.

I snorted through my nose and complied, letting him take my hand. "Yes."

22

FINISHING THIS LATER

{ *Lavinia* }

"**Y**es."

Jesse beamed in excitement and pulled me away from the kitchen and up the stairs. The pieces of wood creaked slightly under our weight, filling the silence while I trailed behind him, still hand in hand.

"This is the second floor," he said in a dull announcer voice. He decided to give me a tour just for fun, despite my having been in the house on a few separate occasions.

My lips cracked into a smile as I followed the sweeping motion of his free hand to see the wide landing.

"Yes, this is nice," I noted, dropping his hand. I strode across the room to the circular turret and ran one of my hands along the soft chairs overlooking the side yard.

"Impressed yet?" came his low voice behind me before his arms wrapped around my upper body. I leaned comfortably into his embrace and tilted my head backward to see his face gazing down at me.

"Always."

The lines around his eyes creased with the upturn of his lips; he attempted to reach far enough to kiss mine. But my head couldn't angle that far backward, so his chin collided with the top of my head, sending us both into fits of giggles.

"Are you—?" I barked out a laugh and couldn't finish. I turned around to face him, and at the sound of his loud laugh, my breath hitched again in my throat.

"Are you okay—?" I tried again.

"I'm"—another laugh—"fine, honey."

Smiles danced on our bright faces when he stole my hands again and leaned down to kiss me—and he was successful this time. Possibly too successful. Our lips parted, as we were still smiling too hard to focus on kissing.

"What was it you wanted to show me again?"

"Oh." He remembered something. "Up here."

Jesse dropped one of my hands and led me out of the hallway into another set of stairs that I knew led into the third floor—his bedroom—that I hadn't been to before. The ceiling opened in the center of the room, and the setting sun's rays shone through his skylight onto our bodies and across the dark floor.

I remained close to Jesse's side, still clasping his hand, and noticed the rest of the furniture against the light grey walls. A desk covered in papers and mason jars filled with brushes, pens, and pencils stood on the far wall among frames propped up on the floor.

On the same wall lay a dresser and a small coat rack; the opposite wall held Jesse's bed, covered in white and grey pillows. My head stopped swiveling and came to rest on him again. It came as no surprise to me when his eyes were fixed upon my face.

"Still impressed?" His face was purposefully nonchalant, but I knew how much appearances mattered to him, especially neatness. And his room was certainly not neat.

"Always." A smile grew on my face.

Jesse's free hand rested on the dip of my back and gently pulled me close to him. Our lips found each other in a matter of seconds, and we settled into a comfortable rhythm while his fingers moved to pleat the fabric of my dress.

My eyes opened occasionally to meet his trusting gaze. While the sun shone across his hair through the skylight, my eyes traveled to track its movement.

"Dinner's ready!" Grace shouted from downstairs after a few moments, though it was distant enough that I wasn't sure if she was on the stairs or still in the kitchen.

Jesse slowly peeled away and stared down at me regretfully.

"She's at the top of the stairs—" I stared in wonder at his accuracy, to which he continued, "She's done this before."

"Oh?" My tone shifted.

"Well, not with—you know," he stammered.

"I do?"

"Yeah, I mean…" Jesse trailed off.

"I haven't been the only one—"

A flush spread across his cheeks, unaware I was baiting him. "No, I mean she yells up the stairs all the time, so now I know—"

He let a beat pass and stared at me, narrowed his eyes, and sighed.

"You're kidding me, aren't you?"

A grin crept onto my face. I couldn't help it. Jesse's eyes began to shine, and with a shake of his head, he snatched me close to his chest again while flashing me a mischievous smile. My hand strayed to his tie, which I straightened before moving my hand to the nape of his neck.

His face stared blankly down at mine, but I began to play with the ends of his curly, dark hair. He reached his free hand to hold mine against the back of his head, and he pressed another kiss to my hair.

"Hurry up, lovebirds!" Grace's voice was closer than last time.

"She always ruins our fun." I pouted.

Jesse puffed out a breath. "She's at the bottom of these stairs."

"Who's she?" I said snidely and sauntered away from him.

"Shut *up*," he groaned, catching up to me and smacking my arm. But when I glanced at him on the stairs, he caved and looked at me, his eyes crinkled.

"Please tell me we can continue this argument later," he continued from behind me.

"What argument?" Grace's curious voice floated to us before entering our view.

Jesse and I answered at the same time, "Nothing."

Grace turned on her heels to walk across the second floor and run down the stairs. Jesse and I shared a glance.

"I'm not the oldest for nothing, you two."

"We're twins!" Jesse shouted defensively.

"She's still older," Liam's voice shouted from the kitchen.

"By a whole two minutes," came Grace's proud reply to Jesse's grumblings.

BY THREE YEARS

{ *Lavinia* }

The doorbell rang for the third time, and Grace got up from her stool at the island.

We had finished dinner, and two other teenagers had already arrived, Alexandra and Bryan. Grace opened the door, and she and the newcomer exchanged words and hugs. It was only until they came closer that I identified the bubbling artist and theater kid whose locker was next to mine.

"Kanya!" I smiled and waved her over to the counter.

She flickered a bright grin in my direction and said hi to the group before she followed Grace up the stairs. The girl wasn't in a costume, and by the bag swinging in her hand, I concluded that Grace was showing her the upstairs bathroom to change in.

I turned back to the conversation, and Jesse sneaked his hand into mine. Smiling to myself, I realized the discussion had turned…well, heated. It involved Liam and Bryan favoriting basketball and football while Persephone and Alexandra agreed on hating any sport with the exception of tennis. Alexandra was standing on the other side of the counter, and Bryan was at the end. Persephone's hand lay in

Liam's lap.

While I didn't have much opinion on the matter, it was interesting to listen to. Bryan and Alexandra continued to argue—good-naturedly, of course—until Grace and Kanya entered the kitchen once again.

This time, Kanya was completely dressed in the exact costume I had imagined Grace in just a few days ago: she was wearing a leather skirt and matching jacket, complete with a velvet, strappy top underneath. Her legs bore fishnet stockings and platform sneakers while her natural hair was pulled into a ponytail high on her head. The purple extension waved with her hair as she swung her way into the kitchen excitedly.

"Calm down, you two!" Kanya laughed.

Bryan and Alexandra's conversation ended abruptly when the doorbell rang again. Grace and Kanya both went to the door and began welcoming more people.

A few moments later, music began playing at a low volume through speakers around the house. I took a deep breath to steady myself for more people and more noise.

You can do this.

"Hey," Jesse said softly.

I hadn't noticed that he was still close to me because our hands had separated a few minutes ago when he had gotten up to greet someone. But there he was with caring, brown eyes staring down at me.

"I'm all right for now," I whispered in response.

Jesse nodded unsurely, but I was thankful he knew to keep a watchful eye. I didn't have to worry about Persephone, of course; her social battery never seemed to drain. Her eyes would be on Liam the entire night, which brought me more comfort.

He'll watch her too.

Once satisfied with my condition, Jesse reached for my hand and gave it an encouraging squeeze before turning to Grace a few feet away.

"Is everyone here? Who else did you invite?"

She paused and peered around the room in thought before deciding on an answer. "Only a few more. May, Aaron, Kat, and Ben." She counted on her fingers.

Jesse made a face of displeasure, to which Grace rolled her eyes. I tilted my head in curiosity at the names, trying to figure out what disagreement was between Jesse and one of them.

I've met May and Kat before, and they're both more harmless than Tigger. Aaron's the only one in economics who's talked to me, and the first thing he said was a soap opera joke, so—

"What's so bad about Ben? Who's that?" I asked Jesse, careful to keep my voice low.

"Oh, he…Everyone makes him out to be this big hero. He's not. He and Grace, well…" He shrugged and adjusted on the stool slightly. "I don't trust him."

"I don't understand why she would invite someone who hurt her. I wouldn't," I said with a bitter shake of my head.

Jesse's kind gaze implored for me to be gentle with myself when remembering those things, but he knew how close and painful it was. My shoulders shook once reflexively, and I squeezed Jesse's hand in silent communication.

I could vaguely see his eyes glancing around before he brought a comforting arm around my shoulders, and I let my head fall into the crook of his neck.

"You don't have to say anything."

I took a shuddered breath and lifted my head, sweeping my hair behind my back. I swallowed once, met his eyes, nodded, and sighed.

"She wanted to give him another chance," he began softly, his arm still holding me close. "I trust her and her ability to communicate boundaries. But I don't trust him."

I nodded again, and after hearing my name from across the room, I turned my head. Persephone was waving me over to the fireplace, a phone in one hand. But it wasn't her phone—I stared curiously. We stood at the same time and met Persephone and Liam in the living room.

"Come pick some music!" Perse bounced in excitement.

I sidled up next to her, peering down at the abundance that was Grace's music library. Jesse leaned over my shoulder and Liam over Persephone's, and I thought of how perfect we must have looked to anyone who glanced this way.

"Ooh, this one, this one!" Jesse reached a finger over, clicked on an album, and the first song brought a wide grin to his face.

Grace and Kanya turned from their spot by the door to pay attention to the song.

The door opened, and in stepped May, Kat, Aaron, and another boy I presumed to be Ben. The foursome laughed before moving past Grace and Kanya.

Something must have been exchanged between Jesse and his twin from across the room, because without hesitation, Jesse snatched my hand and dragged me out onto the open floor.

"No, I am not dancing!" I protested, pretending to shove him off.

"That's ironic coming from you," Grace tittered.

Her and Kanya were now next to us, and both girls joined us with their hands to create a circle. I gave her my best glare in response but let her hand stay in mine.

"Wait for us!" Liam complained. Moments later, he and Persephone joined our circle, and the rest of them—excluding me—began to dance.

"Don't be such a party pooper, Lavinia!" Kanya smiled.

"Fine. Wanna see some dancing?" I sassed.

"Yes!" they collectively exclaimed, though I wasn't sure how much of it was making fun of me and how much of it was actual excitement.

I laughed and spun around, doing a few twists, and soon enough, I wasn't the only one dancing. Hands were exchanged and dropped, but our group of six remained shouting and dancing. Every few minutes, someone would trip and fall, and for a moment, a small portion of us were silent before bursting into laughter again.

Persephone and Liam began to move around outside the group, thinking no one was paying attention to the occasional kiss he would press to her lips that flushed her cheeks. But I gave them a slight shake of my head, noticed only by Persephone.

Soon, I was gasping for air. I fell back from the now full floor of dancing teenagers to the dining room, where I caught my breath and filled a cup of water. I gulped it down.

"So—" said a voice that made me jump.

I turned to see Ben, whom I hadn't met yet, so I gave him a polite greeting.

"Sorry about that." He chuckled apologetically. "I'm Ben."

"So I've heard." I kept smiling. "I'm Lavinia."

He picked up a cup and filled it with punch, glancing at me. "So I've heard."

"Oh? From which twin?"

"Not me," Jesse interjected. He stepped behind me and gave Ben a stink eye but turned to me, reaching out a hand to rest on my back.

"Yup." Ben chuckled awkwardly. "Grace introduced me to Persephone earlier. She's nice—and looks a lot like you."

You should see her *twin. He's good at punching people. Although, he didn't succeed against Alek the last time.*

"And younger than you. By three years," Jesse shot back.

"Oh, stop squabbling, boys." I rolled my eyes.

"Unfortunately for you, she isn't single," Jesse muttered under his breath.

I stared at Jesse hard, his brown hair falling into his eyes, before turning back to Ben, noticing his dyed blond hair and brown eyes. They severely contrasted the red tracksuit he wore. I didn't bother guessing whom his costume was referencing.

"And neither am I." I flashed Ben a sardonic smile and turned out of the dining room, my water still in hand. "Nice meeting you."

I heard his mumbled reply behind me while Jesse and I walked to the kitchen.

"Well, he's annoying," I said flatly.

Jesse sighed. "You're telling me. I've seen him with three different girls in the back of the school within two days of breaking up with Grace."

I chose to ignore how or why he was in the back of the school, which, to my knowledge, was only used for questionable activities like smoking—or what Ben enjoyed so much.

"Jeez," I exclaimed, rolling my eyes. "He's worse than Alek."

"Who?" Jesse gave an innocent tilt of his head.

"Never mind," I corrected before Persephone came up to us, three slices of cheese between her fingers.

24

SAFE PLACE

{ *Lavinia* }

"**H**aving fun?" Persephone mumbled through her first bite.

"Besides just meeting Ben, yes."

My sister scoffed and dramatically rolled her eyes in reply, which swayed her ponytail full of wavy, red hair back and forth.

"He's interesting, isn't he?" She stuck another piece of cheese in her mouth.

I reached for the last piece in her hands and ate it before she could stop me. "Mm-hmm."

"Hey!" She frowned.

Jesse laughed. "You can get more cheese."

Persephone groaned and flamboyantly broke the two of us apart on her way to the dining room—to get more cheese.

Jesse turned to me. "Dancing wasn't so bad, huh?"

"Nope." I popped the "p" sound and took his hand, striding over to the kitchen nook.

We stood side by side at the window. Through the indoor lights, I could only make out the shapes of many cars behind mine in the long driveway.

"I'll have to leave last, won't I?" I heaved a sarcastic sigh, as if it were torture to stay late.

"Oh, like that's so bad." His eyes widened in fake offense and captured me into an embrace. I snickered and let him pull me closer until my face was inches away from his suit jacket.

We waited together in a comfortable silence, his chin resting on top of my head, until the song changed to a slower ballad. At that moment, Jesse lifted his head and regarded me with his soft, brown eyes.

"I don't think I've ever told you how much I love you…"

"You have," I said cheekily, to which he rolled his eyes.

"Well, I'll say it again. I love you, Lavinia Markov."

"I love you too, Jesse Price," I whispered. "Always and forever."

"No matter what, Nia?"

"No matter what, Jesse…I promise," I said, almost biting back my words. But I said it anyway.

Before our faces could meet, Grace called out his name from the other side of the kitchen. I kept my eyes on him, but he slipped out a few choice words for our predicament and faced his sister. She said something to him that I didn't pay attention to; I was too busy staring at him.

"I'll be back." Jesse let go of my arms, leaving to assist Grace.

I sighed in content and faced the window again. I almost cursed myself for uttering those two words: *I promise.*

But I didn't. If he had heard me say that, Jesse would have told me to live my life the way I wanted to and not in the way fate kept pressuring me to. But fate didn't pressure; it forced. Fate didn't stop at anything.

If I was being honest with myself…I was scared. Scared that fate would use that against me.

Scared that when I left school tomorrow, what if I never came back? That our hearts would break beyond repair? Scared that after tomorrow I could never see him again. Worst of all…I was scared I would never have a chance to love him again.

But I shook those thoughts out of my head and acted as happily as I could manage.

I don't think anyone saw through it.

Jesse's hand landed on my back, startling me out of my head.

"Yes?" I turned to face him. *That smile—*

"Some poor girl got juice on her shirt. Come with me to get a new one for her?"

"Oh! How'd that happen?" I gazed sympathetically at the girl behind him. Grace was standing next to her, glancing at us momentarily.

Jesse rolled his eyes so far, I thought they would stick. Then, he sighed. "Ben said it was an accident. But since she just leaked his—"

I raised an eyebrow.

"We all know it wasn't an accident," he finished.

I rolled my eyes before smiling sarcastically in the vague direction of Ben's whereabouts. "Let's go," I responded.

While we walked past the girl and into the stairway, Grace told me where to find the shirt. Jesse trailed behind me as we made our way to her room. He was silent as I found the clothing, and we both left the room to meet Grace and the other girl outside the bathroom door.

The shirt exchanged hands and the girl went to change, but Grace turned back to us.

"Put some stuff on her shirt and put it into the washer, Jess. And then set a timer and put it into the dryer so it can be done before she goes home."

We nodded. The moment her heels began to click down the stairs, the girl— whom I now remembered being Rhiannon—exited the bathroom and gave a thankful nod to Jesse and me before handing him her old shirt.

"Is the laundry room up here?" I asked.

Jesse's reply was a single hum, so I followed him into the small room. He opened the washer, laid out the shirt, and pulled out a spray to get the stain out. I walked past him and hoisted myself up to sit atop the dryer.

"Making yourself at home, I see," he said and gave me a crooked smile.

"Well, what else am I supposed to do?"

He laughed and finished with the shirt, shutting the lid of the washing machine. He pulled out his phone, set the timer, and slid it back into his pocket.

"You know, now that we're here…" Jesse said with a mischievous glint in his eye. He took a step sideways to stand directly in front of me. My legs were slightly parted while my hands supported my weight behind me, and my heels bounced off the edge of the dryer as I swung my feet.

"Yes?" I raised my eyebrows.

He took a step closer to me. "…we can finish our argument."

"Why do I get the feeling you've done this before?" I mused.

Jesse's only response was another small step forward.

I glanced at his suit. "Our costumes fit the theme of this conversation perfectly."

"Oh?" His head tilted back.

"Mm-hmm. History repeats itself; these dresses are coming back into style."

"Suits are always in style," he stated, his large hands now resting on my legs, just below my hips. I bit my lip and thought of the perfect reply to bait him further. Only a few more seconds passed of intense eye contact before I thought of one.

"Always attractive, too." My hands lifted to play with the knot of his tie for the second time tonight.

At least now I don't have to worry about Grace interrupting again.

"Mmm. You think so?"

"Oh, for sure."

Jesse's smile grew, his eyes showing almost none of the brown color I had become accustomed to in this dim light. My pupils must have been the same way, and as I adjusted my legs to enclose around him, he let his forehead rest against mine.

Even my feet went still. After I had given him a small nod of permission, Jesse swiftly pressed a kiss to my lips. I instinctively tightened my legs around his hips and yanked him closer by his tie. My heart began to pound in my chest, and if I hadn't been closing my eyes, my vision would have swum.

Peace.

On this earth, we pushed against each other like waves on a shore—my heart beat, steady as a tide coming in. Like the ocean beat the sands unforgivingly, we pressed together as close as we possibly could.

But my mind was silent—the continual chaos I had become so accustomed to ceased whenever our lips joined. And it was peaceful. Calm. No matter how bad the craving was for each other, how hard we pulled each other closer, I felt at peace.

It was a rare peace. A peace I hadn't felt with anyone else. And I couldn't get enough of it.

Long moments passed until finally, I retreated for more air. I let out a gasp, and my breath jumped again when Jesse pressed a gentle kiss to my cheek, then my jawline, and when he came to my ear, he paused.

"Keep going, please," I whispered.

He did. And just when we made our way back to the party, his alarm rang.

At the end of the night, Jesse gave me a sweet goodbye and "See you tomorrow" and wished Persephone and me luck to make it home.

Home.

I hated that I still thought of that hellhole as home. In my heart, it belonged to him.

And while I fell asleep that night, hair still in my barrette, my thoughts were still swallowed by my love for the only boy who brought me peace.

FINALLY FIGHTING

{ *Persephone* }

I sighed, glancing out the window at the increasingly cloudy sky.

The outdoor field trip had been cancelled, so we were free to go after this class. The problem arose that Lavinia would still have classes, which meant Parker and I either sat outside or in the library—both were going to be dull options. But at least Liam had to wait too.

The rain filled the room with dull background noise. The heavy drops panged the windows incessantly while the clouds grew. When I could leave, I knew I was going to sit on the granite steps and be drawn into the storm…if this class was ever going to end—Mr. Always Wears Tacky Blazers And Socks was blabbering on.

I silently tapped my pencil on my wrist and occasionally doodled something that popped into my head. While the class dragged on, I checked the clock to no avail, of course, since only thirty seconds would pass in between my harsh glances.

An eternity passed before the bell rang. Noise erupted, which disturbed the sounds of rain, and everyone became a flurry of sweaters when they rushed out of the room. I scooped up my tote, stuffed my notebook and textbook inside, and

139

tucked my pencil behind my ear.

It fit securely in my low bun, though a few vibrant wisps threatened to escape. I waited the rush out for a few seconds before getting out of my chair. Parker trailed behind me but didn't keep up.

What a slow walker.

I rushed to my locker, unlocked it, and flung the door open. Footsteps rapidly filled my ears as they hurried in my direction. My muscles tightened, and I reached into my locker to flip open the blade of my favorite knife. I sneaked it into my sleeve.

A firm hand grasped my shoulder and another on my arm. I flipped around, twisting the wrist on my arm—but I was met with the pained face of a familiar blond.

"Perse, it's just me!"

I let go of Liam's wrist, shooting him an apologetic glance. "Sorry."

He returned my gaze and I stuffed my bag in my locker. After hearing something crack, I lifted my bag up and saw the granola bar I'd bought yesterday. I pulled it out, peeled off the wrapper, and bit off a chunk.

I turned around again to see Liam's eyes boring into mine.

I finished chewing. "Now what? You're just gonna guilt-trip me?"

"That was the goal." He winked, to which I rolled my eyes. "I was actually thinking about yelling that I'd rather spend fifty minutes with you in biology than by myself in math."

"Lower your voice," I hissed. He had announced that last statement far too loud for comfort. "Have you forgotten that you could be seriously hurt if anyone found out about you, Jesse, *or* Grace?"

That's putting it mildly.

Liam sighed. "Yes, of course I do. But I still don't want to keep it a secret."

He grabbed my hand that wasn't holding the delicious granola bar.

"I want everything to be perfect so I can shout to the world that you'll always be mine." He pulled away with the widest grin I'd ever seen.

Calm down, Perse, I insisted to myself. *Lavinia would smack us if she were here.*

"I want that to be shouted everywhere too, Liam, but…nothing is perfect. I don't have control of my life. I'm still…" I hesitated because I knew the truth was too colorful for him. "…tied down. But you can trust me when I say this: one day we'll be able to tell as many people as we like about us. Promise."

I shouldn't have said that.

Our sweet moment was spoiled from that nagging thought. I hummed, and thankfully, he didn't seem to notice the hollow joy in my eyes. After just a moment of silence, I stood on my toes to give him a quick peck on the lips.

I let his eyes distract me while I shut my locker and took his hand. Liam led us outside of the brick building. It had begun to rain harder, and while the first few stairs were dry from the roof, we kept going until deciding to sit on a soaked, granite step.

I leaned my head on his shoulder and let myself find some semblance of peace.

Less than a minute of loving silence passed us by when I heard running footsteps behind us. Liam and I groaned simultaneously when Parker, who was already soaked through his collared shirt and graphic tee, came into our view.

"Are you crazy?" Parker scolded, mostly at me. "You'll get freezing cold out here! Persephone, contrary to your beliefs, there are drier—and safer—places to have alone time. I mean, really, haven't you learned anything?"

I narrowed my eyes at him, unamused. "Are you done now?"

He huffed, blew his wet hair out of his eyes, and folded his arms. "I guess…but you shouldn't be out here by yourselves! You don't know who could see you."

This time, Liam spoke up. "No wonder you two are related! Hey, she said something like that to me just a few minutes ago. You know, before you interrupted?"

"Boys," I gently reprimanded.

Parker sank onto the step beside me, grumbling to himself. Something about me being too concerned for him. I sneaked a glance at Liam, whom I discovered was already looking at me.

"What?" I whispered.

Before I could speak again, a shattering of glass erupted from behind us. Parker shot up without hesitation and dashed into the school. I flung around and stared after him.

"What the hell was that?!" Liam screeched.

"Does it look like I know? Stop gaping and follow me!" I hurried my words and pulled him up before I darted forward.

We were both out of breath by the time we ran through the doors and up the stairs, but we came to a halt as the confusion surrounded us.

Students were running and screaming. Some were under desks or behind open doors, and some were banging on closed doors to get inside of classrooms. It was chaos. I saw a flash in my vision, then noticed Parker—he carried two students into a classroom. In the seconds I stood gaping, he ran the other direction.

Care to explain, Parker?

I used my powers to shock him into a stationary position inches away from me and sent him a confused look.

"There's a shooter!" yelled a faint voice across the office hall before Parker nodded in confirmation and dashed away.

My eyes went wide. Like it was choreographed by fate, gunshots and screams rang out from the other direction. Liam and I ran to Parker in an attempt to catch up.

Time to put on a show.

26

WHY DOES IT MATTER

Before I could react, the shooter lifted his gun and snatched May up by her shirt.

In the confusion, Parker and Liam had disappeared from my side, and the man in my vision just around the corner turned slightly. His half-smiling—and disgusting—face sneered during her mad struggle to escape, rainbow hair swinging.

May's face contorted into one of sheer horror when the gun moved to her head in slow motion. I stood completely still, as if a single breath would kill her in an instant. I was afraid to move.

I was afraid to save her.

The shot rang out and her body hit the floor. I choked out a blood-curdling scream of shock, and the shooter whirled, Parker running past me.

I blinked: the shooter was on the ground, and Parker stood in front of me. I looked down at my brother and saw the gun clutched in his hand, his rings glinting around his knuckles. Not a moment passed before I shook off the lingering feelings of May's death with my powers. The short man moaned in pain and crawled toward us.

"I thought I hit him hard enough!" Parker groaned.

I shrugged and stepped forward, lifting my hands up to use my powers to push the man to the floor. But then his jacket shifted, showing the skin of his wrist. A black tattoo was inked on the skin. My blood went cold.

I flung my head around to Parker with a look of surprise. "Do you see that?"

Parker frowned and peered close at the man. "Is that—?"

The symbol tattooed on the man was none other than the X-crossed guns, the very same guns issued to all Ivankov agents. At the end of both the barrels was shading, a swirling pattern meant to represent smoke. If there was any doubt before to his identity, I knew by the small "I" in the middle of the tattoo exactly whom this man worked for.

"They're here for us…" I realized, looking up at my brother.

Oh no. Oh—

"Liam," I whispered.

Parker's blue eyes widened. "And—"

"Jesse and Grace! But…why the whole school? Why not just us?" I sputtered.

Parker nodded, confusion spreading across his face, but then he froze.

"Where's Lavinia?"

My blood ran cold at the images my mind conjured. Images of Lavinia saving Jesse or Grace and sacrificing herself to any Ivankov agent that came her way filled my terrified puddle of a brain. I shuddered at the thoughts. Parker and I tensed.

If they wanted to get rid of someone, Ivankov would never just bring one agent. I should know. Parker and I whirled around to see five more large men in all black with guns. Conveniently, they were all pointed at us. I assumed they were loaded.

The tallest man stalked toward us. "Where is he?" he rasped out. "Where's that boy?"

I swallowed nervously before lifting up my hands in surrender.

"What boy?" My voice purposefully trembled.

Knowing Parker would try something dumb, I shot a glance at him in warning. I knew we'd have to trick them. Somehow. The man who had spoken stopped just inches from my face. His eyebrows were drawn together, eyes squinting, and his face showed a twisted smile of hate.

Without any warning, he slapped my face.

"I know who you are, *Markov*," he spat. "Tell us where that boy and his brother are, and *maybe* I won't tell Ernest I saw you here. Then you might survive."

With my cheek stinging, I took a deep breath and nodded while forcing Parker into stillness with my powers. I silently pointed my thumb behind me. It was, *of course*, the opposite direction of where we had last seen Liam.

The man glanced at Parker for confirmation, to which he replied with a forced nod. The agent jerked his head in that direction and led the other four to follow him.

I didn't wait for anything else to happen, so I pushed the back of my hand pressed against Parker's midsection. We quietly backed away. Immediately after we rounded the corner, we whipped around and sprinted to where we had last seen Liam.

◆ ◆ ◆

I ran in front of Parker and Liam as fast as my legs would carry me, but a loud noise affixed my feet into the ground. A beat passed in complete silence, and the rain continued to pour, soaking me to the bone.

I turned around slowly, afraid of what I'd find, and realized with sudden terror that the sound was a gunshot. Ernest stood in the middle of the backfield, just past the track, holding a gun in a wide stance.

Liam was now close in front of me; Parker and Ernest were closer together, a few yards away. I mentally cursed my brother for not running faster until I concluded what had happened from the hovering bullet—and it horrified me.

Parker had created an aura of his powers around himself using his current emotions. Since my brother stood between Liam and Ernest, the bullet was safely lodged in the bubble of smoke and glowing blue that surrounded him.

It was stunning, and in any other situation, I would be proud of his abilities and amazed at how majestic he looked.

He's an amazing Master.

Now, fear throbbed in my veins. Liam was shaking slightly, and Parker's clenched fists revealed his raging anger.

I could protect myself and Liam if I managed to create a bubble with my powers, but I had only seen Lavinia pull that off. She was far more advanced than me. I wondered how Parker knew how to do it. Taking a step toward Liam, I whispered for him to take a few steps backward to me.

"Don't you *dare* touch him!" Ernest's gravelly voice screamed, and he aimed his gun at us.

"Get down!" Parker shouted.

Seconds flashed by and Liam was by my side when we knelt on the ground. I squeezed my eyes shut, and upon not hearing another shot, I slowly peeled them open.

The bullet had whizzed above our heads to land in a tree trunk from the forest behind us. Parker stood, protective aura gone, between Ernest and my and Liam's huddled figures. I kept still and tried desperately to get my mind to give me ideas on how to get out of this.

Then, Parker took small, steady steps to Ernest. Ernest moved his gun to aim at Parker, simply staring at my brother in confusion. He started to ask Parker something but shut his mouth.

"What are you doing, Ernest? What do you even *want*?" Parker pleaded, his voice almost too soft for me and Liam to hear. He was desperate to know the truth.

Though Lavinia and Anastasia had successfully desensitized themselves to everything we'd gone through, Parker and I were a work in progress. Ernest and Margaret were the only parental figures Parker and I had ever experienced—it was hard to hate them or even to let them go. I understood Parker's emotions. I did. But Lavinia…

I bit my lip in worry; I still didn't know her whereabouts. She should have shown herself by now. Parker continued to walk toward Ernest and expected an answer. Ernest almost wavered and slightly lowered his gun, but then he brought it back up and hardened his expression.

"Why does it matter?"

The rain continued to pour, and Parker stopped walking. I could hear the fury in his voice as he stared Ernest down.

"Why does it *matter*? Because, *Ernest*, none of us ever know! I never found out why any of us are even here in the first place. I can't remember anything from my own parents, but I know you're not it. So why? You chose *us*, remember? So why do you hate us so much?"

Ernest stared at him, at a lack of words. I didn't know how to react to this, either. I hadn't ever seen Parker react to this extreme—*Has he been holding this all in?*

Parker's voice grew louder. "Why are you so bitter about everything? You never care about anything but yourself! Not even Margaret! How can one person be so *heartless*?"

With every sentence, he grew closer and closer to Ernest. His voice and demeanor were angry and cold…but I knew he was breaking. I could feel it. From where I stood, I could see his fists clenching so hard that his knuckles turned white. I attempted to let myself into my brother's mind, only hearing pieces.

How can he hate us so much? What did we ever do to him? He wanted this, so—

His voice was close to breaking as he shouted, "Are you even listening to me—?"

"Oh my *God*, I don't care!" Ernest screamed. He looked wild, rain plastering his hair to his forehead. His eyes flashed. "I don't care! I never did! Why can't you all see that? You ruined everything!" His voice grew quieter. "I was of a comfortable rank, and then, because of you three, I was demoted to handler. I wish I could imagine a world without you. It would be so much better. I wouldn't have to be burdened with keeping track of you or your sister."

That was the first time Ernest glanced at me since they started arguing. I felt a pang of guilt, although I didn't know why. I could see Parker's jaw tighten and shoulders tense. I knew Ernest wouldn't stop there.

I need to do something…anything!

"The only one of you that did anything for me was Lavinia! She was the perfect child! Never complained, always did what she was ordered to do."

Our world grew silent before the sky thundered. The rain ignored our troubles and continued to soak us. I shivered at his stinging remarks, though we both already knew what he thought of us. Liam exhaled a tense breath from next to me as the alarms from the school continued to ring. More police cars, ambulances, and fire trucks surrounded the school.

Students scurried outside to meet all their saviors, unaware that the people responsible were standing hundreds of yards away. Not a single person noticed us standing by the tree line.

Parker seemed calmer, though his hands still shook. I wasn't sure if it was from anger or cold. But Ernest continued his rave.

"You two never meant anything to me. Everything I ever wanted and needed was solved when your sister was trained!" His voice was hoarse and screaming as he finished cruelly, "You're both worth nothing to me! You hear me? Nothing!"

Liam's gaze landed on me, uncertain of my reaction. I swallowed hard and looked back over at him, shrugging. He turned forward again, his lips separating in realization. I followed his eyes and was met with a surprise:

Lavinia, in all her rage, was creeping up behind Ernest. She paused from hearing his outburst. Her face was hard and focused while her hands hung by her side. One sported a knife, covered in blood. Jesse was a few inches behind her, and she knew he was there but let him follow.

Please don't bring someone else innocent into this.

But they kept coming.

27

DEAD TO ME

"**Y**ou two never meant anything to me. Everything I ever wanted and needed was solved when your sister was trained! You're both worth nothing to me! You hear me? Nothing!"

The words that stung all of us froze me while I stared at Ernest's back. At that moment, Parker's face fell, and he glanced over Ernest's shoulder and noticed me.

Don't—my brother quickly focused back on the man between us to not reveal my presence.

Jesse reached me and hesitantly put a hand on my shoulder. If he was trying to calm me down, it wasn't working. My heart beat in my gut.

Should I stab Ernest and risk him shooting the twins? Or me? Stab him and risk him shooting Jesse or Liam? Or both? I put my hand to my chest and used my powers to slow my heart rate, taking a deep breath.

My eyes met Parker's again, this time with confidence. I was going to save them.

Get them out of here. I'll take care of Ernest.

His breath caught, just enough for me to notice. *It's a gun over a knife, Nia.*

I almost laughed. *It's me over him. He trained me himself. Now stop arguing and wait for my count. Call Anastasia and then find Grace.*

The only confirmation I got from my brother was his eyes training back on Ernest's fuming face. Parker took a step forward, and I hurriedly and quietly shrugged Jesse's hands off my shoulders and readied my knife.

5...4...3...

Parker visibly swallowed and took another step. He could do this.

2...1...

It all happened in a matter of seconds.

My brother shouted to Persephone and then the boys to run to safety at the edge of the woods. I lurched forward to grab Ernest's hands in my arm and held him tight against me. Grace came into my peripheral vision, running toward her brothers, and as soon as Parker noticed her, she vanished from my sight.

I brought the knife to Ernest's neck while his gun fell to the wet grass under our feet.

"Don't even *think* about it," I whispered harshly, holding him in an iron grip.

He panted hard. I was almost offended that he was surprised that his own agent, years younger than him, had rendered him useless.

Ernest struggled against me. "I've taught you well, daughter," he choked out. "Needless to say, I'm pleasantly surprised."

"Don't call me that." I pressed the knife closer to him, drawing first blood. The downpour of rain forced it to swim down his neck and chest, staining his shirt. "You had nothing to do with it," I gritted through my teeth. "I worked because I was trying to stay alive. Just like you never wanted the twins, I never wanted any of this. To have to fight every day—like my parents once did."

Ernest suddenly grunted and almost caught me by surprise. I held him tighter.

"They never had to fight!"

"They gave *up*!" I yelled, breaking his skin further. "They got used to it!"

"They never even tried to escape!" Ernest returned the volume of my voice.

"That's because they knew they'd die! They were *cowards*. And so are you," I glowered.

I threw him on the muddy ground and snatched up the gun with one hand, aiming it at his face with both hands. Instinct took over, and my finger hovered on the trigger, ready at any moment. He frantically scrambled to sit up, and I grinned at his terror.

"I don't care if I'm a coward because I know that you're the same! You're a coward just like your parents," he sneered.

I adjusted my grip on the gun and hardened my expression. "No, I'm not. The difference between us is that I'm going to do something about this. I'm going to try my damned hardest to get me and *my* siblings away from all of you. They're not your kids and they never will be. No matter what happens, I'm not going to give up." I took a step toward him, water seeping through my shoes as I whispered, "I won't *stop*."

"Stop it!" an unexpected voice screamed. "Don't do it!"

I lifted my head to see Persephone scrambling against Parker's arms. She let out more pained cries, and her blue eyes were bloodshot as Parker tried to shush her. The rain, even through the trees, was staining her face further with tears.

A surge of pain swelled in my heart to see her struggle with herself. While she hated the man I held at gunpoint, she didn't want to hurt him. Even after all he had done to hurt us.

"We'll never get out of Ivankov if I let him live," I shouted to her.

I steeled my resolve and faced Ernest. Our gazes met, and I prepared to shoot. His brown eyes that I had become so accustomed to hating were stone cold. It was like he didn't care that his life would soon be stripped away.

But before I could pull the trigger, a voice rang in my head with a distant memory flooding me. I struggled to block the scene playing in front of my eyes, but I knew that once it began, it wouldn't stop. The control over my powers waned away:

I strode into the roped-off area of the gym and took off my sweatshirt. As I threw the fabric onto the ground, he focused his eyes onto mine and leaned back into his fighting stance. Our fists raised. I swung at him, he ducked, and I swung again.

I groaned as he rolled his arm into my side, turning me onto the ground. His knees fell to the floor on either side of me, and his hands closed around my throat. The breath flew from my lungs, but the struggle was too great.

I tapped out and gasped for air. He shook his head and let go.

"Again."

The next seconds crawled by as I steadied my feet. I glanced over at the group at the tree line. Parker held a phone to his ear, though he was staring back at me while his lips went still. Jesse's brown eyes stayed on mine, a frown drawn onto his lips, and he nodded to me.

The breaths in my lungs were short and few; I continued sparring Ernest. It had been a half hour in the frigid Russian winter, and without the heat on in the gym, the cruel torture had been worsened.

He motioned me to get up and resumed his stance. A fist flew at my ribs, but I swung my legs to meet his hand and into a powerful blow on his stomach.

I let out a satisfied breath when he sank into the mat. I rushed to pick up the gun on the side of the ring and pretended to pull the trigger on him.

He flashed a wide grin and picked himself off the floor. "Now that's what I call a successful Markov!"

I took a shaky breath and then looked directly at Ernest to lock my jaw. I bore a hole at the center of his skull and pulled my finger tight on the trigger.

The alarms pounded my eardrums as the rain cascaded heavily upon my head, soaking my trembling hands. I snapped my finger close to my hand, and the muffled shot rang out. I shook off the momentary ache in my shoulders at the impact.

I let the grip of my powers slip away from me. I didn't need to quiet the sounds of our presence anymore. Ernest's body now lay dead on the leaves. His eyes were glassy and lifeless, a frozen expression of fear on his face.

His feet were crooked and his arms lay by his sides, covered in dirt. The rain began to erase his existence. I felt…relieved? *No, not that.*

I felt free. *Finally.*

Not a single tear dropped onto my face at that moment, only rain wrapping my heavy, auburn hair onto my shoulders. I moved my stare up into the forest at the group that stood there, silent.

Liam's and Persephone's faces were close together in a hug, Liam's eyes trained on the scene while Grace stood in shock. Her brown eyes were filled with lingering betrayal, focusing on Ernest's limp body in the grass.

I exhaled in relief as the adrenaline left my body and calmed my breathing.

Grace stared at me, then turned back to her brother.

They're safe.

Jesse's and Parker's gazes remained fixed on the body as they held hands for comfort. I would have smiled if it weren't for my attention jumping elsewhere.

"Lavinia!" Liam shouted over the downpour. He let go of Persephone, frantically pointed behind me, and began to sprint in my direction.

Mind slowing, I turned around.

Margaret. She has a gun.

"She has a gun!" another voice screamed.

Air was thrust out my chest; a shot rang out. She failed to hit me, but I wasn't about to find out if she could get it right. My legs took over and drove me to the forest in an attempt to dodge the oncoming bullets.

Rain blurred my swimming vision, and I barely made out Jesse's figure in front of me, hand outstretched and screaming. Footsteps thundered behind me, quickly catching up.

I cursed in frustration when my foot caught on something. My face landed in the mud, filling my mouth with grass. Pain shot through my ankle, but I gritted my teeth and slowly rolled to my feet.

"*No!*" two voices yelled.

I was closer to Jesse now, but my eyes were clouded with the rain's dirty handiwork: I couldn't tell who was shouting and who was being held back by whom.

"Go!" I yelled back to them, stumbling to turn around to face Margaret.

"Hurry!" a new voice screamed from behind me, though I wasn't sure if they were talking to me or to my crying sister.

Anastasia, I realized. *She'll save them.*

I paused for only a moment, wiped the dirt out of my eyes, and cast a glance behind me.

Go, Jesse. Just what we promised. I love you.

Margaret whirled on me, but I hit her as hard as my arms could swing. She fell back and dropped the gun. I scurried to step on her chest, reached for the gun, and cocked it without hesitation. The trigger seemed to pull itself, and just a few moments passed before she gasped for her last breath.

But a burning hole swept through my shoulder, and at that moment, I realized the thick, red stain on my shirt was the result of the double shot—the exact time I deprived Margaret of her right to live, someone had decided to punish me.

"No," I whispered in dread. "Jesse, *no!*"

I lurched backward, and the gun plummeted out of my grasp as the earth fell out from underneath me. An unidentifiable figure loomed threateningly over me, shouts filling my ears. I didn't have time to turn around in an attempt to outrun the man.

Before I could think of anything else, my world went black.

28

YOU SAVED ME

{ *Anastasia* }

"**S**tay awake, Nia," I muttered under my breath.

Her shallow breathing was the only response in the quiet space. I had shut the door on the Prices and a crying Persephone. Only Parker remained next to me in the empty room, on the other side of Lavinia, while we tried to wake her up.

I met his blue eyes filled with concern and leaned down to meet Lavinia's lips. I plugged her nose and closed my eyes to fill her lungs with air.

Maybe if she—

"Wake up, please," I whispered, pulling back. My heart sank.

Parker pulled me off of her, trying to calm me down. He sat next to me and resumed his pressure on her wound. Blood stained his favorite silver rings.

"It's better she doesn't wake up yet. She'd be in more pain," he explained gently.

I panted heavily and stuttered mostly incomprehensible words, to which he nudged me without taking his hands off the gaping wound in her shoulder.

"Listen to me, Anastasia. Are you listening?"

I didn't reply.

"Can you hear me?"

I managed to nod while staring into Lavinia's ashen face. Her closed eyes were sunken so far that I thought they might fall into her skull, and her limp hands lay lifeless by her side. I could only hear Parker's soft voice and her almost inaudible breathing.

"We need to keep her asleep when we get the bullet out. She'll bleed out unless we close the wound, because I can't stop all this blood myself."

I glanced down to his red-stained hands pressing below her collarbone. Her shirt was still wet from the rain, and a tear slipped out of my eyes to contribute, as if she wasn't wet enough.

"After we stitch her up and give her medication, we can take her to the hospital. If it's safe. Do you have what we need to do that?"

"Yes," I mumbled blankly. I had outfitted my safehouse—whose location was unknown to everyone at Ivankov but myself and Lavinia—with everything needed in case something like this ever happened.

The small cottage was set back from the road, surrounded by trees, and had windows in almost every room. When I could spare a weekend, the cottage was a welcome reprieve with the many plants—some fake, some that required little upkeep—and plentiful books and silence.

I just didn't think I would have to be the one to save my best friend. My sister.

"Can you do it?"

I hesitated. I knew how to pull a bullet out of a wound and sew it shut, and I had done it before—on myself and once on someone else. But that was in my leg, which wasn't as dangerous as the important arteries close to Lavinia's wound.

"Anya, I can't do it," he pressed, meeting my eyes. "I would kill her. You can do it."

"I can't—"

"Yes, you can. I'll talk you through it."

Silence settled over us for a moment. The only sound that reached us was the hazy voices of the Prices and Persephone huddled in the next room over.

The faint sunlight provided us with enough to see in the small room filled with bookshelves, but I would need more if I was going to save her.

I needed to save her.

"Stay here, Parker," I said, standing up.

He replied shortly while I hurried out of the room, passed the rest of the group, and ran past the stairs. I opened the small kitchen cabinets containing everything I would need and quickly gathered it in my arms—needles, medical thread, bandages, pain medication, and a few metal tools to pry her skin open and remove the bullet.

My head spun as some of the things clattered to the floor, and I tried desperately to think of who was the most level-headed one to assist me.

"Grace!" I shouted. A few moments later, she appeared. "Come help me with this." I gestured to the pile of supplies on the ground and in the cabinet. "Grab as much as you can."

Grace nodded and flipped her long, dark hair out of her face, bent down, and gathered the bandages and boxes in her arms. "We need all of it?"

I nodded to her, and she followed me back to the library. When we stepped into the room with Parker and Lavinia, Grace stopped momentarily at the sight of the unconscious girl.

"Here." I dumped the things next to Parker, where I was previously sitting. "Go back for the rest of it, Grace."

She rushed off without another word, leaving Parker and me to tend to Lavinia.

"What do we do first?" he asked me.

I took a deep breath and stared down at her chest filled with dying breaths.

"Tell Jesse to get scissors," I said. Parker looked up at me and nodded in resolve, waiting for me to hold down her wound before he got up.

"We're going to save her, Anya."

I hope so.

THROUGH THE DARK

{ *Jesse* }

The sound of a door closing snapped me awake.

Liam and Persephone were still sitting next to each other, wide awake, as Anastasia came over to us.

"She's gonna make it."

Relief spread through me, and a fresh tear slid down my cheek. Without thinking, I jumped and wrapped my arms around Anastasia. She tensed under my embrace but quickly recovered and returned it with an awkward pat on my back.

I pulled away, apologizing. "I didn't mean—"

"No, it's okay." She tiredly rubbed a hand over her face. "We're not thinking clearly."

"She's going to be okay?" Liam asked quietly.

"She'll live, and that's enough for me," Anastasia amended.

Persephone let out a small gasp, though this time—unlike the previous outbursts—she was filled with relief.

"I don't know much beyond that," Anastasia continued, holding her arms out to the moving Persephone. The two enclosed each other in a close hug, and I glanced at Liam. His eyes were fixed on them.

"Will we be able to take her to the hospital?" I asked.

Anastasia pulled away from Persephone but kept her close.

"Anya," Persephone started, "we have to, she'll—"

"I know, Perse," Anastasia whispered, smoothing Persephone's hair. She turned to me and sighed. "We're going to. But we'll have to wait until tomorrow."

"Why?" Liam asked.

I chuckled wryly. "In case you forgot, there's kind of an entire organization that knows they're missing. And Anastasia's the one who has to take the fall."

"Not the entire organization," Anastasia corrected at Liam's chastened expression. "You forgot I killed the guy who shot Nia. It's simply a matter of them missing from after school. And it isn't even too late for that, but you're right. I have to go back and fix this mess."

"What are you going to tell Higgins?" Persephone asked. I didn't know who that was, and by the looks of Liam's face, he didn't, either. I assumed it wasn't important.

"I'm not going to tell Higgins. I'm going straight to the Master's Board."

Whatever the reveal meant, Persephone's mouth dropped open, and she took a step back. She looked horrified.

"Perse, they'll believe me! Do you have any idea how long I've been with Ivankov? How loyal I've been to them for this exact purpose?"

Persephone frowned. "Yes, but you're not one of them—"

"Ernest, Margaret, and Pamuk all trained me themselves. We were friends, and now, thanks to Lavinia, they're dead."

"She was *protecting*—" Persephone hissed.

"And I'm protecting *you*, Perse," Anastasia begged. "I'm protecting all of you. So excuse me while I do everything I can to save you three *and* these idiots"—she jerked a thumb toward Liam and me, and I would have been offended if it weren't true—"by risking everything to talk to the Master's Board."

Persephone was quiet, though I wasn't sure how much of it was out of anger or tiredness. I was exhausted. But I wasn't the one who had lived all of this before.

"What are you going to tell them?" Persephone asked softly after a few long moments.

Anastasia hesitated only a moment. "I'm going to tell them that as your in-team, I have the authority to authorize you for missions and organization-related activities. Which is true. I'm also going to tell them that today, after school, I picked you up instead of Ming."

Persephone tilted her head.

"Which is also true. I told Ming I was taking you three on a mission, and when I was almost there, Parker called me. I didn't foresee *this* happening."

"You didn't know they were coming after us?"

"No. In order for me not to know about it, it would have been a Board decision. Not an agent or in-team one."

Persephone nodded in understanding. But I didn't get any of this.

"So," Anastasia continued, "instead of taking you on the mission, I'm going to take Lavinia to the hospital a few minutes away."

Anastasia turned to me and Liam before Persephone could protest to not going with them. "You three are welcome to stay here with the twins, there's more than enough space. But you can decide what to tell your parents."

"Thank you." I nodded to her. "I know we'd like to, but…I don't know what we'd tell them. I'll have to talk to Grace."

Just after Liam echoed my thoughts, Parker stuck his head out of the door and found Anastasia with his diamond blue eyes.

"Anya," he said frantically, "she's awake."

DEATH IS NOTHING

{ *Jesse* }

I turned the corner of the hallway, coffee in hand.

The hospital café might not have been completely up to my standards, but it was better than the expired grounds at Anastasia's safehouse. She had let us take turns coming to the hospital with her to be with Lavinia ever since her return two nights ago.

Parker and Persephone took turns yesterday, and I was the first for today. The first night Anastasia was gone, though I was comfortable in my own bed, I couldn't sleep. In the morning, Grace and Liam and I gave our well-rehearsed story to our parents—that Kanya had been fatally wounded in the shooting and, while we were fine, her parents weren't in town to stay with her at the hospital.

Honestly, I was surprised they believed it because Mr. and Mrs. Phan were certainly in town. But my parents remained unaware, so they let us "stay with Kanya." The car ride back to the safehouse crawled by—but this morning crawled even slower.

Once Lavinia was awake, I assumed Anastasia would let us all be there at once.

For now, I was grateful just to sit with her. I reached Lavinia's door, turned the knob, and opened it while taking a sip of my coffee.

There she was, asleep in her bed like she had been the past two days.

She's had enough sleep by now, why won't she just wake up?

I wanted to see her again. To tell her I love her.

I sat down in one of the plastic chairs on the wall next to her bed, shivered, and shrugged my sweater back onto my shoulders. Heaving a sigh, I leaned against the back of my chair to rest my head on the wall and let my eyes close.

I lifted my coffee cup to my lips. My mind emptied as I let the hot coffee warm and calm me. Sleep sounded very nice right about now.

"Hey, you."

My eyes flew open to see Lavinia awake and trying to sit up.

"Nia," I breathed in relief.

A smile danced on her lips as she croaked, "Get over here and help me."

"I can see you're feeling better." I pressed the button to incline the upper half of the bed. "How was your two-and-a-half-day nap?"

"Two and a *half?*" Her eyes went wide. "What about—?"

"Yes, two and a half." I laughed, took the hand of her good arm, and pushed her other hand to rest on her stomach. She tried to hit me.

"But what—who—how did I get here?" Her eyebrows furrowed in confusion.

"Calm down, honey. Calm down. I can call a nurse—"

Lavinia frowned like a toddler and stuck out her bottom lip. I let out a laugh, and though she acted offended, her lips split into a smile.

"Ooh," she winced, using her bad arm's hand to press into her stomach.

I let go of her hand. "What is it?"

"No, no, it's okay, don't call a nurse yet, it's just"—she hissed out a pained breath—"getting shot isn't a breeze. Even if I did sleep for two and a half days."

"You would have been in a lot more pain if you woke up earlier," I quipped, "because Anastasia took out the bullet herself. Parker helped and Grace watched."

If Lavinia's eyes weren't big before, they were now. Her sharp jaw fell open in surprise, and then she paused. She closed her mouth, opened it, and closed it again, to which I smiled.

"You look like a fish."

"Shut up," she snapped jokingly, slapping my arm with her good arm's hand, the right hand. The shot had hit her beneath the collarbone on her left side, in a diagonal line above her heart.

"You—" she tried again, breaking into laughter. "She took it out herself?"

"Yup!"

She giggled softly, trying to calm herself down since the movement was jostling her shoulder. We laughed for a few minutes, stopping occasionally but being unable to hold it in when we made eye contact again.

I pulled up my chair next to the bed and took a sip of my coffee before setting it on the floor next to the chair. I knew she would have questions about how she had gotten here. Eventually, she sobered herself—only a small smile played around on her bright face.

"So," she started, "I got shot. Anastasia took the bullet out, and then she took me to the hospital. What happened to the person who shot me?"

"Anastasia killed him."

"Oh."

I reached past the railing on her bed to grasp her hand. "Yes, dear. She drove us to her safehouse, and that's where she took the bullet out. Then she went back to Ivankov, fixed the rest of the mess, and came back. That's when she took you to the hospital."

"But how did she—?" Lavinia shook her head and tightened her grip on my hand. "Why is Ivankov letting this happen? We could—"

I let her take a breath. Her grey eyes wandered around the room, taking in the clock across from her and the single window across from me. She focused again and met my gaze, sighing.

"They could kill us for this, Jesse. I could get sent to—" She stopped herself from whatever she was about to say and took another breath. "I killed not one, but *two* agents." A tear filled her clear eyes, though I suspected it wasn't for the loss of the Labzinas. "And they weren't just any agents. They were handlers. My handlers."

"I know, honey," I whispered, sweeping my thumbs over the back of her hand in comfort. "But you're going to be safe here, for a while, at least. I promise."

"How?" she whispered in a hopeless tone.

"Look at me, sweetheart." When she did, I sent her a comforting smile.

"Anastasia was going to take you three on a mission, and she was on her way when Parker called. Ming never saw what really happened. Both Ernest and Margaret are gone, and so is the guy that shot you. Pamuk, I think." I paused.

Lavinia let out a sharp gasp, and she instinctively gripped my hand tighter.

"Who is he?" I asked.

"He—" She shook her head wildly, as if it would clear the bad memories of that rain-filled afternoon. "I thought he was a friend. He has powers like I do, only he can…" Lavinia's eyes dropped to the blanket at her feet. "I guess it doesn't matter now. He's dead."

"He also tried to kill you," I pointed out.

"No!" She shook her head again. "If he wanted to kill me, he wouldn't have aimed for my shoulder. He wouldn't have missed."

Her voice dropped to a tense whisper; she gazed at me again and implored for the rest of the story. Two and a half days was a lot to catch up on.

"No one else knows what really happened, so after you stabilized in the safehouse, Anastasia left to go inform something called the Master's Board about your mission. She didn't say a word about it when she got back."

At the mention of the Master's Board, she remained unfazed.

Persephone thought it was a big deal. Why doesn't Lavinia? She must know more about them. Or just doesn't care.

"Did I wake up when I was at the safehouse? I remember—I remember something, but…"

"You did, for a few minutes. It was right after your surgery, and you were in a lot of pain. Your eyes were open, but you weren't really there. The first thing I remember you doing was crying, and when Parker gave you…well, whatever he gave you, you fell asleep again. And now, today, you woke up again."

"Two and a half days later."

"Yes," I said.

Lavinia fidgeted slightly. While I had never been in one, I had been around hospitals and their beds enough to know that they weren't comfortable. At all. It had taken me a few hours to adjust to seeing Lavinia in one, even…

"What is it?" I asked her softly.

She sighed and stared at our interlocked hands. "Why did you come back for me?"

"What?" I froze.

"Why did you come back?" She met my eyes. "I remember that too. You…You came back for me."

"Just because you told me to go doesn't mean I did. Why wouldn't I come back for you?"

"Because I'm not worth dying for." Her eyes dropped.

Lavinia had sent a pang of guilt through my heart with those words. I couldn't help but jump to think, *Why would she believe that when I've told her otherwise so many times? Why would she think that she isn't worth that much to me with how much I tell her I love her?*

"Look at me right now, Lavinia Markov."

She met my eyes in a small motion of shame at my reaction.

"Remember when I told you that it's impossible to find someone who doesn't hurt you? Just a few days after I first told you I love you?"

Lavinia nodded and took a shaky breath. I knew she was still in pain, even if she would never admit it. Her powers accelerated her healing, but it only went so far.

"And I told you that sometimes you find people who are worth the pain. You find someone you love so much that you forget about everything else around them; they're the only person that matters. And when you find that person, you would do anything for them."

"I remember," she said quietly.

"So you should remember that I told you that you were that person for me. You are worth every single moment of every single kind of pain I could endure because I love you. I will wait forever for you. No matter what happens to us, I will spend every last second of my life on Earth dedicated to loving you."

Lavinia kept her eyes on me. I searched them for the woman I knew and loved, and she was there. She was in there. Even after almost being denied life and after withdrawing its blessing from two other people, she was there. She would always be there.

"Death is nothing compared to what I would do for you."

"I…" she started.

There were tears on both our cheeks, falling freely as the things we knew so well about each other went unsaid. We didn't need to say them. I didn't need her to be okay and tell me she believed me because I knew she didn't. Not yet. Not completely.

But I would die for her to believe that I loved her that much. Because I did.

FIND HER, FOUND HER

{ *Jesse* }

Lavinia laid her head back and watched me.

I returned her gaze and gave her hand a gentle squeeze. Her eyelids drooped after a few minutes while we sat in silence. When her eyes closed fully, I stood up, pressed a kiss to her forehead, and let go of her hands.

I settled back into my chair and folded a leg underneath me. Moments turned into minutes while I watched her sleep with a peaceful expression on her face until the door slowly creaked open. I turned my head to see Anastasia standing still, staring at Lavinia's unmoving body.

She took a slow breath in and let it out, just now noticing my presence. Her feet shuffled tiredly to pick up the other chair, and she set it down opposite me.

"Did she wake up yet?" Her voice was filled with sleep as she gazed at the floor.

I leaned back in the hard chair. "Just a few minutes ago."

Anastasia's head snapped up. "She did?"

I nodded in response and glanced at Lavinia's face. She was breathing heavier now but still in a peaceful sleep. Anastasia sighed.

"Did you—?" She rubbed her green eyes tiredly. "How much did you tell her?"

"As much as I know."

"Hmm. She must be exhausted."

"She was," Lavinia said, cracking her eyes open.

"Did we wake you?" I asked quietly and took her hand.

"No, it's okay." She shushed me, turning to Anastasia. "Even if I did sleep for two and a half days."

"To be fair, I didn't have the best supplies," came Anastasia's smiling response.

"You're also not a doctor."

Anastasia gasped in fake offense. "Like you could have done it to me!"

"I have." Lavinia leaned her head against her pillow and grinned.

Now this interested me. "When was that?"

"Oh, a few years ago, right?" Lavinia's head shifted slightly to Anastasia's direction.

"Not even." She paused. "But you also did it in a moving van."

"At least I wasn't driving."

"Who was driving?" I asked. "And why didn't they do it and let Lavinia drive?"

"Pamuk, actually." Anastasia nodded.

Oh.

Lavinia gave a small sigh. "I don't want to know how it went, Anya. He…"

"He didn't deserve it," Anastasia finished, meeting my eyes.

"No, he didn't."

The girls fell into silence. I began to wonder if I should leave them be. After all, Anastasia's known Lavinia her whole life. There were bound to be things Anastasia noticed about Lavinia's current emotional state that I didn't.

"How did it go with you?" Anya asked.

Lavinia rolled her eyes. "How do you think it went? I pulled the trigger twice on people who spent every moment of their time making my life miserable and blaming my brother and sister for not living up to the standard as well as I did."

"But you still had to do it. It's going to take a toll," Anastasia said.

"We've been trained to not let that happen, Anya."

"That doesn't mean anything. We're human."

"I am painfully aware of that fact," Lavinia chuckled dryly, "because the wound in my shoulder is going to keep me in this cursed place—which I hate—for a week or more."

You could never hate hospitals as much as I do, I thought without hesitation.

Lavinia glanced at me, and I was afraid she'd heard it in her own head. But she looked away a second later, and I silently sighed in relief.

Maybe she doesn't know the whole story. Yet. I wanted to tell her.

"You might be able to get out of here in a few days if you can walk around a bit," Anastasia declared brightly. "Then you can spend the rest of the recovery time at the safehouse with everyone else. I got us a total of two weeks. I even made bags for you all so you wouldn't have to sleep in the same clothes."

Lavinia's eyes widened. "What did you tell them to get *that* amount of time?"

"I just called Higgins this morning to tell him you were injured. He doesn't know where the 'mission' is, so he believed me when I told him we wouldn't be back for another two weeks. He told the Master's Board, don't worry."

Lavinia nodded and glanced at me again, thinking for a moment. "Where did I get shot, exactly? I mean, the probability of bleeding out if you're shot in the shoulder is pretty up there because of the axillary artery and vein—"

"Don't worry, smarty pants, you did fine." Anastasia paused. "Although, you came close. Pamuk hit you right underneath the axillary artery, above your heart. A centimeter in any direction and you would have been dead in minutes."

Lavinia cast a glance toward me. "I told you so."

"I didn't know any of that!" I held my hands up, both of them breaking into laughter.

"I guess I didn't get lucky, then. Even if he's dead now, I'd like to make a public thank-you to our lovely friend Pamuk. He's far more useful than he'll ever know."

We went silent for a few minutes before Lavinia pointed to the necklace sitting on my lap.

"What's that?"

I bit my lip and met her eyes. "It's Kanya's."

Lavinia's face fell. "Please tell me she's not—"

"We don't know yet. We still can't find her. Grace is going crazy."

"I don't blame her," she whispered. "Where did you find the necklace?"

"Grace found it in her locker. She snuck there before coming outside, which was when she found us." I hesitated. "I'm keeping it so she doesn't worry even more."

"I can look for her," Anastasia piped up. Lavinia and I stared. "What? I'm an international spy. Finding a teenage girl is easy."

"Not if she's dead," Lavinia tactfully pointed out.

"Thanks for that, sweetheart." I grimaced.

Anastasia rolled her eyes and got up from her chair. "I'm going to get everyone else. They'll be excited to see you, Nia."

Lavinia smiled brightly, perhaps the largest one I had seen yet.

"And after I drop them off, I'll find Kanya. Jesse, have someone text me her parents' names and address."

I nodded and watched her walk toward the door, turning back to Lavinia.

Anastasia's back was to us before she opened the door and waved her hand in the air in a loose gesture of annoyance. "You two better kiss or something before I get back."

The door shut and I smiled at Lavinia, who licked her lips once, waited, and then rolled her eyes.

"C'mere, you," she mumbled.

"Gladly," I beamed, standing to meet Lavinia's face. I hesitated a moment, not wanting to hurt her, but her brows furrowed in annoyance.

"Hurry up already, hot stuff."

"Fine," I muttered with a sarcastic roll of my eyes. I pressed our lips together gently.

Our hands tightened together, and her familiar peace overcame me. My stomach tumbled in a way that burned giddiness into my brain instead of growing the overwhelming pit of fear and dread I had gotten used to feeling the past few days.

She was finally safe. And she was kissing me, so what else could I ask for?

She grinned widely as I pulled away. "Happy now?" I asked with amusement.

"Very. Now go"—Lavinia hit me in the arm—"and let me sleep in peace."

I laughed and let go of her hand, leaving her be. The necklace was now in my pocket while I trotted down the stairs and found my way to the cafeteria. The room was full of visitors and family, so I didn't pay any mind to the people swelling around me.

I found a cheeseburger and a banana, paid, and found a small booth to sit in. A couple sat across from me with only their heads visible over the booth walls. Their dark hair bobbed up and down, and the small cries of the woman drifted through the air in my earshot.

Wait a minute.

I peered around the edge of the booth and tried to be casual. I didn't want them thinking I was being creepy. The woman's tear-stained skin was a slap in my face. I shot up and rushed to the couple.

"Mr. Phan?"

Kanya's father turned to face me, his hands still clasping his wife's trembling hands over the table.

"Jesse!" His deep voice was filled with relief at my presence. "Why are you here?"

"A friend of mine was—" I hesitated and cast a glance at Mrs. Phan. "She was shot at the school. We're...visiting."

Mr. Phan nodded solemnly at my news and told me he wished the best for our friend. But why were *they* here?

"Where's Kanya? We couldn't find her, and...Grace is—"

"She's gone, Jesse," Mrs. Phan choked out. "Our little girl is dead."

My heart dropped. I knew before she finished speaking, but...for Grace's sake, I had kept hoping. I wanted to believe she was home safe. That she was okay.

But she wasn't. And yet another person a member of my family loved was dead.

IN THE FACE

{ Jesse }

"**A**re you still in the car?" I asked when the phone was answered.

"Yeah, I'm almost there," Anastasia replied. "What's up?"

"Kanya's dead."

Her line went silent with the exception of the cars on the road whizzing past her. I took a broken breath through my pained chest.

"How do you know that?"

"Her parents are here. I just saw them in the cafeteria."

"Lavinia's still asleep?"

"Yes. But probably not for long." I glanced back through the door's glass at her sleeping figure. "You know how she can feel other people's extreme emotions unless she blocks it out."

"I know. She's vulnerable right now and won't be able to control it at first."

"That's what I thought. So I'm going to let her realize on her own. But…someone has to tell Grace. And Liam."

"Do you want me to tell them before we come?"

"I think…" I took another breath. "I think she'd take it better from someone she can't blame. She doesn't know you, and—"

"I'll tell her," she offered without hesitation.

"Thank you, Anastasia."

"I'll be back in twenty minutes, okay?"

"Okay."

"And call me Anya."

Before I could reply, she hung up. I smiled to myself, but really, I was dreading for the rest of the group to arrive. I didn't want to truly feel the news I had just received. I didn't want to believe it was real, and I wanted nothing more than to support Grace, but it was going to be hard.

She went through everything silently. We rarely talked about our struggles because we already knew about them. But this was different. She would break from this like nothing before, and she might have watched me break like this, but she wouldn't know what to do with it herself.

I wasn't so sure I wanted to find out how she would break.

♦ Persephone ♦

I wanted to walk over to Anastasia and slap her in the face at the news.

But instead, she ushered Parker and me out to the car and told Grace and Liam to take as much time as they needed; we would wait for them. The second we closed the doors, a cry sounded from inside that broke my heart. A shriek of nightmare-induced terror, more like.

Although it was only ten minutes before a tear-stained and red-faced Grace climbed into the front seat, Liam trailing behind her, those silent moments crept slowly.

Liam sat next to me, Parker on my other side. While we drove to the hospital, the only communication between the five of us was Liam's hand finding its way to rest in mine. I clutched it soothingly as a few silent tears slid down his face.

I couldn't pretend to know how he was feeling, but I could support him.

When we reached the hospital and went inside, Anastasia led us down the familiar path to Lavinia's room, where we were met with Jesse's grim face.

"She just woke up again," Jesse said.

None of us replied. Parker and I met each other's eyes, though, and I squeezed

Liam's hand again. Anastasia shifted on her feet.

"I'll take the twins in," she stated with her eyes on me and Parker.

"Grace and Liam and I can go talk to Mr. and Mrs. Phan," Jesse offered.

"I'll stay here," Grace murmured, "and tonight, I'm taking us home."

Jesse and Liam stared at her in shock, and my heart sank into the gaping pit of my chest. Anastasia glanced at each of us for a moment and nodded once.

"I'm sure that she's waiting. Come on." Anya opened the door and greeted Lavinia.

I dropped Liam's hand before leaving the rest of the group behind, following Parker into the hospital room. Lavinia was sitting up in her bed, clearly tired but fully awake nonetheless.

"Hey," she greeted and waved us over with her good hand.

Parker met her first and wrapped her in the tightest hug he could manage without hurting her, to which she laughed and pushed him away.

"How was your nap?" my twin smiled.

"Oh, just lovely," Lavinia drawled with a roll of her eyes. "My favorite part was undergoing the knife by someone who—"

"Hey, she knew what she was doing!" Parker exclaimed. "And I helped!"

I came to the other side of Lavinia's bed while Anastasia sat at the end. Lavinia playfully hit Parker and turned to me instead.

"At least you didn't have to watch all that blood."

"I was too busy crying, actually," I admitted, embracing her gently.

"How touching," she beamed. Then she paused and angled her head past Parker to see out the door's window.

"They're out there, aren't they? Why aren't they in here?" she asked, turning to the three of us surrounding her bed.

Parker and I met each other's blue eyes and turned to Anastasia simultaneously.

"Grace is taking the boys home tonight."

"What? Why? Didn't they tell their parents—?"

"Kanya died." Anastasia sighed. "Jesse saw her parents in the cafeteria, and…I can't blame her for wanting to be home."

"Then…" Lavinia set her head back and stared at the ceiling, giving a helpless wave of her hand. "Do you think the boys will come back?"

Her last question was a mere whisper, more to herself than to the rest of us.

"They might. Jesse has a license, doesn't he?"

"Yeah," Lavinia whispered and focused her eyes back on Anastasia.

"Then ask him before he leaves."

Lavinia looked down at her lap and folded her hands. A few silent minutes passed before her head twitched to the side and her eyes grew wide. Tears began slipping down her face, and she struggled to breathe.

Confusion filled me, and Parker's lips drew together in a frown; Anastasia shot up and shoved him aside to be close to Lavinia.

"Hey, hey, I'm right here, it's okay," she shushed.

Lavinia gasped for air, and her terror-filled eyes met Anastasia's, trying to speak. "It's—It's—Grace, I—"

"You're feeling what she's feeling—what Jesse and Liam are feeling. It's okay." She pressed her forehead against Lavinia's and gripped the sides of her face.

"But how—?"

Anya's voice softened. "You can't control it sometimes, remember? We've done this before."

Parker backed up until he reached the door, his steps silent. I took his cue and slowly followed him.

"But it didn't feel like this…"

Lavinia's voice broke while I followed Parker outside and shut the door behind me. Liam stood against the wall, eyes closed, and Jesse and Grace were nowhere in sight.

"I know," Anastasia whispered just inside my earshot.

If what Lavinia was feeling was only a fraction of the real pain, I didn't want to know what Grace felt like.

♦ Jesse ♦

Grace sat down hard on the lounge's couch and kept her eyes off of me. I didn't want to pry or ask what had happened earlier—when Anastasia was the one who had broken the news to her. I was too afraid the answer would bring too much to the surface.

Grace breathed in sharply and adjusted her hands, fiddling with them on her lap. I took slow steps to sit down beside her. Her eyes were filled with tears, but it wasn't until I sat down and looked at her that she let them break through.

She gripped the sides of her arms, sniffling, "I wish this never happened."

"Everyone does," I whispered.

Grace shook her head and closed her eyes. "If Ivankov never knew about us— if we had never met the Markovs—Kanya would be alive. She'd be…"

I stiffened at her tirade.

"She'd still be here." Her voice broke as she turned to stare at me. "And I'm mad. Mad that after everything I've done for you and for Liam, I have to go through this too. It—" Grace stopped and fixed her gaze on the wall. "It would have been easier to bear if she just died, but instead…" She trembled. "It's their fault. It's all their fault, Jesse, and they all know it."

Voices screamed inside me, telling me she didn't mean it—but I shut them off. I gave in to my anger because I knew she did mean it. She blamed Lavinia for this. Her words stung because really, without Lavinia…this wouldn't have happened.

Grace and I both had lost someone we loved at the wrong time, and yet…she helped me then. But now, it was a different story. I was supposed to help her no matter what, and now?

I didn't know whom to choose. Did I even have to choose? Lavinia was a totally different situation than my sister, and she had her own family that could help.

No matter who it was, Grace needed someone. Someone to help. And I knew how to do that.

33

YOU'RE HOME

"**D**o you ever think this is my fault?"

Liam looked at me incredulously over his sandwich. His eyes went dull, his lips tightening as he swallowed and put the bread down on the foil.

"No. Because it's not."

I scoffed. "But if I hadn't stopped Nia, then…maybe we would have escaped before Pamuk got there, and—"

"Are you even listening to yourself?" He gaped at me and reached a hand out. "Margaret still would have found her. Pamuk still would have shot her. And by then, Kanya was long gone." His voice fell to a whisper. "You couldn't have stopped anything."

"I…" I shook my head at him. I didn't really have words for him. Nothing but—"I think I love you, Liam…"

Did I just say that? Did I—?

I let my eyes widen, his mouth falling open and his hand tightening in my grip.

I shouldn't have said that. What is wrong with you, Persephone-Willow

Markov? You got a screw loose?

"Good to hear, 'cause I think I love you too."

Oh.

I gave him a small laugh, and my breath caught in my throat. He smiled again in return and grasped my other hand firmly. A piece of hair fell into my face, so he let go of one hand and put it behind my ear.

"You're right," I said softly. "No one could have stopped it."

He adjusted to the side to face me directly. The booth seats were comfortably wide, which allowed the two of us to have room on one side.

"I know." Liam kept his eyes trained on mine, but for just a second, his gaze wandered.

"You can kiss me if you'd like," I teased in a whisper.

Liam leaned closer, pressing his lips to mine shortly. I raised my eyebrows to challenge him. It was a bit too short.

"You asked," he pointed out before pushing our lips together again.

I froze for a split second. My eyes slowly shut, and I let my hands travel up his back, holding him close. He kept going, gliding his hands to my face and tracing the end of my eyebrows.

We stayed together, intertwined until we were forced apart for air. I let my lungs fill again and smiled at the red-faced boy in front of me. I was quite sure his head was as fuzzy as mine.

I glanced over his shoulder. "That couple looked ready to come over and tell us off."

Liam wrapped an arm around my shoulder, glancing momentarily in that direction. But I kept smiling and let his warmth comfort me.

Just for now. I closed my eyes.

♦ ♦ ♦

"We're going, Liam." Grace's voice traveled to my ears.

I sat up in surprise and noticed Jesse and Anastasia trailing behind Grace, Anya swinging her keys. Liam sighed from his spot on the couch next to me. He and Jesse had already visited Lavinia, but I had hoped Grace would have waited a little longer.

I guessed not.

"See you soon. Hopefully," Liam whispered. He pressed a kiss to my forehead before he got up.

Grace stalked out of the lounge with Liam and Jesse in tow. Anastasia waited by the door until they were out of earshot before speaking to me.

"Parker's on a walk; I'll be back after I drop them off. Grace has to get her car from the safehouse."

"Okay," I mumbled.

"And Perse?" She angled her head back through the doorway. "Jesse and Liam will be back if they can. This isn't over yet."

I hoped she was right. But too many things had been going wrong lately—I wouldn't be surprised if this would too.

BIRD IN THE SKY

{ *Lavinia* }

"**B**e gentle," Anastasia chastised.

I swatted her hand away and stood up by myself. The past few days, I had gotten back on my feet—literally—and while the pain was excruciating at times, it was manageable. Because of my powers, healing worked faster, but unfortunately, medication wasn't effective unless in lethal doses. I picked my battles, though.

"How are you feeling today?" the nurse tittered inside. "You did an amazing job moving around yesterday. You even changed your shirt by yourself."

"Yes, I know," I groaned and let her prod around me. I sat still at the edge of the bed.

"Oh, lighten up, Lavinia," she chided.

I rolled my eyes at her and turned to stare at Anastasia. "Why did you let her in?"

"Because she knows what she's doing."

"I do, in fact," the nurse said proudly.

"Yes, but can she remove a bullet herself?"

"No." She laughed. "But you're avoiding the question. How are you feeling today?"

"Better."

She lifted her small chin. "Better, like, all the time? Just until you move? Less pain?"

"It's not as bad." I sighed. "I still get pangs when I move it fast without thinking."

"But it's good you forget about it"—she bustled around me, moving cords and carts—"because that means the pain is lessening. You're healing very fast."

Trust me. I know.

I was thankful that my powers weren't detectable through tests because, if they had been, I would have long been arrested. In my body, clotting occurred faster, scars faded easily, muscles stretched comfortably, my skin was pleasantly clear, and I was rarely tired to the point of exhaustion.

If I could, I would return everything Ivankov had given me. But this…

"How did you sleep last night? Any discomfort?"

"No more than usual," I replied lightly, coming back down to Earth.

Just a little nightmare.

"That's what I like to hear," the nurse beamed, setting all the equipment in their original positions. "I'll be back with your lunch."

"Can't wait." My eyes rolled backward again.

She turned to leave, clicking her tongue at me. "I'll miss you, Lavinia. I don't tell that to all my patients."

"Of course not," I drawled as she closed the door.

"You could at least pretend to be normal." Anastasia chuckled.

"Well, I don't have much practice. Especially not in hospitals."

She grinned and helped me swing my legs back onto the bed. I leaned back, sitting upright, and shooed her off.

"Go away," I muttered.

"I know you can't wait to be out of here, no matter what you tell her. You can't wait to have good pasta and taco salad instead of the limp salad here."

I groaned in hunger. "And your chocolate chip cookies…"

"I'll make them right after we get back." Anastasia winked and closed the door behind her.

Finally. Quiet.

Being alone was the one place where I could let my guard down fully. Even here, surrounded by people and impossible for Ivankov to touch, showing any evidence of my powers—no matter how insignificant—scared me far more than I wanted to admit.

I never had to deal with the fear of being discovered because where I grew up, Masters were celebrated. They're the most elite type of agents within Ivankov. But I didn't know what it was like in the real world.

Were Masters feared? Were there different names for them, and did they express themselves freely within society? Who hated them? Were they used by the government?

My head spun with questions I never would have entertained a few weeks ago. But meeting someone who changed my life like Jesse had…That had its effects.

I let my mind wander and rested my gaze on objects of interest around the room—the small bug on the far wall, the dots on the ceiling, the streaks of paint, birds outside the window, the pretty vase. I started to breathe deeper, taking the time to close my wandering eyes and clear my head.

Too much was going on…*I don't know what to think.* People I had known forever weren't who I thought they were, and where I once felt free, I now felt trapped. Trapped inside my own head, trapped inside my memories.

My memories had torn me apart for as long as I could remember. I'd not known what to do since then. Even now, I didn't know. I'd tried so hard to put on a mask: an "I'm fine" mask.

I'd put on that mask for my siblings for them to never realize what I went through. What I went through for them and what they should never have to go through. I wanted so badly for them to never know what I'd endured, but that mask was coming undone. Slowly, thinly, like a film of soap floating out of a pot you're washing.

I had tried so hard to appear like someone else to them. To appear like someone who knew who they were, who had a sense of worth and identity. But instead, underneath that mask, I didn't know who I was.

I didn't know because in between all of my messy childhood, I had to grow up too fast. I had to grow up in order to not fall apart every day. And all these years later, I still had to fight the urge to fall apart every day.

I wished I could say that in a few years I could rise up. I wished I could say that I could rise gradually and find myself. I wished I could say that I could change, and eventually, I would know who I am.

I wanted to say that I could do what I wanted and live my best life, loving whom I wanted to. I wished I could say that I would walk confidently in the future like none of this had happened.

But for right now, I was stuck fantasizing about what life would be like if I could ever truly be myself.

35

UNEXPECTED

"But when are the cookies going to be done?"

"I just put them in the oven!" Anastasia rolled her eyes.

I pouted and attempted to cross my arms. I hissed a breath when pain shot down my injured arm, Anastasia rushing to my side.

"Stop it." I batted her hands away with my good arm. After my shoulder lay still and my hand rested on my lap, the pain receded to a dull ache. "Go back to the kitchen and clean or"—I waved my hand around—"something."

She gave me a dirty look, placed her palms on the arms of my chair, and leaned down to hover her face above mine.

"Fine. But you're coming with me."

Without another word of protest, though I did scream at her to put me down, she lifted up my chair and swung through the cottage to reach the kitchen as easily as if I were a baby. We were met with a surprised Parker and Persephone, who, to my chagrin, began laughing at the sight.

"Oh, come on, you guys," I pouted most seriously. "Be nice to me! She just—

"

"I know what I did," Anastasia defended.

She flipped her long hair out of her face, turned back to the counters, grabbed a paper towel, and began to clean what I assumed to be her baking mess. The woman made lovely cookies, but not without proof of baking ingredients everywhere.

"I'm as sober as a church mouse," Anastasia declared with a groan when she dropped the bag of sugar. The white granules covered the floor and the front of her pants.

She frowned as we giggled at her language slipup. "Is that not how you're supposed to say it?"

"No," Parker laughed. "It's 'quiet as a church mouse,' silly."

"My point still stands."

I rolled my eyes. "Well, can't help you there. I can't even drive right now!"

"At least *I* can pick you up."

Persephone couldn't contain her giggles, though Parker at least attempted it. He gave up when I sent him another look of discipline and joined Persephone.

They were the most annoying family ever. *I'm gonna miss this.*

♦ Parker ♦

"Well, she's back now. More annoying than ever," I said into the phone.

On the other end, Sarvesh laughed. "The safehouse truly is safe, then?"

"For now. Even though Anastasia forgot my medication and Lavinia's toothbrush."

We didn't want to think about what it would mean if it were discovered that we had never gone on a mission in the first place or that the Prices had seen us since the shooting fiasco. I, for one, didn't want to think about what it would do to Lavinia and Persephone if Ivankov got to them and succeeded in their original mission. Especially if my sisters couldn't save them—the effect of their guilt alone would cripple me by association.

"Do you ever think…?" I started. "Do you ever wonder why Ivankov went after Liam and Jesse's classrooms, but not Grace's? And that the shooters could have taken out Lavinia when they had the chance…but they didn't?"

"Why, do you?"

"Yes."

"Well, I…The obvious answer is that Lavinia is far more valuable to them than Jesse or Liam is. Far, far more. She's one of the best we have."

"I know that," I whispered in frustration. "But the agents they sent knew better. They were trained better than to be defeated and not take out their original targets."

"Maybe they weren't the targets."

"You—"

"I'm just saying, Parker, maybe they wanted to bring Jesse and Liam in and use them."

"Use them for what?" My voice struggled.

"To get Lavinia to cooperate—use her memory-manipulating powers. On Grace."

"But why would they want her to—?"

"Parker, you need to think about this." Sarvesh dropped his voice. I sighed and nodded even though I knew he couldn't see me. "Think about how Grace was spared entirely. Not even threatened in the slightest. But Jesse and Liam were targeted— either to be disposed of or to bring in—and that's not an accident. Ivankov knows you aren't as involved with them as your sisters are."

"That's true enough," I muttered with a roll of my eyes.

"I can't explain why they didn't break into the home and kill the whole family, including the parents. Maybe that has something to do with it. But I know that Ivankov wants them, dead or alive, and they don't stop when they want something."

The line went silent when the painful words resurfaced memories for both of us. But things started to make more sense now.

"You think Ivankov was trying to use Liam and Jesse to turn Grace to their side because she knew too, and that…one of their parents, they…?"

"We have to consider the fact that one of them could be an agent."

My heart sank into my stomach. "Talk to you later, Sarvesh."

Before waiting for a response, I hung up, returned my phone to the pocket of my jeans, and hurried back inside.

"Anya, Nia, we—" I caught my breath and ignored my twin's questioning stares. "—we need to talk about Grace."

36

MAN IN THE SUNGLASSES

{ Anastasia }

Cold air flooded around me, sending a shiver down my spine.

I gladly shut the freezer door, turned back to the cart, and set the frozen vegetables inside.

That's the last of it.

I weaved the cart through the aisles to the front of the store and to a register, politely flashing the cashier a smile while I loaded the items onto the conveyor.

I mentally ran through the order of items so that the heaviest ones would be at the bottom of the cart. It was a habit instilled in me so nothing would break. A one-time single mark on a container was all it took for me to remember never to put cereal below fruit again.

The cashier and I exchanged friendly words while the bagger began to load my cart. I hadn't forgotten anything, not even the two kinds of cereal Parker would eat—Lucky Charms and Cocoa Puffs. And Lavinia's cheese. And the chive cream cheese for Persephone.

I chuckled to myself at their food choices, but I knew what it felt like to have such little autonomy that choosing your food was a lovely luxury. I still knew what it felt like.

Someone is watching you.

My gut lurched at the all too familiar feeling of uncertainty. But I was certain someone was watching. I reached for my wallet and paid the cashier an even amount, scanning my eyes around the store in an attempt to identify the person.

There.

A man stood at a register in front of me, facing my direction. A woman was paying for their items; her long, black hair rested loosely around her shoulders. The man wore sunglasses and a brown jacket and stood three inches taller than the woman. As he stared, his eyebrow twitched.

That's either a tell or a...

I looked away from the man, took the receipt from the cashier, and put it in my wallet.

Lavinia, I panicked. She had worried when I told her I'd be going out for groceries and only "agreed" to let me go if I let her track my mind and connect us if something went wrong.

What is it? Even her voice in my head was concerned.

What Masters twitch their eyebrows to activate their powers?

Silence.

Nia?

I'm here, I'm just—that doesn't make sense. The only Masters who can do that are—that's impossible, Anya.

I'm not asking for possible. I'm asking what Master can do that. I resisted the urge to look behind me when I passed the couple's register and kept moving toward the exit.

Are you sure it's a Master?

I would say that by the looks of the man in sunglasses and the Korean woman next to him following me, yes, they are Ivankov agents in the very least. And who would they dare send after me unless they were a Master?

You have a point.

I know. So, tell me, who—?

He's a Tracker.

And that means?

The doors closed behind me, and I crossed the parking lot to the car.

You should've taken my class with Pamuk.

I frowned.

Anyway, he can track your movements with his brain. His vision will distract him, which is why he's wearing sunglasses. Is he blind?

Didn't see a cane.

Then the woman must be his handler or his partner. Trackers never travel alone because, well…

Because?

They're kind of on everyone's top list. They're important. Only a few in the world exist.

Great. I scoffed under my breath. No doubt Lavinia heard me anyway. *I'm being hunted by one of the rarest Masters in the world.*

Actually, those are Sensors, Lavinia corrected. *You'll need to purposefully think about anything but the safehouse or us. Or the Prices. Think about going somewhere else. Pick another store or a coffee shop and wait him out.*

He's a mind reader too? Then how is he—?

No, he's not. Plus, I'm protecting this conversation. Think of him like a human lie detector and a seer of sorts. He can only find out and track what he wants to know.

But if he wants to know everything, then—

Trackers' powers are protected by their handlers. They can control what the Tracker sees inside their mind to only the information they need. Otherwise, they'd melt in an overload. Like a computer.

Oh. I finished putting the bags into the car. I shut the boot with a loud thud and got into the driver's seat. *Somehow, that's not very comforting.*

I'm sure they're only looking for information on us, Anya. If they find out that nothing is amiss and that we're truly on injury recovery for a mission, then they'll leave. Buy yourself an hour at least.

All right. I sighed and started the car. *You better be right about this.*

I'm always right.

♦ Lavinia ♦

"You're sure you don't know who they are?" Anastasia asked Sarvesh over the phone.

His response caused her to sigh. A moment later, she hung up.

"Nothing?"

"Nope." She rolled her eyes and fell back on the bed.

Parker and Persephone sat silently on the chairs perpendicular to the bed. I leaned against the headboard, comfortably resting my bad arm on a pillow, and stared out the single door leading into the small backyard. The curtains were drawn away from the glass and toward the bookshelves lining the cottage walls on either side of the door.

The morning had crawled by slowly ever since Anastasia left, and though she brought back wonderful food, it had little comfort. I had a sunken feeling in my stomach all morning and it hadn't subsided, not even after Anastasia returned.

I didn't want to think of what connection it could have to Jesse's phone going straight to voicemail when I'd called it earlier.

They should be in school. The thought was only a small solace.

Ever since they left, I had been running over every possible situation that could occur because they left the safety of the hospital and the safehouse.

I was beginning to think we'd made a terrible mistake.

37

LOCKED PATHS

{ Lavinia }

The twins soon left to fix themselves lunch.

Parker said it was good for me to start moving around on my own and that if I needed help in the kitchen, he would offer it. But he wouldn't make it for me.

What a brother.

Anastasia now lay on the carpet on her stomach with her hands above her head. She looked quite pathetic from my vantage point on the bed, and as she groaned and rolled over, I smiled.

"Be quiet," she muttered, closing her eyes.

"Stop worrying."

That got her attention. She sat up and stared at me. "You're one to talk."

"Maybe you should go eat something and forget about it for a few minutes. You're too stressed to think about this logically and consider what Parker told us last night."

"I don't like it when you're right." But she was smiling when she stood.

"Well, I'm always right, so—"

Anastasia waved a finger threateningly in my direction. "You're pushing it."

I was left in silence as the door closed. Sweet, sweet silence. I turned my head to stare at the clock above the door and watched the hands tick by, minute by minute. Positioning myself on my good side, I lifted my hands out from underneath the blankets.

I played with my powers by pulling some of my memories into my hand and watching them dance around. The orbs that contained them sparkled and glistened, begging to be set free. But I kept them close and stared in fascination at the changing colors and sounds.

They were good times. Happy times. I let my eyes close. I drifted off until I felt a crick in my neck start to grow.

"Ow," I mumbled, snapping my eyes open. Only a half hour had passed during my nap.

"You hungry yet?" Parker's voice asked, his head popping through the door.

I groaned tiredly and closed my eyes again, head falling back on the pillow.

"No, no, no, no naptime," he scolded, walking to the bedside.

"But I want to sleep." My voice escaped the pillow with a small whine.

"Then you won't sleep tonight," Parker whispered.

"Go away."

"No," he declared and ripped the pillow out of my grasp.

I gasped in fake offense but let him pull me into a sitting position with my good arm.

"You're going to get up, make yourself a sandwich, and sit down at the table and talk to us. Talking, remember that? Socializing? Because we're your family— remember us?"

"Gross. Family."

"Don't even. You love us."

I sighed. *I do love you all, Parker. But I just can't…*

"What is it?" His hand left my arm, and he sat next to me.

"This whole…mess." I waved a hand around in exasperation. "It's exhausting. Even before I was shot, it…"

"I know what you mean."

My head turned to look at my brother, whose eyes were trained on the wall across from the bed and through the door. The glass's corners were frosted over from the chilly air. Still, the sun sang while a few brave birds danced around the bushes devoid of summer flowers. The trees surrounding the cottage were bare, and a few pine trees were dispersed amongst them.

I surveyed the small room full of shelves, plants, books, and the occasional basket overflowing with knickknacks. A quilt that looked twice as old as Anastasia lay across the end of the bed, under my legs.

Where did she even find all this stuff?

"Not even the birds have to worry about what they're going to do tomorrow." Parker laughed, though I suspected it wasn't out of humor.

"We have a roof over our heads. We have full bellies. And we have each other." I reached across his legs and took his hands.

His eyes stayed focused on the outside world. "We won't always."

"We will never be able to stop what we were meant to be, Parker. But we're all destined for the same thing, and that means we'll be together…until we die."

Parker turned to face me now, a tear dripping out of his blue eyes and onto his pale and flushed cheeks. "Even death can't separate us. Our love is far stronger."

I bit back the harsher truth I wanted to say. "Death's powers have much greater holds on us than our own. No matter how much you try to stop it, it destroys people. Death is permanent, and it is painful. It doesn't care about how much you love me."

My brother cast a glance at our interlocked hands and then back up to focus on my face. It pained me to say and to even realize it for myself, but I needed him to know the pain he'd feel when he lost someone close to him. If he ever lost me, this could be his only solace.

"Parker, nothing could keep me from loving you except death. But you'll have to learn how to live without me if you ever lose me."

Parker released one of his hands and extended a finger to gently wipe a tear that had fallen from my eyes. His lips wore a small smile, one of sadness.

"Then I'll remember every second we have. I'll wait as long as it takes, no matter where we go, to protect you. No one should feel the pain of losing you."

38

INFALLIBLE HEROES

{ *Jesse* }

I sprinted down the staircase, swung around the post, and sauntered down the next flight.

The kitchen was empty, but the sun shone brightly through all the windows.

I hate it when Dad opens all the curtains.

Music played softly in my ears, so I reached down to my phone and clicked the volume button up on the playlist Lavinia had sent me last night.

A yawn opened my jaw wide before I rubbed my still-clouded eyes and opened the fridge. *Hmm.* I decided on the plastic container of strawberries that I knew to be Grace's and a banana off the counter.

I slid both items into the small cooler pouch of my backpack, zipped it up, and propped it on the island counter. Liam's footsteps descended the stairs before I heard his grumbling. He wandered to the fridge, eyes still closed. I chuckled at his outfit of a tattered *Star Wars* t-shirt and grey sweatpants.

"Did you sleep in those?"

"Shut up." He slapped me with a piece of lunch meat before stuffing it in his face. I snorted under my breath and picked up his homework assignment on the dining room table.

"You left this in here!" I called.

Liam snatched the paper out of my hands and turned on his heels to pick up another one in the living room.

"Jesse! Liam! Where's your sister?" Mom yelled from upstairs. Her head of dark hair soon appeared at the banister, and I leaned against the bottom rail, taking out my earbuds.

"She isn't in her room?"

"No, and I texted her a few times while I was getting ready, but when I went to check, she wasn't there. She isn't getting food?"

"It's just me and Lee."

"Hmm." She sighed. "Is the car gone?"

Liam leaned out the breakfast nook window and shook his head. "It's still there. Dad's car isn't, though. Did either of you hear him leave?"

"No," Mom and I both said at the same time.

"I just saw him in the bathroom, he—" She disappeared into her room and reappeared a second later, phone up to her ear. It was ringing. And ringing. And ringing.

"Where the hell are you, Tom?" she shouted into the phone as she walked down the stairs.

After extending her tirade a few more words, she hung up the phone and pressed her thumbs to her temples.

"Mom," I said gently, taking one hand away from her face. She turned her worried eyes on me and bit her lip.

"Uh, guys?" Liam called before she could reply.

Mom and I turned to see him with both palms against the window, a few papers now on the floor. Cars were speeding down our street and into our long driveway. They were all black, and the two huge SUVs that opened revealed men dressed in black tactical gear.

"Run!" Mom whisper-yelled, tearing Liam away from the window and rushing to lock the front and kitchen door.

We sprinted up the stairs, and my heart leapt into my chest. Mom pushed us until we reached the bottom of my floor's staircase, when Liam stopped in his tracks, whirring around.

"We can't just jump out his window!"

"Adrenaline can do many things, Liam. *Go!*" Mom hissed from behind me.

Liam fled to the top of the stairs, and I trailed behind him. But when I reached the top and Liam continued to open my window, I realized there was no sound behind me.

"Mom, what are you doing?" I called back down the stairs in a whisper.

She took a few steps up and motioned for me to keep going. "I need to make sure you're both safe. I'll hide out, but if they come looking for you two, I need to—"

"Stop trying to be a hero," I snapped.

"I am not *asking*, Jesse Reid," she returned with a glare. "I can do this, and I damn well will. Get out there and onto the backside of the house."

Noises sounded from the first floor, and she gave me a heavy shove. "Don't come back inside until they're gone!"

"Mom—"

But she was gone. I rushed over to Liam, who was standing outside the window on the porch roof, and pushed him through.

"Wait, where's Mo—?"

"Go," I hissed through my teeth.

We jumped onto the porch roof, and I flung the window shut. I glimpsed over the side of the house and over the driveway at all the cars. Hatred rose within me and twisted my stomach into knots while bile climbed into my throat and brought a foul taste to my mouth.

I hate this.

The cover of the back of the house, even hidden on the roof, caused beads of sweat to grow on every bare inch of my skin. My fingers shook against the touchscreen of my phone; I dialed Grace's number and held it up to my face.

"Nothing?" Liam whispered, his back turned to me. He glanced at me before turning his attention to stare off the side of the house.

"No," I returned before dialing her again. And again. And again.

But Grace didn't answer, and neither did Dad. We couldn't see the cars from our hiding spot in the shade, which meant we could only hear them leave. Liam and I met each other's eyes and stood up, moved to the window, and opened it.

Mom wasn't in the house. She wasn't in any open space, any hiding space, any small or cramped area where she could have been suffocating. She wasn't in the building she was supposed to be safe in—the building we were all supposed to be safe in. Instead, she was missing and in the hands of some psychos with guns.

The only evidence we found of the men's presence was a small piece of paper, half the size of a business card, with a single symbol on it. It was a simple sketch of two handguns, crossed over each other like an X.

The only peculiar thing I noticed about the card was that at the tip of the guns was drawn what looked to be a puff of red smoke. But it was clear to me that it didn't represent a smoking gun.

I wasn't sure what it meant, but from the glow I had seen on a certain auburn-haired friend's hands that looked like that smoke, I knew I needed to find out.

I need Lavinia.

THE DARKER TRUTH

{ *Lavinia* }

A knock broke the silence, and we all looked at each other in confusion, food still in our mouths.

I met Anastasia's green eyes, panic rising within both of us. Her eyes widened, and she quickly swallowed her food, stood up from the small table, and passed into the entryway. One slender hand motioned at Parker, and the other rested on the doorknob.

Parker rushed to Anya and took her gun from its place on her lower back, preparing himself behind her to come to our defense. Persephone glanced at me with fear in her blue eyes.

The knock sounded again. This time, Anastasia opened the door. Before I could see who our visitors were, she sighed heavily in relief.

"Parker, put it away." She opened the door to reveal Jesse and Liam.

"You should have told us you were coming!" Parker scolded, though a smile played on his lips while he slid the pistol in between his jeans and the small of his back.

Liam stood in the doorway, hands fiddling nervously in front of him. Jesse brushed past Anya and Parker to kneel on the ground beside my chair, his jaw clenched.

"What is this, Nia?" he asked softly, taking one of my hands. With his other hand, he placed a small piece of cardstock in my hand and met my eyes.

I hesitated and searched his face before I swallowed and looked down to the card. A sharp breath shuddered my lungs.

It's—

"Where did you get this?" My jaw tensed, and I stole a glance at Anastasia.

Jesse's eyes fell to my lap. "It was the only thing left behind."

"You mean—" Anastasia started.

Liam spoke next with a glare in her direction, stepping inside. "They took our mother." The room fell silent while Liam paused. "We hadn't even left for school when over a dozen cars pulled into our driveway and out stepped men. With guns. Jesse and I hid on the porch roof on the back side while Mom hid inside. She—"

Liam stopped and let out a small sigh. A tear rolled down his face, eyes cast to the floor. Persephone stood from her chair and peeked at the card I held. She recognized its bearer, clamped her mouth shut, and finished her walk to Liam.

Parker stood in place, staring at me, while Anastasia took Persephone's seat beside me. The two by the entryway spoke in hushed tones while Jesse turned to me again.

"Does this belong to who I think it belongs to?"

I locked my eyes shut and bit my lip to stop it from trembling. It wasn't from sadness, and that surprised me. It was anger and hate like I had never felt before as my guts turned inside out and my heart jumped right through my throat.

But he needs to hear the truth. Not just yours, but the truth that's too scary for normal people. The truth that you wish you never had to hear, much less live through.

"It was Ivankov who took your mother, Jesse. To protect their secrets."

His breath caught in his throat. He lowered his eyes again, this time cursing while he stood to pace behind me. Parker and I met each other's eyes, and he gritted his teeth together.

Don't, I mouthed to him.

But he spun on his heels and sprinted up the stairs, slamming the door shut to his room once at the top. Even Liam and Persephone grew quiet at his outburst. Jesse slowed his pacing, and Anastasia turned her quiet eyes to rest on me.

"Is he—?" Liam asked.

No one answered him until Jesse stopped beside me and glanced down. "He needs you more than we do."

I shook my head. "It wasn't his mother that—"

"No, Lavinia, it wasn't," he snapped. "But it was his mother and father who died protecting all of you, and the only other father he did get to have just told him he was worth nothing. So yes—" He paused. "—he needs you. Far more than I do."

"He's right," Persephone said, "Ernest hurt us both, and Margaret may have tried to kill you, but you're still alive thanks to Pamuk. I can…I can deal with those thoughts and feelings with my powers. Parker physically can't."

I turned to Anastasia for some kind of help, but she shook her head at me. "Some people can't get through this kind of life by themselves, Nia. Parker's one of them."

I breathed a sigh and stood slowly from my chair, ignoring Jesse's outstretched helping hand, and glanced back to Anya. "He's going to need to be." *I won't always be able to protect him.*

I kept my eyes on the steps beneath me as I climbed the stairs and grasped the railing with my good hand. At the top, I turned left on the small landing and stood at his door.

"No," came his muffled voice.

"I didn't even ask yet." I rolled my eyes. No answer. "Can I come in?"

"It's unlocked."

I reached out and opened the door. Parker was sitting in the armchair in the far-right corner of the room, inside the nook, with several of his ringed fingers tracing his jaw. I was thankful he had gotten the blood stains off of them easily. His head of blond hair leaned back against the dark green paint. His eyes were a much lighter shade of blue than the decorative flower stickers along the top of the wall near the ceiling.

I took a breath and walked to stand in front of him between the window and the chair. "If I sit on your bed, this will make for an awkward conversation."

He rolled his eyes, knowing full well his bed was on the opposite side of the room and almost out of sight. He unfolded himself out of the armchair.

"Fine."

I took his seat and tucked a leg underneath me, training my gaze on where he now stood in front of the glass balcony doors. His arms were crossed, and he still breathed heavily.

"Parker, I—"

Without warning, he spun. "I should've killed him when I had the chance!"

"Don't bring that up again," I spat.

"I'm not, Nia, I'm talking about just then—before you killed Ernest—it should've been me."

"Well, I'm sorry for not waiting," I snapped.

"It's not your fault," he sighed. "I shouldn't have let him keep talking. I could have done it before you or Margaret or Pamuk ever got there, and then you wouldn't have—Mrs. Price would still—"

"What, I wouldn't have gotten shot? They wouldn't have taken Mrs. Price anyway?" I raised my voice with a lame gesture to my shoulder. "Parker, you need to stop blaming yourself. Persephone needs to stop blaming herself, and even though Anya hasn't said anything, I know she blames herself too."

"But it's—"

"No buts, Parker! It's no one's fault except the man that shot me, Pamuk—who was my friend, in case you forgot—and even now, I don't blame him, because he didn't kill me! I don't think you all realize that I'm still alive and well, though in pain, and you don't *need* to blame yourself for anything!"

He stared at me, stunned, before recovering and shaking his head. "I didn't mean to scare you or anything, just…"

"You didn't scare me," I said flatly. "You think seeing you mad scares me?"

"Well, it…" He chuckled wryly and met my eyes. "I guess it doesn't."

"No, it doesn't. What does scare me, however,"—I lifted a hand and pointed to him—"is seeing Anastasia mad at me."

"That doesn't happen often, though, right?"

"You'd be surprised," I said lightly and hesitated. "Parker, I'm…"

When he sat on the rug at my feet and made eye contact, I tried again. "I feel all the anger you're feeling. But you need to keep it, hold it in, and fester it…until we get to where you can let every ounce of it out and destroy them with it."

"Them? Ivankov?"

"Yes." I paused and closed my eyes for a moment. "I don't know when or how or even if it will happen, but there will be a day in the future when we can make Ivankov hurt as much as they've hurt us. Worse, even."

"We're not the only kids ripped away from normal lives, Lavinia. There are thousands of others, some Masters, some not—Sarvesh, Viktoriya, Alek, Hannah, James, they're all…"

"Just as broken as us."

"Yeah. And the worst part about them is that they don't have *any* family. We have each other, and we have Anya. We can get through it together, but everyone else…"

I leaned my head back onto the wall, letting Parker's hands gently enclose mine and taking comfort in the cold metal of his rings pressed against my palm.

"They'll never be able to break free," I finished.

40

HELL AND BACK

"**S**he never answered her phone, so when…" Jesse breathed.

"…when they all left, I took her car and drove us here. I didn't trust anywhere else to be safe."

Persephone glanced around the living room and set down her plate. "Other than the obvious, why would Ivankov break in? What could they want with Mrs. Price?"

Liam nodded from his spot on the couch next to her. "Right, doesn't it make more sense for them to find you four?"

"Not since they think we're on injury-mission recovery," Parker said, leaning against the wall with his arms folded. "We're safe for now."

His tight lips were downcast, his eyes grave and unforgiving. Not a single word was said to him when the two of us came back down the stairs, which I knew he was grateful for. We simply began eating again and let Jesse and Liam tell the full story.

I didn't want to say what I was really thinking. Not with Jesse and Liam here. I wished Anastasia would shoo everyone out and confirm my suspicions, but instead, she adjusted her legs in the armchair across from the main couch and took a breath.

"There's really only one plausible answer. But it's not a good one," she warned, looking at Jesse. He glanced at my blank face before staring back at Anya.

"Any answer is a good one at this point," he shrugged. "What is it?"

"Don't, Anya, not now," I said softly. There was no point, though, since everyone heard.

"Why, what is it?" Liam leaned past Jesse's head of curls to meet my eyes.

Anastasia stood and put her hands on her hips, wearing her most serene expression on her angled face. She looked as much of a goddess as she ever had in that moment, with dark hair swirled around her shoulders and face, her green eyes piercing whomever she chose.

"No matter any of our opinions, there are facts," she began. "Facts tell us that Liam and Jesse were targeted at the school for the reason of their knowledge about Ivankov. Grace was not targeted. This morning, the house was raided by Ivankov agents. Jesse and Liam were there, Grace wasn't." She took a few steps toward the windows at the front of the cottage.

"Those two events have that in common," I said, "so we can't ignore the fact that to Ivankov, Grace is important not to damage."

Anastasia gestured to me in confirmation before slowly walking in the other direction. "This morning, Jesse told us that Grace's car was still in the driveway and that she had been in the house that morning. So had his father, but now they were gone, and so was his car."

"And common sense would say that Grace and Mr. Price left together," Persephone said, like it were the easiest thing to understand.

"Yes." Anya nodded. "And because Grace was taken out of the equation by Mr. Price and not Liam, Jesse, or Mrs. Price, the facts tell us there are two different reasons for Mr. Price's behavior. One reason: Mr. Price had received a distraction somehow and was innocent in removing his daughter from the home." She paused and held up a finger. "The other reason: Mr. Price received orders to preserve Grace's life because Ivankov knows they could turn her into a valuable asset with Lavinia's memory manipulation powers, if she cooperates,"—her finger pointed at me—"and they wanted to take Liam, Jesse, and Mrs. Price into captivity to ensure that."

The room was silent until a single crow cawed outside in interruption. I kept my eyes on the tall woman standing in the middle of the room, ignoring Jesse's and Liam's gaping expressions, Parker's rolling eyes, and Persephone's head in her hands.

Jesse took a deep breath and fumbled with his hands in his hair before standing to meet Anastasia. He almost equaled her height, though even if she were much shorter than me, I doubted she would seem like it—even compared to Jesse's anger.

"You're saying it's possible that my father is an Ivankov agent?"

"I'm saying it's highly probable," she corrected.

Jesse scoffed. Without another word, he left the rest of us sitting in silence to stalk through the hall and kitchen, out of sight.

I stared at Anastasia, unmoving. "You're sure about this?"

"What other reason could there be for Grace *and* their father to go missing from the house, far outside their normal routine, just before Ivankov agents storm in? And then, when Jesse and Liam are nowhere to be found, they only take their mother?"

◆ ◆ ◆

I knocked on the door of my room but received no answer.

"Jesse?" I called softly.

He opened the door. His hair was unkempt, presumably from running his hands through it. He had probably been pacing or—

"I know she's right, it's just…"

"I know." I nodded. "I know."

Jesse stepped past me out of the door with a single glance in acknowledgement. His pace was brisk, setting off an alarm bell inside my head.

He's right to be upset, Lavinia, it doesn't mean he's gonna—

I hurried after him and stopped at the living room arch to watch Anastasia turn at the sound of his steps. I silently cursed her for not reading my reaction.

"You can't just believe what you want to believe," she said calmly. *What a diplomat.* "You don't know the pain of finding out someone you thought was good was really just another one of your demons. Another person who's responsible for your pain and the people you love. The stuff you've profited off of!"

Jesse stiffened, and though I could only see his back, I imagined that his face did not bear a smile. "You think that if I didn't know sooner, I wouldn't have killed the bastard myself? You think I'm not pissed off right now? That I don't want to believe that someone I love could be so treacherous?"

Parker's hands began to glow with his powers, and I met his eyes to send him a warning. This was something they needed to work out, and I, for one, did not want to be the one to get in between the assassin and the boyfriend.

"You know what this life is like," Jesse stated with an eerily calm anger, "so you can put yourself in my shoes. I could be ready to put a bullet in my father's brain if it means saving the rest of my family, but you want to know who's hurt more than us? The people he's lied to?"

She waited for him to continue.

"He's been a part of the demons that have haunted the girl I love for all her life. The monsters that have twisted her into someone who had to survive are at fault, and he's one of those. My own father is partly responsible for the hell she's been through, and it's not just her. It's her family. It's you."

Anastasia let her eyes glimpse me in sympathy and Jesse followed, turning around. He trained his stare on me, letting a tear fall down his face.

"I didn't know about any of it. When I was growing up, you were being tortured by something my father might be a part of, and I couldn't do anything about it. *That's* what hurts. I don't want to believe it, because…"

My lips moved before I could stop them. "Jesse, don't—"

"No. I'm allowed to be angry at myself, just like I can be angry at him for ruining your life. Because we've all walked through hell and back,"—he laughed sardonically and waved at our peculiar group—"and all the while, I could've been as happy as I've ever been—with you. And he's to blame."

The tears soaked my cheeks and continued to fall until they reached my lips. He stepped closer to me and took one of my hands.

"Then let's make him pay," I whispered.

41

GOOD ENOUGH FOR ME

"**I** know it hurts whether you'll admit it or not. Ernest and Margaret."

Jesse's hands fell through my hair, and the water retreated as he put the shower head back in its place. I turned slowly to face him.

"It shouldn't hurt. I'm used to it."

"And you don't realize you *shouldn't* be used to killing someone?"

"I know that," I whispered, letting our hands connect again. "But I feel bad sometimes. I feel bad that I regret it."

"It's pretty normal to regret having to kill someone," Jesse said and scoffed. "It was never your fault to be in this mess."

Sometimes I wonder.

He took his gaze off of me and let it wander around the shower; I looked at him, letting my response be the water running down on us. I pondered that through all our messy moments, through the many conversations we've had, there had never been anything quite like this.

It was one thing to see him this bare on top of me, but it was another thing to be standing beside him in the shower when he brought up the fact that I'd just murdered, though in self-defense, the only parents I could really remember.

Some parents, I thought bitterly.

I surmised that I could say with confidence that most other almost seventeen-year-olds didn't have those types of conversations with their significant others while stark naked under a shower faucet.

I wonder what normal people talk about.

Jesse's dark eyes found me again, sure as the sun rising. "Do you ever ask yourself what you would be like outside of this life?"

"Every day," I responded without hesitation. "Every time I have to take a life, I think of what I would be like if I had a father to teach me how to ride a bike and a mother to teach me hymns and grandparents to sneak me candy. What my brother and sister would be like if I'd grown up teasing them about their crushes and their lack of fashion sense."

"My grandfather used to carry mints with him wherever he went." Jesse's face widened into a smile. A sweet, sweet smile that swelled peace within me.

The corners of my lips lifted slightly. "From what I remember about my mom, so did she."

We stood in silence for a few moments, letting the shower fill the space with a gentle hum of water hitting his side and my front. I thought of the scars of mine he was seeing…the first time he wrapped my arm in his bathroom.

I had seen one of his scars then: he had fallen as a kid and split open the skin behind his ear. While my shoulder was used to the heat now, it would be a few weeks before I could put the scarred skin under the water.

"You know," Jesse sighed, "not everyone else is as good as you might think they are. Everyone's flawed."

"But they're normal. You're normal."

He raised an eyebrow, but even though it was a joking response, I frowned. "You're as normal as I've seen, Jesse."

"Right, because I haven't shot anyone or was taken at birth, I'm normal?" He scoffed.

"It wasn't at birth."

"Same difference. It's a terrible thing."

"I know. Which is why"—I let out a sigh—"I'm not normal. None of us are. And even with all that…"

"You have me, at least." He reached a hand into my hair again, and I let him adjust my stance to stand back to the water.

"I know. But there's still so much missing with how terrible I feel."

"Terrible, like?"

"How bad of a person I am."

Jesse's hands went still, and he waited for me to finish.

"I've tried so hard to be good, even with everything they put me through. I wanted to be good for Parker, for Persephone, even for Anastasia—who's twice as messed up as I am—to just feel something other than survival. Just once." I turned and the water hit my stomach, just avoiding my shoulder wound. Our eyes met again as Jesse nodded in confirmation, in solace. "But I don't think I'm very good at all. At least, not without you."

"I don't think I am, either." He smiled faintly.

His wet hair was flat against his head, unlike the familiar curls I had touched so many times before. But I stared at him in wonder. Wonder at his innocence compared to mine, though it wasn't very innocent at all.

But even with all that, he was still good. He still chose to be good.

"You're the best I've seen, Jesse Reid Price. And that's good enough for me."

{ Anastasia }

I stared out the upstairs study window while the raindrops fell heavily on the roof.

It was late, which meant the twins and Liam were asleep in the other three bedrooms of this floor and Jesse was still in Lavinia's room behind the kitchen. I was alone, and it was quiet. Just the way I liked it.

My thoughts drifted to everything I had to tiptoe around lately, one of the largest being that I had to hide the Markovs from Higgins and the Board. But while it was my job to analyze people and factor Ivankov's best interests into their future, I hadn't expected things to get this messy when I came to New York.

I was fourteen when I completed the graduation mission of the Black Box program in St. Petersburg, which was when I requested my position to be in New York—not Russia. The other girls and my trainers were surprised, but I kept insisting. When they finally agreed four years later, I was grateful beyond belief.

217

I had been told there was a team of children ten years younger than me who needed a strong hand of guidance and a figure that would represent Ivankov's standards to the fullest. But I had other reasons for wanting to accept the job.

I became an in-team to the kids from Latvia. We were a messy family at first, but soon, I trained them well. There was Agent Everton, whom I still didn't like; Agent Moren; Agent Kuhn; a handful of others; and a lovely Master—a spitball of fire known as Agent Markov.

Her siblings were in a lower team, but at eight years old, these kids had been in Ivankov half their lives or longer. Most of them anyway. Moren had been born into it and had transferred from the Black Box. Kuhn was only three and Markov was six when they were taken. I had come up with a little story that Everton wasn't actually born—he was sent up from hell.

Markov was the toughest to train, the angriest, and the least favorite of her team members. I never let it show to the other in-teams at the compound that she was something of my favorite, since they all hated her too.

But it was only because she was better—better than all of them put together. She wasn't as good as me, but I attributed that to her age. I had vowed to make her second only to me so that she could defend herself and her family when I couldn't help her any longer.

Despite my best efforts and years of training telling me otherwise, I had gotten attached to the Markovs from the time I met them. Over the course of that time— eight years later—I was a friend to them. They had known and remembered what it was like to be ripped from their family, and so did I.

There wasn't any way I could reverse the damage, but I could give them a friend. I was powerful within Ivankov, far more than even Lavinia knew, but I couldn't just leave them or the Markovs. Though it was devastating, I didn't know anything else.

This was the life I was used to, and I was comfortable. Even if it was the most corrupt life imaginable, this was what I knew. This was what Anastasia Rabinova, in all her depressed glory, would do all her life. I'd be here until I died.

The ringing of my phone startled me, and the raindrops sliced through my ears as I came back down to earth. Sarvesh's contact shone brightly in the dim room. I pressed the answer button and lifted the phone up to my ear.

"Hey, you got anything?"

He answered with a chuckle. "Sure, hello to you too, Anya. How've you been, Anya? How'd you sleep, Anya? Do anything without me, Anya?"

I rolled my eyes. "Good evening, Sarvesh. How have you been?"

"Good. How about you?"

"Not bad, but I'd be better if you answered my question. Do you have anything?"

"No, sadly. Just the normal buzz and the boring, Ivankov-filled life we lead. Normal training stuff. Oh, and everyone's happy you 'sent the Markovs on a mission' so they can wait longer to move."

I pictured him making air quotes while spinning in his desk chair and smiled. "And no one suspects anything?"

"Nothing. A few assignments that Alek and Vik complain about, but that's nothing new."

I let a silence grow between us for a few moments.

"You're trying to tell me something, Anastasia. What is it?"

"We know Mr. Price is an Ivankov agent. They kidnapped Jesse and Liam's mother, and Grace is missing. Probably sitting next to her mother in a cell or in a comfortable room with her dad a few hundred yards away from you."

"Wow. That's…"

"I know."

Sarvesh sighed deeply and hesitated for a moment. "I could find them if you want me to."

"You can?" I sat up straight. The moonlight shone in my face as the clouds parted. The rain slowed and I leaned forward, the cushions filling in the space.

"Sure. Cameras and files are just as easy to crack as going into the prisoner levels myself."

I chuckled. "Only, you don't have to lie to a computer."

He snickered when I poked fun at his people skills. "That's the one thing you haven't taught me quite as well."

"Hey, I taught you fine, you're just not applying yourself to get good at it."

I shook my head, and we both let our laughter fade into silence. The door of the study opened, and Jesse's face peeked through. The hall lamp glowed behind him and engulfed the study in light.

"I'll check in tomorrow morning, Sarvesh. Have a good night."

"Sleep well," he echoed and hung up.

"What is it, Jesse?" I asked quietly. Parker's room was on the other side of the hall and he slept lightly, while Liam's bed was just on the other side of this wall.

"Just wanted to let you know that I'll be staying in Nia's room, so you don't have to stay on this couch. You can have your room back."

I sniffed. "Her bed is big enough?"

Jesse hummed. "Yeah. I'll be on the inside so her shoulder isn't bothered and she can get out without much difficulty."

I stood and opened the door fully while he stepped back to allow me room. I met his eyes and angled my head.

"Be gentle with her," I warned. Whether he was going to think I was talking about her injury or not was up to him.

Jesse rolled his eyes and made his way back down the stairs. "I won't bother her shoulder while I'm the little spoon, if that's what you mean."

My lips cracked open wide in an unexpected smile as I opened my door and flipped the light switch on.

He treats her well, doesn't he?

42

THANK YOU FOR THE MEMORIES

{ *Lavinia* }

The room was dark, and the only sound was faint breathing rising and falling.

But it wasn't next to me.

Still foggy, I muttered to Jesse and reached out with one arm to inch closer. My hand landed on the cold sheets—he wasn't there.

I jolted awake. I had heard myself breathing, and it took a few blinks of my heavy eyelids to grow used to the room to realize that Jesse wasn't here at all. I frowned. I considered that he had just gone to the bathroom before I got up.

I wrapped his sweatshirt that was sitting on the floor around my shoulders. I found him sitting on the bottom step of the stairs with his knees drawn up and head resting in his hands. My socked feet slid noiselessly across the floor, and he drew back in surprise when I sat down.

I wasn't sure what time it was. The outdoor lamp in front of the kitchen window cast a dim glow over the hallway in front of the stairs.

"You comin' back to bed?" I whispered, letting my head rest on his shoulder. He tensed, so I drew back. "Is everything okay?"

I couldn't see his face clearly, but the shadows that flickered were enough. His gaze was focused on the floor below him. He wasn't seeing it, though, and his eyes were clouded over—like he was still sleeping.

I inched a little farther away from him, and that very moment, I noticed the subtle signs of panic. His face was lined with tension and small beads of sweat, his breathing was rough, and his fingers were itching his knees repeatedly. He looked warm, uncomfortably so, and though he tried to control it, his feet were shaking.

For the first time, I didn't know what to do or how to help him. I had never been around Persephone's anxiety attacks, and Anastasia, though she trusted me, had effectively coped otherwise—healthily or not was another conversation.

"Can we stand up?" I asked softly, reaching a hand out.

I wanted him to know I was trying to help. I wanted to avoid reading his feelings or mind because I knew I could help without it, and it would be intrusive.

He hesitated for a few moments before taking my hand. I stood up and pulled him with me, looking him in the eye. He met my gaze shyly and bit his lip. I studied him for a moment and then led him back to my room.

Jesse moved slowly beside me, but I could tell there was a difference in his breathing, and his hand felt less sweaty as we walked. Our silence was comfortable to me, but when I let my powers connect us through our hands, I knew he was still alone.

He felt alone. He felt anger and love, but most of all, I was taken aback by the sharp fear that chilled my blood. Pain, almost physical, clung to my heart and pushed against my rising lungs.

The powerful waves of love and fear rushed over me, and then, while I sat next to Jesse on my bed, realization struck me. That connection I had at 2:00 in the morning, what seemed like weeks ago, was him. He had had a nightmare, and I was connected to him, so I had woken up in pain.

Anastasia had held me much in the same position as I held Jesse now, cradling his head in my arms after he rested it above my chest, almost to my shoulder. She had asked me if I could have fallen in love with someone and become connected to them in their sleep. I didn't want to believe it then, but there was no denying it now.

Jesse's breathing was staggered. He knew I could feel it, and despite that, he didn't speak. He didn't try to explain or make excuses. He simply lay by my side.

"Can I help?" I whispered into his hair, playing with a stray piece between my slender fingers.

I knew what was wrong, and I knew exactly how to help, but I wanted him to ask. It wouldn't mean anything if he didn't want it. I couldn't help him unless he sought it out.

Jesse mumbled something into me, but I couldn't make it out. I hummed in question as I pressed a kiss to his hair.

He turned his head to rest more comfortably in my arms. "I had a nightmare."

I deliberated on staying silent and letting him continue. "Have you had one before?" I asked softly.

"Yes." His voice was a mere whisper. "Lots of times. Almost every night."

His words were broken up, like he wrestled with what he would say before every word—every secret he revealed. He didn't want me to know.

"Are they the same?"

"No."

I paused. "Have you had *this* one before?"

Jesse didn't say anything. I connected our hands again and circled his palm with a fingertip.

His voice was barely audible, and he winced when he let the answer escape his lips. "Yes. It was about you."

"Do you want to tell me, or would you rather me pull the memory?"

He knew a lot about my powers, but he didn't know I could remove the memory if he wanted me to. I decided to ask after he told me about it. He didn't need that now.

"I can't—" Jesse's voice broke. "I can't tell you."

"Why not?"

"Because—I just, it's…"

"It's all right, Jesse." I held him closer. "You don't have to tell me a thing."

"But I want to. I just can't get it out. How am I supposed to tell you that I have nightmares every night, that every time I fall asleep is torment? Every moment I'm awake is another moment I'm not infected with those—those *things*. Those reminders."

"Reminders of what?"

"Of"—he sniffled—"her dying."

I stiffened. I had realized everything else, but I didn't know what the nightmares were. I didn't know what he had to go through every night. Who…?

Who did he lose?

I had lost my parents and any semblance of a normal life years ago. I had lost myself. I didn't know what life could be like without Ivankov until Jesse came along.

But what had he lost?

"Who?" I whispered.

"She—She died, right in front of me, and I had to…She bled out…and her blue eyes, her soft hair, covered in blood—she…Everything was fine, and then it went down in flames. Her hands went cold while I held them, Lavinia. I had to—"

I fondled the edge of his shirt sleeve and ran a finger across his cold skin. I looked down at him; his face focused on a spot on the wall, and his hand rested on my stomach. There wasn't much for him to grasp of my t-shirt, but he brushed his fingers between the folds of the fabric.

"I loved her so much. And she…she died. And I had to live in a world without her, without anything good, in so much pain. I had to survive. Grace had to pull me out of bed every morning to make sure I wouldn't…And then, when you…When I met you…" He shook as another breath left his lungs. "You helped me, without knowing, to fall in love with life again. To see the pretty little things. To see new things. And just when I was starting to figure everything out, I fell in love with you. And you've kept me here."

Jesse turned onto his side and wrapped his arm around me, curling close. His breathing slowed, his face pressed into my side. I could feel his pain wash away as I flickered my fingers in his hair, gently pulling the memories from his mind.

"And I never thought you'd bring me pain," he continued, shaking. "But every time I fall asleep, I see you. Dying. And I was the one who did it."

I further pushed his memory and whispered, "No, you didn't, I'm still here."

"But every night—"

"I'm right here, Jesse. I'm not going anywhere," I promised softly.

"Nia, I—I can't deal with this pain anymore. I can't take it."

"I know, sweetheart. But don't get lost in it. There's so much love waiting for you to experience and feel. You don't just have me. You have Grace and Liam and so many other people that would do anything for you."

Jesse's response was a small sniffle. I knew there was more we didn't say, and I knew it would take him a while to believe me—that it was really going to get better. It always gets better for people like Jesse.

Not for you, though.

"You know," he sniffled again, "every time I see something that reminds me of her, I have a panic attack. Almost every time. But it depends on what it is."

I paused for a moment and let my powers fade. "How often does it happen?"

"Almost every day. Before school, mostly."

My body stiffened when flashes of memories sprung through my mind, all of Jesse greeting Grace or me at school—his red eyes, puffy cheeks, scattered glances, sweat on his face, tousled hair—all signs of panic and distress I'd never noticed. Ever.

I momentarily shook it all away, adjusting my hand on his hair. "And that's why you're late so often?"

"Yeah," came his breaking voice.

A tear fell on my cheeks. I smiled sadly, closing my eyes, and dropped my head to rest on his. Jesse let out a broken sigh. I held him closer, as close as I possibly could without hurting my shoulder, and squeezed my eyes shut like it could erase the nightmare we were living in.

"I..." he said almost inaudibly. "I'm going to love you forever, Lavinia Markov."

A real smile played on my tired lips this time when I whispered an "I love you" in return, kissing his forehead.

"Death is nothing compared to what I would do for you, Jesse Price."

A few more of his tears stained my side. He sighed, and soon his breaths slowed when he fell into a deep sleep.

I would stay awake for as long as it took so he wouldn't go through that torment again. So he could feel peace. So we could both be the other's peace.

If Only we Could Stay

{ *Lavinia* }

I adjusted my shoulder against the pillow and snaked my good hand underneath it.

The soft texture made me sigh in contentment as I moved closer, leaving my eyes comfortably shut, and heard a sudden grunt. I lifted my head up to see that the pillow was, in fact, Jesse. And he was not asleep anymore.

"Oh my—I'm so sorry," I whispered, and my eyes widened.

Jesse chuckled softly and pressed a kiss to my hair. "It's fine."

His eyes, usually dark and peaceful, shone of worry from the events of last night, so I gave him a small "Good morning" smile. The sun shone through the glass door and window, highlighting the skin around his eyes that was still swollen and red.

Jesse's smile didn't quite reach his eyes when he said good morning, but I yawned widely and grinned in return. His arm around my torso pulled me closer and he turned on his side, back facing the wall. His other hand moved to rest by my head, where he reached out and touched a few pieces of my hair between his fingers.

"How'd you sleep?" I said softly, gazing up at him.

It was a routine question but a question nonetheless. Jesse yawned down at me, letting his fingers slip to the side of my face. His hand was warm and comforting.

"Better than past nights. Better because you're here," he amended with a small chuckle.

"I'm glad." I searched his face.

He gazed at me while we took a moment to understand what he really meant—but what he didn't say.

Because you feel safer with me by your side, my mind echoed.

"And how did you sleep?" His somber mood lifted slightly.

"Wonderful," I beamed, "but I'd be better if you kissed me good morning."

He scoffed but then leaned closer so that his lips lingered an inch away from mine. "I can help with that."

Jesse pressed our lips together, then adjusted from his side to prop himself up, an arm on each side of me. I took his head into my hands and pushed his hair back as I kept him close, our lips still locked.

"Are you two up?" a voice yelled from the stairs.

Our lips separated, and he rested his forehead on mine. We waited in silence, but Anastasia called out again. I rolled my eyes and shoved Jesse off of me the best I could with one arm.

"That's Anya."

He darted his gaze to the door and back to my face. "I didn't hear anything, did you?"

Footsteps softly plodded outside the door, and a knock sounded. I gave him a look of "I told you so," and he rolled his brown eyes in return before he got off the bed and opened the door.

"Yes, Anastasia?"

I closed my eyes for a moment and opened them to continue enjoying my view of the boy standing in front of the door, leaning against the frame. He was wearing dark grey sweatpants and a black t-shirt that exposed his toned arms—especially since his stance, arm high against the doorframe, slid the sleeve farther toward his shoulder.

I ignored whatever know-it-all response Anya dealt to Jesse and waited until he closed the door and looked at me in silent expectation.

"Well?"

"She said she's making breakfast and expects us to be there soon."

"How soon is soon?" I queried.

He stretched his arms above his head, lifting his shirt to reveal part of his stomach. "She didn't say." He winked and jumped back onto the bed.

"But what is she making…?" I whispered as his face hovered above mine.

He paused and thought for a moment. "Pancakes."

"Ooh!" I smiled widely.

"Never heard you squeal before, much less over food."

"Oh? You must not be aware of how much I love pancakes, then," I sassed.

"Mmm. Waffles are better."

I gasped in fake offense and slapped his arm with my good hand. "Get off of me, you big pancake hater!"

"Never," Jesse grumbled jokingly. I grinned in bliss at his mood improvement compared to last night, and pancakes would excite him even more. So I indulged him further.

♦ ♦ ♦

"So," Parker started, swallowing the last of his pancakes. "Now that the gang's been back together for a little while now…"

Anastasia stood up and collected some of the plates to take them to the kitchen. "Please tell me you don't want to play games and watch sitcoms," she called out over her shoulder.

We all laughed, but Persephone shook her head. "We don't even have a TV."

"Huh. Wonder why," Anastasia said dryly, reappearing in the living room.

"We do have games, though—found them on one of the bookshelves of the upstairs study," Liam offered.

"You're not helping my case." Anya sent him a sideways smile.

"Hey!" I defended. "I can do a lot more now!"

"Well, we could always…"

All eyes turned to Jesse.

"We could do what?" I asked.

"Make a plan to get Mom and Grace back from Ivankov," he finished with a glance in my direction.

I froze, recovering after a moment of silence. "How would we—?"

Anastasia folded her arms and sat back down, crossing one leg over the other. "All we have is me, Lavinia, two newbies in the field, and two near strangers to violence. Do you know what we'd be going up against?"

Near strangers to violence? I thought wryly. *She has no idea.*

She scoffed and swung her hair out of her face. "The base is an expertly designed fortress with cameras at every corner, biometric locks on each door that are almost impossible to bypass, hundreds of life-experienced guards that are constantly rotating, and not a single place to hide if you get caught along the way."

"You've snuck out before, haven't you? With the party?" Jesse's eyes swiveled between Persephone and me with his rhetorical question.

My sister spoke, her voice light. "We've only done it once—with all the curfew rules and locks and trackers, I'm surprised we could."

Anastasia chuckled. "Actually, she's been out plenty. So have I."

I sighed internally, pursing my lips in thought. A plan was doable, but it would be difficult.

"You're talking about missions, though, aren't you?" Parker frowned. A pause. "Aren't you?" He folded his arms and fiddled with a ring.

I stared at my brother and mimicked his accent. "Nope."

Parker groaned and ran his hands through his blond hair, upsetting it into a larger mess.

I smiled. "There are ways in and out that many people know about! You and Persephone excluded."

"Back to the topic at hand," Liam said, "you're saying there are ways in? It's possible?"

"It's more than possible. Just dangerous." Anastasia pursed her lips.

"So we should at least try," he pressed.

"Did you not hear the part about the biometric locks and cameras?" Persephone gaped. "And, you know, the armed and experienced guards?"

"You think I can't outsmart them?" Anastasia lifted a corner of her mouth.

Parker held up a hand. "Hang on, you two, I still think it's stupid!" Everyone's eyes rested on his stern expression. "It's dangerous. It's risky. We can't just 'try,' because if we get caught, we're done for. Having an international assassin *and* three

Masters on our side isn't enough, because Ivankov has ten more expendable agents for every one of us. They don't care who they send to stop us so long as we're stopped."

"It might be stupid, Parker, but we could figure it out," I insisted, feeling a smug smirk grow. "And it's not like you're going to stay behind and not help us. You might as well agree now."

He grumbled, stood, stalked to the kitchen, and disappeared behind the stairs.

"You're all acting like you can't just come back from your 'mission' like normal and find a way to get Mom and Grace out then," Jesse scoffed. "Why break in?"

He has a point.

Anastasia spoke slowly. "Ivankov won't wait that long to extort Lavinia into using her powers on Grace. Higgins will contact me in a few days, I'm sure, to bring the Markovs back early. The longer they have a prisoner in custody, the more of a risk they are."

She also has a point.

"Oh."

"It's now or never. We don't have many options," I said regretfully.

"So—what's the plan?" Liam asked.

Everyone's eyes turned to Anastasia.

♦ ♦ ♦

"That entire plan hinges upon one thing,"—she paused—"and that is discretion. We cannot alert Ivankov of our presence, or we will be doomed."

"Doomed. Got it," Jesse nodded with a sober expression.

"I'm serious." Anastasia gave him a stink eye.

"Of course you are!" He returned with a smirk.

Parker rolled his eyes. "C'mon, Anya, move along."

"Fine." She glared at Jesse momentarily. "Our goal is to not turn any heads. No guns"—she glanced at me and Parker—"and no knives,"—she glanced at Persephone—"or our cover will be blown."

"Oh, you're no fun," I pouted.

"Don't care. You will only defend yourselves if absolutely necessary. Parker will go everywhere Lavinia goes *first* so she can erase the memories of anyone you

231

come into contact with. But only if necessary. Understood?”

We collectively nodded in confirmation.

“Under no circumstances are you to engage with any agent or guard you see unless it’s Sarvesh or me. He’ll be waiting on sublevel three to meet you and lead you to Grace and Mrs. Price—if he can find them.”

“And if he can’t?” Liam whispered.

“Then there is no plan.”

44

BLUE-EYED

"**A**ll done!" Parker called out.

I opened the door and stopped in surprise at the two teenagers standing in front of me. Parker was facing Lavinia, though she was looking out the window.

"You still look like you."

Lavinia let out a giggle. "That's because you've been staring at me for all fourteen years of your life."

"True enough."

Lavinia's eyes rotated to rest on my face while I searched her new appearance. I stammered but then found my words. "I never knew your powers could do all of that."

"I live to surprise," came her brand-new, crooked smile. "After all, I can control all types of matter and energy. That includes human bodies, as weird as it sounds."

Her bright blonde hair, long and curly, lay freely down her back, and her eyes flashed a bright green instead of their usual grey. The eyebrows decorating her face were thinner; her narrow jawline now showed filled-out, pink cheeks; and her thin shoulders barely carried her small frame and protruding hips.

"This is different. Very, very different," I gawked.

"Well, it was Parker's idea to change my build and shape, because apparently, 'someone who looks like a high school mean girl should have a matching body,' and I 'look too nice' with my own figure with this hair, so…" She scoffed and flailed a thin hand with painted fingernails.

"I'm not wrong, am I?"

"Sadly, no." Lavinia frowned. "Even for the few weeks we *did* go to Northview, you do not want to know how many girls in the bathroom stood in front of the mirror and compared themselves against their friends."

Parker and I shared a glance of skepticism, though we knew she was right.

"That, and…"—she scrunched her nose—"how many times I got told my curves would be better suited to baggier clothes so I would look skinnier. They weren't helpful."

My lip curled. "Really?"

Lavinia smiled softly with an expression almost foreign to me and waved a hand in dismissal; clearly, the remarks by thoughtless brats didn't faze her.

She gave a small twirl and swung her hair around. "But you like it, though?"

"I like the real you better." I laughed. "Without the blonde hair."

"At least I didn't go blue-eyed." She waved a finger at me and took my hand. "And what about him? Did I do a good job?"

We turned to Parker, and I processed the differences in his appearance: his eyes were a light brown, almost hazel; his wavy, blond hair was now jet black and shorter; and his face was drastically changed as if Lavinia had changed it blindly. He was the same height, which I assumed was because Lavinia couldn't change it easily, and his build was slimmer than usual. None of his fingers held his usual assortment of rings.

"He let you cut his hair?" I widened my eyes. Parker's expression grew horrified, and Lavinia interrupted.

"Actually, no! When I reverse everything, it will grow back instantly. It looks good, doesn't it?" Her face shone with pride. "I've never done something this intricate before."

"It does look good." I gave her an approving glance. "I can barely tell it's the same person."

Parker folded his arms and leaned on one leg. "Really?"

"Well, except when you do that. And your voice is the same."

"I could've changed it," Lavinia said while she looked up at me, bending her hand to sit comfortably around my waist. "But it seemed like a waste of precious time if I can just erase everyone's memories—as a backup plan, of course."

"Of course." I nodded solemnly. "And Parker has such a nice voice. Hate to ruin the accent."

"Sure." Parker rolled his eyes and brushed past me, out the door. "If that's what you think."

Lavinia and I shared a laugh and she turned to face me, now placing her other hand around my torso to pull us close.

"Still like the real you better," I mused, and her lips lifted.

FOURTH WALL: I'M SORRY

{ *Lavinia* }

"Testing, testing, this is Anastasia." Her voice crackled through the comms.

I situated the small earpiece inside my ear, and Parker copied the motion. We were waiting outside the West Wing entrance, just far enough away to not be seen, heard, or noticed but close enough for our earpieces to connect to Anastasia's and Sarvesh's.

"This is Lavinia, you're connected," I answered.

"Sweet!" Parker's voice was abrupt in both my ears.

"Parker, chill." I rolled my eyes.

"Testing, testing, this is Sarvesh. You guys good out there?"

I sighed and checked the two loaded guns in my holsters and the knife tucked in my jacket. "Nervous, but good."

"Your head's in the game, right?" Anastasia confirmed in a level tone.

"Yeah, of course."

"Focus, you two. Don't turn into Grandpa over there!"

"Sarvesh, it's my job to tell her and Grandpa to shut up, don't steal my spotlight," Anastasia teased.

"Keep the line clear," I scolded. "No chattering. I'll be waiting for the text."

"Yes, Mom," Sarvesh and Anastasia responded sassily. I rolled my eyes.

I held my phone in my hand, and after almost scaring myself with my unfamiliar reflection, I waited patiently for the screen to light up with the text. Parker hummed softly from beside me and adjusted his position every few minutes. He muttered under his breath, and when I raised an eyebrow to ask what he said, he shook his head in dismissal.

"Parker, we have to time this right, or it won't work. If you're ever going to be patient—now's the time."

My brother exhaled a weak sigh and nodded. Just when I glanced back to my phone, the text lit up my screen.

It's go time.

I pushed myself up and began to stalk to the entrance, Parker trailing close behind. When no one was watching, I would lead, but he was going into the facility first.

"The eagle is flying," he murmured from behind me.

"What the—?" Anastasia started.

Parker gave a light laugh and, upon the glare I sent to him, cleared his throat. "Just, uh, thought it was funny. We're going in. Carry on."

As Parker led the two of us into the building, we stopped at the appropriate checkpoints for approving Ivankov official weapons and tactical gear. Our covers protected us, and we strode up to the door we needed.

"We're here for a prisoner transfer," Parker said in a monotonous tone to the agent, gesturing disinterestedly to both of us. "Agent Agapov and Agent Krupina."

The agent held up a hand in a waiting gesture and pulled out a small keypad from his jacket, checking the information we had given him. He looked up at us, down at the keypad, and back up at us. His eyes narrowed, and a few tense moments passed before he waved us through.

The door unlocked, and Parker and I stepped into the bright hallway. It was a small rectangle space with two doors on either end and one elevator door in front of us. I reached out to push the button, and once we were safely inside, I glanced at Parker.

I muttered, "I still don't know why Anya had to choose a cover whose name means 'grains.' I mean, she could have been more creative. At least yours sounds cool."

Parker cracked a smile, breaking the serious agent façade. "Mine means love."

"My point exactly."

But I knew the agents she had chosen had great purpose, one of them being our genetic similarities so we would pass retinal scans. That had been my main focus while changing Parker's and my appearances—only a few prisoner cells needed fingerprint verification, and I wildly hoped we wouldn't need to unlock one of those.

By the time my irritation started to dissipate, the elevator door opened on the other side of where we entered to reveal a dark hallway hiding a shadowed silhouette.

Sarvesh.

"Hand that to me." I gestured to the flashlight in his hand.

"Why?" he wondered. When I stared him down, he rolled his dark eyes and handed me the flashlight.

I took a hold of it with both hands and streamed my powers into it, brightening its glow until we could see every cell in our natural range of eyesight. I pushed past Sarvesh and followed Parker's soft footsteps down the cold corridor.

"Stupid Master privileges," Sarvesh muttered under his breath behind me.

Sublevel three was exactly how I remembered it. Dank, musty, and cold. Really, really cold. The cell walls were bars of freezing metal interwoven with a Kevlar protective shield. Cells on sublevel four and lower were soundproof.

"You're sure they're here?" I asked Sarvesh, keeping the flashlight pointed beyond Parker.

My brother strode with purpose, and his occasional glances to the sides of the hall into the cells told me he was checking every one of the limp and sleeping bodies for anything familiar. I didn't need to read his mind to know he was looking for our parents.

Even if they've been dead for years. He won't stop hoping.

"I checked the records," Sarvesh started. "If their parents aren't here, they're already dead."

"That would be a shame," I muttered.

I wondered how this many prisoners were kept alive for years. Ivankov wasn't kind to prisoners here or anywhere else. Unless…

The Rejuvenator Ivankov had control over was in charge of the Assassin, and if it weren't for them, I was sure Ivankov would be very different today. I only knew that a Rejuvenator could wipe memories like my powers could, but how they did it…it was a mystery to me, along with whatever else they were hiding.

When we descended farther into the long hallway of cells, the smell grew pungent in my nose and the air grew colder. Every few hundred feet, the floor would drop down a step. I counted sixteen steps in total before I got my brother's attention.

"Parker?" I prompted, but his only response was a shake of his head.

Sarvesh muttered something about bringing backup, which slowed my pace just enough so that we were walking briskly next to each other. I cursed Parker's long legs.

"Anya's going to be in position, and so will Jesse," I informed. "This is the hardest part."

"I know, but…" He trailed off and let his dark eyes search past Parker. "I don't trust me and Parker to get them out by ourselves if you have to be the distraction."

Anastasia's voice sounded through the comms. "I assigned a member of the team to do an intake and assessment on a few prisoners and I'll be coming down to sign off on their reports. We'll be plenty of backup."

"Who did you choose?" I asked incredulously, staring at Sarvesh.

"Oh, no one special. Just me," a new voice chirped over the comms, a little too excitedly and sarcastically.

My heart sank into my stomach. "Alek, what—?"

But at the same moment I was about to cuss him out, Parker snapped his fingers. "Found her!"

◆ ◆ ◆

The cell Parker brought us to was darker than the rest, but I dimmed the flashlight back to its normal glow so as to not blind the unmoving body lying on the cold floor inside. The girl's jeans and sweater were tattered almost to shreds, and the clothing clung to her thin frame. White sneakers on her feet were no longer white, and her dark hair was mangled around her face.

Is she even alive? The worried voice in my head attempted to keep going, but I shushed it, sensing her heartbeat.

"Grace?" I whispered, waving the flashlight over her.

She didn't give any response, so I handed the flashlight to Parker and motioned for him to get out of the way. I unlocked the cell door and thanked my powers—and my skill—that my fake eyes passed the retinal scan for Agent Krupin.

I took small and quiet steps to kneel in front of her, gently extending a hand to tap her shoulder. The girl reflexively shot her feet out in an attempt to kick my shins, and her hair flew out of her face to reveal terrified eyes and tightly knit brows.

"Grace, it's just me! It's Lavinia!" I whispered furiously.

Her feet grew still. When she recognized my voice and not my face, hair, or eyes, she made a throaty sound—almost like breaking wood—and crumpled onto the ground. I groaned, lifted her up, and braced her on my side to slap her awake.

"Grace! We need to get out and you need to be awake. I can't carry you."

Sarvesh's footsteps came to a stop as he returned to the front of the cell. I met his eyes, and he nervously shook his head. I sighed at the exact moment Grace opened her eyes again.

Parker pushed past Sarvesh to support Grace on his side. She gazed at him in a stupor while he led her out of the cell. I followed him, letting Sarvesh lead the rest of us, and closed the cell. I unholstered my gun and raised my guard in case any agent came in here and realized we had "the wrong prisoner."

"Anya, we couldn't find Mrs. Price, but we have Grace," I said softly.

"You need backup?"

"Not yet. We haven't gotten to the elevator yet."

"Let me know when you're at the extraction point."

"Okay," I mumbled.

I wished furtively for no trouble from here on out, but since we were kind of breaking through the outer wall of the building to escape, I knew we were bound to have problems. I hadn't exactly told Sarvesh the truth when I said that the hardest part was finding Grace. But at least we weren't a problem for the cameras. I had Sarvesh to thank for that.

We exited the main corridor and entered the elevator hallway. Sarvesh stepped into the elevator and waved at Parker and me.

"See you later." The door closed on him.

Parker adjusted Grace, whose arms were still slung around his shoulders, to face me. I unfolded the shirt I had hidden inside my vest and replaced Grace's torn one with it. We had some difficulty changing her pants and shoes, but she was more awake and cooperative now.

But she was just as confused.

"Who—how—why do you look different?" Her words slurred together.

We avoided her questions and offered comforting words instead. Once she was ready to stand against Parker again, we helped her up.

"Now, I'm going to need you to hold still, Grace," I started. "This is going to feel pretty strange."

I lifted my hands to her face and traced her features with my fingers, letting the familiar power surge change her features to someone Ivankov could care less about. Her face and eyes were different and rejuvenated, and as my hands moved to her hair, I altered the color to be lighter and for it to grow shorter.

"What—What are you doing to me?" she asked, wildly confused.

"Keeping you safe. And don't worry, it's all temporary," I assured. Parker led us into the elevator, and Grace stood on her own, close by my side.

"Now, when we get off," I warned, "we're not going out the door in front of us. We're turning right."

"Right," she repeated.

"Follow Parker, not me, and you'll be safe. Jesse has the car waiting to take you back to the safehouse."

"And…L-Liam? He's there too?"

"Yes," Parker responded.

At that moment, the elevator door opened to reveal Anastasia and Alek standing in identical stances, feet shoulder-width apart and arms crossed.

"You two should start a band." Parker rolled his eyes and turned right.

Grace treaded after him, and they disappeared behind the door—it led to a complicated series of passageways and offices that Parker had memorized the route of escape for. I had not. If we still needed help after Grace had made it to the rest of the group, Parker would return.

"So?" I asked the two agents.

Alek frowned as his eyes met mine. "What the hell did you do to your hair?"

"Oh, this?" I held up a piece. "It's fake."

"Good, because—"

"I know you don't like blondes. Get over yourself."

Anastasia rolled her eyes. "Just be quiet."

I put a hand on my hip. "Didn't you say you had to sign his—?"

"Yes, I do, which is why…"Anastasia paused and gestured to the elevator. "…we'll be going back down."

When I stared at her blankly, she scoffed. "It will only be for a minute or two. Then we'll be on our merry way, and you can waltz right out the front door, saying you forgot something in the car."

"You know what I *did* forget in the car?" The doors closed on us. "My sanity."

"Thought you left that in Latvia."

I decided not to deign Alek with an answer.

Thankfully, Parker saved me, his voice loud in my earpiece. "So, Nia, uh…"

I went on full alert. "What is it, what's happening?"

"Just thought I'd warn you three that you're about to get stormed. Grace has a tracker."

"Oh, for God's sake," I groaned, hitting the elevator wall with my fist.

"I'm almost," he grunted, "done with taking it out. It's—"

"You're what?" Anastasia shrieked.

"I'm taking the tracker out! She'll live, it's only in her ankle," he snapped.

Alek barked out a dry laugh. "This is an interesting turn of events."

"You think?" I whirled on him.

The elevator door opened—before I could punch him—to reveal well over a dozen agents in full tactical gear, weapons drawn. We didn't have time to think about our covers.

"Hi, gentlemen." Anastasia grinned.

46

CALL IT FUN

"**I**sn't this fun?" I shouted over the mess.

Alek grunted from somewhere behind me, and Anastasia groaned when, I assumed, she was punched in the gut. My knife was drawn and covered in several agents' blood, their bodies littering the ground at my feet. I stuck it in another agent's side and twisted it, half-smiling at the cry of pain escaping from their lips.

"Why do I get the feeling—" Alek stopped and threw a punch. "—that you're enjoying this?"

"Maybe because I am."

I deduced it was a good sign that there were no alarms ringing, and since the cameras were off, the only reason the squad of agents had revealed themselves was because of an alert for a tracker out of range. I was thankful they probably didn't know who we were.

To be safe, though…

Alek finished off the final agent charging at him while Anastasia kicked another one down. She fell back into her stance as she caught her breath and flipped

245

her hair off her shoulder.

How is it that she looks so good after fighting for her life?

"Lavinia, please tell me…" Anastasia started.

"Yes," I finished for her, waving a tired hand over the fallen agents. Those who still had heartbeats were soon deprived of them.

Alek froze. "What did you just do?"

"Stopped their hearts," Anya answered for me. "It's easier than erasing their memories."

His mouth dropped. "You couldn't have led with that?"

I shrugged. "It wouldn't be as fun that way."

Parker's voice crackled through the comms. "We're all in the car, but I'm—"

"Do *not* come back!" Anastasia and I yelled simultaneously.

"How are you going to get out?"

I tapped the comms off and looked between Anastasia and Alek. "Can we get out this far down?"

Anya scowled in concentration and ran a hand through her tousled hair. "Yes, actually. There's a passageway that leads into the higher-level training grounds outside."

"And that won't be a problem?" Alek raised a blond eyebrow. "You know, since the Assassin is still here and everything?"

"It's the only option."

♦ ♦ ♦

Twice as many agents stormed us when the door opened to the outside. This time, I assumed they had a slight idea of who we were.

How fun.

"Can we—?" Alek grunted. "Can I use my gun now? It's only fair."

"Oh, to hell with it," I muttered, unholstering my gun and then knocking the back of someone's head with the butt of the handle.

"Time for the fun stuff, Anya!" I yelled in warning.

We met eyes, and I aimed the gun just past her head. Within moments, she finished her victim and slid out of the way as I pulled the trigger in rapid succession to take out the agents entering the courtyard behind her.

After a few minutes, the agents were taken care of—either dead or with memories wiped—and the three of us breathed a sigh of relief in reprieve. Because this wasn't a planned escape route, I worried the cameras would be tracking our movement.

"You two have to get out of here." I faced Anastasia and Alek. "I'll be safe."

"You sure about that?" Alek asked skeptically. His dirty blond hair was tossed to one side of his face, and he panted to catch his breath. Poor guy was really doing the most out here.

"Yeah, she's got it. At the very least, *you* need to get out of here," Anastasia said, taking a few steps to close the distance between our group.

"But I can—"

"Do you really want to find out what Ivankov does to their undergraduate agents that they find doing something like this?" she hissed.

"I guess not." He rolled his eyes and turned back the way we'd come. He posed no threat by himself and would make it back to our wing safely. When the door shut behind him, Anastasia and I shared a glance of annoyance.

"I hate your ideas," I grunted.

"Would you rather me have chosen Vik?" she shot back.

"I would have let her die. Or killed her myself."

"I know."

A single beat passed between her silence and another agent entering the courtyard. With the unmistakable swagger of his heavy metal arms and legs, the Assassin stared emptily with his brown eyes at both Anastasia and me.

"Not you again," I groaned, even though I knew he wouldn't recognize me or my voice. He had one purpose as the Master's Board's puppet.

He will kill me if I don't kill him.

The cage around his face resembling a muzzle adjusted with his flexing jaw. He stalked across the stone pathway to meet us.

Glad it's a fair fight: the Manipulator of the Highest Order and the Assassin with metal arms and legs as useful as a machine gun.

I raised my gun and clicked the trigger, only to realize I was out of bullets.

Well, crap.

Anastasia took a step behind me when I quickly snapped open my other holster, pulled out the second gun, and fired above his left arm. He didn't stop.

I shook my shoulders in preparation, thankful for the past few days I had spent healing my shoulder, and ran to meet him. My breath kept even as I dodged his punches and kicks, but I grinned and decided to at least have some fun.

"You know, for a sixteen-year-old, I'm doing a pretty good job of beating an eighty-year-old man." I chuckled while I deflected his punches and ducked under his legs to shoot his back.

The Assassin had been training and killing under Ivankov before they ever became powerful. It was no doubt that because of him, their empire had grown. Ivankov had tried creating their own Master, and when they ended up with the Assassin instead, they decided to keep using him.

It was no mystery to me that they had kept him alive and young using a Master Rejuvenator, though I would be lying if I said it didn't scare me to know that both my siblings and I could be in the same position years from now: brainwashed, alive only physically, and built for killing.

"What, you didn't find that funny?" I laughed, aiming higher this time.

I fired what I knew was my last bullet in the back of his head. I wasn't sure if it made its target or not as he whirled around upon hearing my voice. Although he was currently an uncoordinated mess, he dove to the ground on top of me and caused my gun to fall.

I groaned at his weight and rolled out from underneath him as he tried to punch my head, landing at the spot on the floor where I left. He stumbled to get up, weakening from the bullet I'd put in his back. I took the chance to stand up, get in a proper stance, and whip out my knife.

I stretched my neck around in circles. "Ready for another round?"

Anastasia hadn't made an appearance in our fight, but from the grunts followed by sudden silence, I happily assumed she was taking care of other agents. The Assassin's eyes now flamed in anger.

I wonder if antagonizing him is the best course of action.

A deafening crack sliced the air. Anastasia had jumped from behind the Assassin in an impressive maneuver when his guard fell, wrapping her legs tight around his neck and wrangling his head with her fists.

"You know, Dmitri, I was hoping—" She made a remarkable punch. "—that you would recognize me. So I wouldn't have to fight you."

"He gets his memory wiped by our mystery Rejuvenator friend, remember?" I raised an eyebrow and caught my breath.

He flipped over to the ground and landed Anastasia beneath him on the floor. I took this as my cue and flipped my knife into his wounded shoulder. Before the blade could sink into his marred skin, he snapped out of the way and stuck out a hand to bring me down.

Anastasia grabbed him from on top of her instead while I searched frantically for a gun to end our friend's charade once and for all. I snatched a small handgun off an agent at my feet and regained my composure to aim at the back of the Assassin's neck.

Both of them kept moving, and I stood still. Anya would get him still long enough. I waited a few more moments until she pinned his face down so I could see a still point to shoot. Just when Anya jumped off, I took the shot.

He lay there unmoving as I panted hard and glanced at her. It was silent. No guns, no agents—just us. We were safe for a moment.

He would wake up soon in a great deal of pain and attribute his memory loss to the bullets inside him. If he were normal, his breaths would have run out minutes ago, but unfortunately, these bullets wouldn't kill him.

"Wipe him." Anya caught her breath and got up.

I tilted my head skeptically. "Why don't I just stop his—?"

"Do it," she snapped.

I complied and lazily flicked my fingers over his face. *Good as new.*

"It must be hard to constantly forget who you are, though." I met her eyes. "Imagine not having any memories of who you've loved, who your family was."

"They do it so he can do his job," was her immediate answer.

"It's your job too. And mine."

Anastasia blinked. "Let's get out of here," she mumbled and ran to the exit.

I followed her and sprinted over the bodies littered on the ground. A gasp escaped my lips when a hand grabbed my leg and pulled me down, head hitting the cold floor.

Ow.

"Anya!" I shouted.

A shot rang out. The agent holding onto me went limp, but my face was still burning with the ache of the cold floor. Footsteps ran back toward me, and Anastasia extended a hand to lift me to my feet. I stretched an arm out and shook the throb out of my head.

Anastasia's face was stern and cold, though not at me, thankfully. "If it comes down to it, Nia," she panted, "I have to leave you to fend for yourself."

"So much for backup," I muttered with a roll of my eyes. "I understand."

She nodded and we sprinted to the exit, this time watching our feet. I flipped my comms back on in preparation for her signal. I threw my hands out wide, choked out a cough of blood from my injuries, and extended my powers as far as they would reach to stop the hearts still faintly beating on the floor.

Except for the Assassin. Sadly.

"Are you ready?" Anya shouted over the comms, flinging the door open. Her answer came by way of the speeding car as it stopped in front of us, revealing the rest of our crew.

"Get in!" Jesse yelled, throwing open the passenger door.

Anastasia helped me climb in while I clung to my burning side—that I hoped hadn't been stabbed—and nodded to me.

She thrusted her earpiece into my lap and turned swiftly to run back inside. Upon her signal, I flung my better hand out the window and used my powers to knock her out once she was inside. I nodded to Jesse.

He gave me a look of confusion, and realization sank into my pained chest: *Parker.*

The neighboring door to our exit was hurled open, and Parker ran through, a gun in each hand. An agent followed him in pursuit as we yelled in support. I couldn't get out of the car fast enough, and when the door finally opened, two shots went off.

Parker collapsed. I slid to the ground, frozen, and Persephone screamed from inside the car. Reality crashed around me with a scream sliding out from my dry throat while Jesse rushed out of the car and to my side.

Another shot went off, and he fell beside me.

One more, and my eyes succumbed to the dark chaos within me.

ALL WILL BE REVEALED

{ *Lavinia* }

Pressure pounded against my head, and I groaned.

My heavy eyes started to open, but the room swam. I shut them quickly and tried to get my bearings on where I was. The space was small, damp, and cold.

I choked out a cough, lungs spasming, and reeled forward. The front of my head gave me a sharp pain in warning of my injuries. Clearly, I hadn't been shot with a real bullet. My eyes snapped open as a voice whispered intensely, but the chaos made me shut them again.

"Lavinia! Are you okay?" the voice cracked.

I gritted my teeth in pain and managed to nod. I slowly opened my eyes, fought the urge to black out, and saw my sister's worried face through the dim light. Her red hair snagged the clothing at her shoulders, and her blue eyes shone wide.

I shifted with great difficulty, inch by inch, to lean my back up against the back wall.

"Perse, where are we?"

"Back where you found me," another small voice squeaked. I twisted my head and gave a silent groan in pain to see Grace huddled in the other cell next to me.

"Are you hurt?"

"Not any worse than I was before," came her muffled voice. "My ankle's bandaged now."

I narrowed my eyes and angled my head to see that my side was wrapped and a single bandage was stuck to my forearm.

Don't remember hitting that.

"What about everyone else, are they—?" I glanced at Persephone.

"Liam and Jesse don't know we're here," she admitted. "I only know because I can sense them. Barely. Their cells are too far away, but they're alive."

"And Parker?" I whispered.

"I don't know." She returned the volume of my voice and leaned against the bars separating us. "I don't know."

I attempted to ignore the ringing in my head and the heaviness that sat upon my eyelids. "I'll rest for a few minutes and then I'll find them."

"Lavinia—" Grace started. When I let my eyes rest on her slouched body, she met my gaze. "I—"

"Don't, Grace," I said softly. "It's none of your fault."

"I know."

Not what I was expecting.

"Excuse me?" I whispered, adjusting my position against the cold wall in an attempt to get comfortable. But it was worsened by headaches.

"Nothing. These cells won't let you use your powers. I woke up somewhere along the way and saw they used some kind of device on you, and once it worked, both our…fake appearances vanished. Back to normal."

My heart dropped to my stomach.

"But mine worked…hardly!" Persephone gaped.

"I think it's only because your cell's security isn't as high." Grace glanced between us. "They took extra caution for Lavinia."

"Of course they did." I rolled my eyes.

Footsteps entered our hearing range, and as they walked to our cells, I craned my head and slid to the front of the cell to see.

"Well, look who decided to show up," I said to the familiar figure.

Anastasia stopped to stand in front of my cell, arms crossed over her new suit of tactical gear. Her clear green eyes were trained on mine.

"Outfit looks good on you." She looked unamused and stepped closer.

I sighed, waiting for her lecture.

Her voice was uncharacteristically quiet. "Parker's recovering, Nia. He'll be okay."

"But what's going to happen to us?" Persephone asked. She was standing against the door of her cell, white knuckles gripping the gaps in the metal.

Anastasia glanced at her and then to Grace before focusing on me. "You've probably realized by now you can't use your powers in here."

"Haven't tried it." I shrugged but winced at the pain in my side. Frankly, I didn't want to know what it would feel like to try and not get anywhere.

"They're splitting you up and putting you against the Assassin when Parker is healed. One of you will fight for your group's lives."

"They can't expect us to—"

"None of you have graduated yet, and half of you aren't even agents. The General can do whatever he wants with the Board's permission."

I frowned, but Anastasia gave me a chastising look before leaning closer, her voice a whisper.

"I tried to find an Agent Price, but neither of them exists in the system. I don't think they're even alive anymore, Lavinia."

I nodded and twisted my hands in nervousness, ignoring the blood-soaked skin. That was not the news I wanted to hear, but it was better than Parker's death.

Or even Jesse's.

♦ ♦ ♦

"So, you know—"

"We've been over this a thousand times, Lavinia, yes!" Grace groaned.

I narrowed my eyes. "Just checking. The last time something like this happened—"

"Could we not talk about that?" she said sharply, her nostrils flaring.

I honored her request with silence and a single nod. The awkward moment lingered before the door at the far end of the hall opened, and my heart sank with dread. It had already been the longest week of my life, and not knowing where Jesse was made it even harder. Sleep was scarce without him.

Heavy footsteps sounded toward us—I counted ten agents—and the lights slowly flickered on with every yard they passed.

The steps grew louder as they neared our cells. Once the agents reached us, they split into three groups of three, leaving one agent to stand still and face the door at the end of the hallway. She was dressed differently than the others; instead of tactical gear and a gun strapped to her thigh, she wore a white laboratory coat.

As the agents stepped inside our cells and took us out, Grace's head was covered in a black hood and handcuffs were strapped onto her wrists. The moment I exited the protective shield of my cell, I felt my powers return in a powerful surge through my body. I knew the faint remaining marks had disappeared and the wound on my side had closed over.

The woman in the lab coat turned around to reveal her black skin shining under the low lights, hands in her pockets. Her face was wide and full, her lips broad, and I guessed she couldn't have been more than a few months younger than me.

Where did she come from?

She nodded to the agent holding my arm and then to the agent next to Persephone. Without hesitation, the agents handcuffed us and snapped a thick band around our ankles. It was more than rubber, definitely electronic, but it felt cold and sharp.

What is it even supposed to—oh.

Several small needles pushed out of the band and into my and Persephone's skin, and immediately after, the energies of my powers vanished as quickly as they had returned.

Damn it.

"It's working, Doctor." The agent holding me turned to face the woman.

She looked at the band proudly and nodded. Persephone's head was then covered by a hood, and so was mine. I listened carefully and slowed my breathing to track our movements throughout the base. The agent holding me gripped my arm tightly and followed the woman while the rest of the group trailed behind us.

The hallway door shut, and we stepped into the elevator. After exiting, the agent holding my arm paused. The elevator dinged, and we started moving again. I had all but memorized the layout of our facility from the several failed escape plans throughout my years here.

I knew it would come in handy.

I had no doubts that our steps would confuse Grace and even Persephone. The medical wing's bright lights and whirring machines made their way into my awareness through the hood, but a sound from another elevator confused me. The elevator inside the medical wing led exclusively to the top few floors of the building.

I didn't realize until we reached the top and stepped off that we were on a floor very familiar to me. Our team's training gyms and living quarters were here, along with a few other teams' territories we never associated with.

It was easier to track our movements now that I knew our exact location. After we traveled down the hall and took a few turns, we ended up just outside a training gym I'd rarely used. The group stopped. The agent gripping firmly onto my arm released me, took off the hood, and shoved me forward.

The doctor stood in front of the metal door and motioned for me to unlock it. I eyed her warily and stepped to the various locking mechanisms next to the door. Once I completed the retinal scan and inputted my agent I.D. number, she bypassed the fingerprint verification to avoid removing my handcuffs.

Smart choice, lady.

The door opened slowly, and the woman led our group inside. Extra agents filed in behind us as we came to a stop on one side of the main training ring. Once the woman was satisfied with our placement, she gestured for Persephone's hood to be removed.

Grace was moved to stand on the other side of the ring, taking Parker's place while another agent forcibly moved him to stand beside me. His appearance was set to normal again. My gaze was drawn to Grace and Liam, noticing a dark haired, freckled-face mess with his gaze trained on me.

I sighed at the sight of him. Jesse's unharmed face wore a wry smile, one of desperate hope, but it broke when he saw someone behind me. I glanced over my shoulder and inwardly frowned at the sight of the two agents of equal height stalking to the end of the training arena.

The Assassin and the Agent Rabinova. What a power couple.

His black hair shone under the lights, while her dark red hair lay around her shoulders in her usual fashion. They both wore black tactical gear, complete with guns strapped to their thighs.

As they entered the arena, the power and confidence they held in their saunter was distinctive. They came to a stop at the edge of the arena before Anastasia took a slight step back. She was signaling the Assassin's superiority over her.

The Assassin surveyed the room, his cold, brown eyes coming to rest on me for a long moment. I returned it with a harsh stare. He didn't react. He simply looked away to focus on the General entering the end of the arena.

I know he didn't remember me, considering the little stunt I'd pulled during our fight, but I doubted that he remembered anything at all. His eyes were always blank and his features were sharp…like he only had one purpose: to kill.

Several men of Ivankov's board of directors—the public front, not the Master's Board—were surrounding the General in black-and-white suits and ties. My face twisted into one of disgust when my eyes fell on the General. It was no secret that he was the Assassin's boss, though he was of lower standing than the Rejuvenator and the Board.

And if the Assassin managed missions and ordered kidnappings of young Masters…I hated to think of what facility the General was in charge of. Of the bodies he was responsible for.

Armed agents heavily flanked the group. As I noticed their military-issued rifles, I looked around and saw that every agent, surrounding the arena and standing along the edge of each wall, carried matching guns.

If you don't win…you're never getting out of here alive.

The catwalks above us were filled with agents and bright lights casting downwards. I lowered my glance to Jesse's now nervous face. I tried to send a message to calm him, but I knew it was useless. My powers wouldn't work until I got this stupid ankle cuff off.

His face was still uneasy, and our gazes remained fixed on each other until the General started to speak. His voice was loud and commanding.

"Lavinia Markov, Jesse Price…you'll both be fighting the Assassin to determine your family's future. If you win, Agent Markov, you and your family will be reinstated as agents of Ivankov. If you do not, your services will no longer be required."

His piercing gaze turned to Jesse. "If you win, you and your family's lives will be spared and you will return to your home. If you do not, the Master's Board will decide your fate. Good luck," he said sharply. He saluted and then uttered a single Russian word.

Loyalty.

I swallowed down the bile rising in my throat, thoroughly disgusted, when I looked around to see everyone except those of us in handcuffs repeating the action. I glanced at Anastasia and saw her tightened jaw; she copied the salute.

I tried to ignore the furious, pitiful, and shocked looks of both Parker and Persephone next to me and Grace and Liam across from us. I took a deep breath and tried to calm my own furious nerves.

Not one of them deserves this mess I've gotten us into.

I snapped myself out of my thoughts and looked across at Jesse, who swallowed in nervousness and waited for the General to continue.

"Jesse Price, you will have access to these weapons"—he gestured to the agent walking toward Jesse, who was holding a knife and loaded gun—"while you fight. No actions or words are prohibited. All is fair. Fight to the death or the surrender of either opponent."

Jesse remained silent as he secured the gun and knife into the holsters that had been strapped to his legs. After doing so, he glanced up at me before looking back to the General.

"You may—"

"Wait!" a voice yelled.

The room went silent. Every head turned to our side of the arena. Parker was half-stepped in front of me with a hand held out in a protective motion. His clear blue eyes were clouded in anger and his jaw was locked. The muscles flexed under his skin.

He momentarily glanced at me in uncertainty before steeling his resolve.

What is he thinking? Is he crazy?

But I knew that wasn't true. He was going to save Jesse for me, no matter the cost—even if it cost him his life. But I didn't want him to.

"I'll do it. Please, let me do it." He lowered his voice and stared the General down.

HELPLESS DROWNING

{ Lavinia }

The General's voice was quiet and firm.

"I'm afraid I can't allow that. Jesse Price will be fighting the Assassin. Stand down. Now."

I almost felt pity for the General at the look of rage on my brother's face tearing into his soul. The tension was thick until the General cleared his throat. He was expecting an answer from Parker, who was emitting guilt in powerful waves from his proximity to me.

He thinks that if he never left the car, we would have escaped...And now he's trying to save us. All of us.

Hope almost withered within me at the defeat that sank into Parker's posture, and I tried to ignore my own guilt attempting to kill my resolve.

"Yes, sir," he said sharply, stepping back next to me.

Why are you giving up? I glared at him, but his gaze stayed trained on the General. He couldn't hear me, not with this cuff on my ankle.

"Very good. Now, Agent," the General called out, causing the Assassin's attention to pivot. "You may begin."

You're not going to win that easily. I gritted my teeth.

"General," I said evenly.

He focused his eyes on me and tensed. "Markov?"

"May I speak to you in private about the terms of this arrangement?" My voice came out light but with a surprising amount of command.

I needed to do something. *Anything.* I had been fighting this my whole life, and it was only for my siblings' safeties that I never defected. Now…there was no other place to hide. It was all or nothing.

He glared. "You are not leaving this room."

"I don't need to. I can create a sound barrier between us and the rest of the room."

"You can't activate your powers with the stopper on your ankle or your handcuffs."

"I know," I replied with a firm nod to the Assassin. "But he can ensure I won't get up to any funny business when you take it off me."

Would he really agree to this? I didn't dare to let hope bloom in my chest again. My stomach churned, flipping in the chaos within me.

The General's face remained skeptical, but he gestured to the Assassin to take them off. I turned around and extended my hands out behind me, winking at Parker's astonished expression.

He responded to my glance with an irritated glower, and I turned back to face the General. The Assassin stepped back after removing my handcuffs and the anklet, nodding to the General.

I lifted my arms and created a bubble around us. Once it was sealed, I let my hands drop. The General had never seen me before—he certainly hadn't seen my power. He was impressed, but still, his tone was wary when he spoke.

"What terms would you change, Agent Markov?"

"Why make both of us fight? There's no need for the Assassin to waste energy with two of us—just have him fight me."

Because I've beaten him twice before—even if he only remembers the first time. I can do it again.

He considered this momentarily. "Why not let the boy fight?"

"He would never win! He didn't ask to be dragged into this," I hissed, more forcefully than intended. I bit back my lip at the harsh truth I had just admitted to myself.

It stung, but I knew Jesse wouldn't stand a chance against the Assassin. He would only survive by some miracle, and unless I brought the building and us all down, that couldn't happen.

Could I bring it down?

I didn't dare glance at the structure to find out; he would grow suspicious. I swallowed the guilt back. I knew it was my fault, but I didn't want to believe it. Fire burned inside me at the General's hardened expression. Not wanting to give up on my family—Jesse being a part of that now—was my fatal flaw.

Fatal to who? a voice inside me whispered. *Shut up, Lavinia.*

"No, Agent," he spat, striding to meet me. "He didn't. You did."

His hazel eyes flamed and he bristled, but he never broke his peaceful stance, hands clasped behind his back. I locked my jaw and fought against the impulse to smite him where he stood.

The Assassin is watching right behind you. He'd kill you first.

"You brought the poor boy and his siblings into this when you foolishly told them of our organization," the General snapped, "and you will pay the price for not adhering to this life. We have taught you to be better, and you have disappointed all of us."

"Then get rid of me if I'm so useless," I blurted. The bite of regret inside me returned when his face stormed, forcing the bile of guilt into my heart.

"You are not useless, Markov. You are one of our best. But we need you to be rid of all *attachments*"—he glanced outside the bubble to Persephone and Parker—"in order to remain a valued and trusted agent—not to mention successful."

I remained still for a moment, hoping to avoid another impulsive comment, and glanced down. With a nod, I looked back up to meet his eyes.

"The terms will remain the same?" I asked, not bothering to hide my anger.

It was eerily silent in our bubble, but somehow, every muscle was fighting me to scream and cry and do anything I could to stop it. My heart pounded in my ears. The General nodded in confirmation, but he might as well have pulled the trigger on Jesse himself.

No, I screamed inside.

"And you will not violate the terms by using your powers?"

"No, sir."

That was a fat lie.

You can't just give up like that…But I might as well piss him off.

I narrowed my eyes at the General and spit venomously at his feet. "I'll see you in hell."

With a sense of satisfaction poorly masking my anger, I flicked a finger, and I knew all memory of anger toward me had dissipated from his mind. I took down the barrier separating us from the vast room without a single motion.

The Assassin reached out a metal hand as I spun around, taking my forearm in his grasp. I tried to tear myself away from his tight grip, glancing at my siblings. Not a single word escaped his lips, nor did his eyes change, nor did he manage to secretly inject me with a needle.

But at that moment, inexplicable docility ran through me at the tightening of his hold on my arm. Frigid, cold air flew up my shoulders and across my chest, spreading through the rest of my body like a wildfire of snow and ice.

"What are you doing to me—?" I tried to choke out, but my throat closed on itself, and my face lifted to meet his dark brown eyes.

Why is he so cold? How am I feeling it?

My thoughts were silenced against my will when his grasp on me stiffened. None of this made sense.

How—?

I couldn't open my mouth to speak. I couldn't rip myself out of his hand, I couldn't move my legs, I couldn't even look away from him.

The Assassin blinked, and at once, I no longer cared. Peace replaced the cold within me and calmed the storm of guilt and anger. My mind fought my legs as he let me go and I strode back to Parker and Persephone.

Unwilling, I stopped between them and faced forward. The Assassin placed the metal handcuffs around my wrist and glared into my soul. I couldn't look away until he turned to take his place beside the General.

I watched them, unable to decipher the nervous whisperings of my brother and sister beside me, and saw the exchange of glances that occurred. The General looked at me in nervousness; I stared right back in subconscious defiance.

But the Assassin coolly spoke something I could not hear, and before I knew it, he met Jesse on the mat in the dead center of the room.

263

49

TELL ME I'M DREAMING

{ Lavinia }

Jesse's right hand gripped his gun.

He had never used one, but after seeing me shoot Ernest dead and after Margaret shot me, he at least knew what it looked like to shoot one. I stood frozen, helpless to the outcome.

Something is terribly wrong—no duh, Sherlock—but I can still feel my powers! The inhibitor device isn't on…Why aren't they working?

Two-fold panic rose in me. Jesse took a step toward the Assassin, and despite my frantic attempts, my powers weren't working. Grace glanced at me; her mouth was drawn into a thin line. She took a deep breath and broke our eye contact as she turned around to watch. I didn't know how she did it.

The seconds crawled into minutes; Persephone still tried to get my attention. But my head was frozen too, and I was unable to speak. I blinked once, and the Assassin dove forward. The men turned into a whirlwind of grunts and punches, but the only thing that rang over and over and over in my mind was a single phrase.

Get Anya to do something.

I fought the Assassin's control over my powers—it was the only thing that made any sense—and focused on trying to control Anastasia's cells. All my power, all the energy flowing inside my veins, all my DNA had been trained to do this. I had been made for this.

I clamped my eyes shut and trained the energy I knew was there straight to Anastasia's body. I couldn't see it happening, but I knew something was going to work.

All at once, like my eardrums exploded, sounds began to flood in. Persephone gasped from beside me and Parker inhaled sharply. Their outbursts caused my eyes to snap open.

At the behest of my control, Anastasia's hand was on one of the Assassin's metal arms. Her green eyes were empty, but they were focused on Jesse. My eyes trailed down the shining metal to see a gun gripped in the Assassin's hand, held at Jesse's chest.

Terror was etched into his face, carved into his soul. My hands flew to my mouth, still in handcuffs, to muffle the sound I'd made. It was too late. The Assassin's hard gaze swiveled to Anastasia, and in one swift motion, when he looked at me, my control over Anastasia snapped.

Her hand dropped and she stepped back, commanded by a force I couldn't see. A force that no one could see. A force that no one could prove, the one that was about to be at fault for—

The world slowed. My thoughts raced, heart dropping. I forced myself to look away, but the unmistakable sound of the gun being cocked pulled me back. I couldn't look at Jesse. The gun's trigger was held by that metal finger, and when it flexed, the shot rang out.

I was pulled. I pushed. I could barely feel the hands on my arms forcing me back as I ran through the agents. I took hold of my powers again, finding it somewhere deep inside. Fire burned on my wrists and the metal of my handcuffs fell to the ground. Nothing was there.

Nothing except for a lone figure, lying there, going cold and empty on the ground.

No, no, no, no, please no...

I drew breath after breath, but it wasn't enough. My lungs were empty. Noise faded from my senses, and though I was vaguely aware of shouts and other cries, I didn't care. I needed to save him.

My body shook; I pushed a trembling hand on the pool of dark blood collecting on his chest in vain. I pushed and pushed, letting what was left of my power flow through me. I tried to fix it, to put his heart back together, to stop the bleeding.

He simply stared. He couldn't really see me. My sobs rattled me, left me gasping for the thin air. I couldn't breathe, but I forced myself on. I kept pushing.

Footsteps faded behind me as a gentle hand pressed on my shoulder, but I didn't turn. Whoever was comforting me drew back, and the sounds of turmoil erupted. Suddenly, I could hear everything. But I forced it out. I had to save him. I had to.

But while Jesse's face grew stiller and my tears rolled onto his body, I extended an arm to wrap around his side and a hand to his face. I willed myself to swallow back the cries, but with every second that his face grew paler, my body shuddered again. Time moved slowly.

Please, tell me I'm dreaming. Tell me I'll wake up with him. Tell me…Tell me he's here. I can't give up on him. I can't. I told him I'd be here. I have to save him…

But Jesse's deep brown eyes called to me, almost silently, as he murmured a few words. I couldn't understand him, and he tried to smile in comfort. Nothing would help. Ringing filled my ears, and my lungs spasmed with hiccups, shaking me.

I couldn't let people see him. I couldn't let him go like this. Lowering my head to his and using what little strength I had left, I took a deep breath. I ignored the blood on his chest coating my sleeve, putting up a small barrier around us.

I tried to open my mouth to speak, but all that came was a moan. He shook his head with a tremendous amount of effort. And although he couldn't speak, I noticed the faint movements of his lips.

I love you.

As another cry convulsed my chest, our tears mixed together on his freckled cheeks, once lively. They were still now.

I choked out, "I love you too…"

A small scream, almost a squeak, slipped through my lips, and I shut my eyes. I couldn't see his last moments. The bubble of my powers faded while I collapsed on his chest, now going motionless. The sounds of chaos flooded me.

There was crying but shouting, too. I couldn't stop the feelings of others raging within me, bringing a fresh wail bubbling out of me. My heart twisted. The hand extended again to rest on my shoulder, this time with a forceful tone directed at the agents pressing toward me.

Anastasia. It's her.

With one last burst of hope, I lifted my head again to see his eyes for the last time. His lips were parted and eyes glossed over, but his face was peaceful. I let another sniffle escape me and leaned down to gently rest my lips on his.

I drew back and smiled at him, my lips broken in a silent plea. I knew I would save him. I would kiss him again, and his lively head of hair would bounce in my vision, if I could just wake up from this nightmare.

I had saved him once before. Bitterness swelled inside me, perpetrating all sides.

Why couldn't I save you now?

The smile faded from my lips. One last thought hastened to stab me before I was the last thing Jesse saw:

Why didn't you try hard enough? You could have saved him.

FINAL PIECE

{ *Jesse* }

"I love you too…" came her quiet words through a sniffle.

Though my lips couldn't move, I smiled inside and felt her peace overtake me. She would be living a nightmare now, but I'd never have to fall asleep in torment again.

I thought of all the love we hadn't had the chance to share yet, all the moments we wouldn't have. I thought of how, eventually, her lips would smile because of another man and that there would come a day when she wouldn't think of me. I would always be thinking of her, though. I would have done anything for her.

Death is nothing compared to what I would do for you.

A silent moment passed as the universe swallowed the last of me.

Don't forget me, Lavinia.

But I would never find out if she did. If she would move on. I gave in to the painful pull of my heart. The thread finally snapped.

Then there was nothing.

51

LIFE WITHOUT YOU

The headache pounded in my sinuses and threatened to wake me.

But the tossing of my body and the strong arms that held me were what jolted me awake. I felt nothing, and after realizing the head of hair sprawled across the strong shoulders of the person carrying me was Anastasia, I let my eyes close again.

I could feel Grace and Liam walking in front of us. They clung to each other through their handcuffs and took small steps. My stomach dropped, the full weight sinking in—not just of my own grief, but theirs.

My eyes snapped open when I was set down inside my cell. I caught sight of Anastasia speaking quietly to the others, telling them that she would be a minute, and then turning back to my cell. She locked the door and glanced down the hall. I closed my eyes quickly before she noticed I was awake and allowed the heaviness of my shoulders to weigh me down.

"Lavinia, I know you can't hear me, but…" she started, her voice tense.

I slid my eyes open just enough to see her sitting cross-legged outside the cell, her hands clasped together nervously and her head leaned on the bars. Her eyes were closed.

Anastasia paused and sniffled, a tear dropping down her face. *That* surprised me.

"I'm so sorry…I'm so incredibly sorry. You wouldn't want me to blame myself, but when has that stopped me before, right?" She chuckled, and more tears streamed down her face. "You don't know this, but a long time ago, I made a promise to you. I made myself a promise that I would protect you and the people you loved…"

I kept my eyes cracked open, and I had to resist the urge to shed my own tears when I saw her hang her head in shame and continue to cry quietly.

"I wanted to be able to keep that promise. But exactly like I've always told you, no one should make promises, let alone ones that they can't keep. And as always,"—she took a breath—"I couldn't. I couldn't save Jesse. I could've bargained with the General and told him we could've gotten information out of him, but I was too much of a coward to do that, and now…"

My heart twisted at her eyes cast downward and eyebrows pulled together. Her nose was red from crying and her teeth were gritted in anger—and almost in frustration—that she was showing this emotion to me.

Her dark red hair rested around her shoulders, wavy, but it was unkempt. Even before today, it was as if she was sleeping listlessly in our previously shared bedroom—restless without me. I shut my eyes tightly and shifted soundlessly.

My face was shadowed away from her, contorting into one of pain. While my powers slipped away from me, I could feel Grace's and Liam's grief slipping in and out of sleep, but Anastasia's myriad of emotions was even stronger.

"Now he's gone. I can't tell you how sorry I am that I couldn't do anything. And I…You know," she sniffled, "Perse and Parker will have to stay here and you'll have to leave…I don't want us to be any different because of this. I don't think I could deal with that…"

She grew quiet after trailing off. I peered up through my eyelids to see her fiddle with her fingers and stare at the ground while she attempted to stop her tears.

"I couldn't live my life the same without you. I wouldn't want to…I love you, so much more than you could possibly know, and just the thought of you breaking hurts me. So to see you here, finally at peace only in sleep, hurts even more, because

I know that whenever you wake up, that hurt will return to you…

"Just know—" She paused. "—that I'm always going to be here. No matter what, okay?"

She waited patiently for an answer that she knew she wouldn't receive. Maybe she was hoping I was awake—that somehow, I would get up, run to her, and cry into her arms. That I would tell her how I could never be mad at her or tell her how much I loved her.

I considered it for a second, but I remained still. It would hurt too much. It *did* hurt too much.

Moments passed until she slowly got up, still sniffling, and sighed. Her steps faded into the dark hallway, leaving me cold and damp on the floor as I choked out slow cries. I curled my legs close to me and tensed to rid myself of the pain.

♦ ♦ ♦

"No! Jesse!" Grace's hoarse voice screamed from somewhere in the dark, breaking free of the deafening silence.

I looked around, panicked. I couldn't see him. Chaos filled my blood and ran me cold. I flexed the gun in my hand. In the chasm behind me, Ernest's voice hissed down my neck.

"You couldn't save him."

"Shut up!" I whirled on him and pulled the trigger, but it wasn't Ernest.

It wasn't Parker. It wasn't Sarvesh or Alek or even Liam.

"Jesse," I whispered in revolt, reaching out to catch him.

But he was already gone. Jesse was dead.

♦ ♦ ♦

I shot up and panted when the dream faded, gasping to fill my lungs with air.

The cold floor beneath me fired pangs through my aching back. I collapsed back onto the ground and let out a breath, yearning for peace and trying to block my mind from Grace's and Liam's emotions. But I was too weak.

I craned my head to the side and saw Grace's and Liam's bodies huddled together. Parker and Persephone were nowhere to be seen. This time, my cell let my powers continue coursing through me. The energies I had become so accustomed to now throbbed in me painfully while the marks encircling my wrists continued to burn from the handcuff's removal.

Grace's and Liam's minds flipped in turmoil even while they slept, and I didn't have enough strength to push their feelings out of my own awareness. I hesitated for a moment before dropping my head down again.

I drifted in and out of sleep as the pain faded. Every few days there was a voice, but the cell doors never opened. There was no escape. I let my walls crash around me as my only friend, the damp floor, held me up.

There was nothing else for me here. Not without him.

A clang of a door rang through the air. I sat straight up before jumping up to the front of the cell; I swallowed down the pain that shot through me. Agents opened Grace and Liam's cell door.

They handcuffed both of them before reaching into my cell next.

The agents holding Grace and Liam each held a needle filled with some kind of blue substance. I didn't bother asking. My throat was dry, and my legs ached when I stood unevenly on them. They weren't used to my weight and almost buckled beneath me.

But I recognized the agent in front of me to be the same doctor, in the lab coat, that had ordered the Master-designed anklets to be strapped onto both Persephone and me. *Before…*

No. Stop thinking about that, I scolded.

Her hair was pinned back into a neat bun, and her hands were tucked into the pockets of her coat, but she extended one and gestured for me to move closer. I furrowed my eyebrows together in confusion. Although I stepped closer, I kept my eyes on the doctor.

"Agent Markov," she said evenly in a sharp English accent, stepping beside me to face Grace and Liam.

I glanced at her suspiciously and looked her up and down. "What?"

I was hardly surprised at my voice—it came out with an uncomfortable scratch of my throat. I didn't know how many days had passed since I last spoke, since…

Stop it.

Her eyes were almost forgiving. She had an ounce of empathy on her face, but as she spoke, my neutral feelings toward her disappeared into the tense air.

"The General has commanded that unless you wish to terminate the remaining Price family—Grace, Liam, and Samantha—you are to alter their memories to remove any trace of Ivankov. And your family."

I swallowed back the lump growing in my throat and wished the burning tears to remain behind my eyes.

First Jesse, and now this? I'll be as good as dead to them.

"I can't alter them to that extent," I explained to the agent, not masking my bitterness. "But I can remove them. What would I put in their place?"

She bristled at my first statement but settled. She thought for a moment while I waited, glancing at the siblings across from me. I grimaced secretly at their pained faces. They were trying to be brave. Liam made eye contact with me.

Please don't erase Perse. I need her.

I have to erase her, but I can leave everything you felt for her. It'll be a different girl.

I wished I could do more for him. He had already been through enough.

A wave of guilt flushed over me from Grace, and I glanced over to see her eyes cast to the floor and a frown on her sculpted features. Her breathing was labored. I saw a single tear roll down her cheeks that used to be full and vibrant. Now, they were dull.

I was almost startled when the agent spoke. "They will remember their brother as a child who died in an accident and their time with your family as a few students who moved shortly after their arrival. They will remember their time here at Ivankov as a school trip, but the details are unnecessary. Once you block them, they will not be able to retrieve them."

I didn't correct her, knowing that if they tried hard enough or received enough retrieval cues, they could remember. But the chance of that happening without me restoring their memories was slim.

I cleared my throat and nodded to the agent. "I can't control my powers well, with being in a freezing cell for days," I said without an ounce of sarcasm. "Can I have water, at least?"

The agent nodded and waved another one off. Only minutes passed, feeling like hours, before the agent returned with a plastic cup of ice and water. I hadn't yet tried to use my powers since the whole…lack of control I'd experienced.

I snatched it rudely from their hand, not stopping to wince in pain at my wrist, and gulped the cool liquid down my aching throat. I finished awkwardly and handed the cup to the agent beside me but hesitated.

"What are those needles for?"

She took the cup and answered evenly, "Once you've finished, the sedatives will be given to them both. They'll be taken back home to their mother."

With only a slight sigh of relief with the knowledge that Mrs. Price was still alive, I turned back to Grace and Liam. I took a deep breath and concentrated, drawing on the little energy within me to pull out my powers, and reached to place a hand on both of their heads.

Before the agents could stop me, the lab-coated woman held out a dark hand. Almost like they were commanded by an invisible force, the agents pulled back and stood still. I looked back at her in surprise, and the glow of her hands—the same red color as mine—was instantly recognizable.

She smiled in response, but I knew she couldn't read my mind.

Another Manipulator. But only of matter…

She nodded me on and stepped closer to put a hand on my shoulder. I felt a surge of power rush through me, giving me strength. Although she wasn't a memory Manipulator, her touch furthered the connection I had made with Grace's and Liam's memories.

I started to seek for myself and my siblings in their minds. I gently drew out the memories one by one and replaced them with threads of fake stories. They would have a hard time breaking the false memories, especially if I wasn't there to undo my work.

I swallowed and shut my eyes to focus and block the pain as I got to the happy memories of both our families—of Jesse when he was a kid, Liam and Persephone sharing tender moments, and Grace's resurfacing grief of Kanya's loss.

When I finished, I took a shuddered breath of relief and released our connection. I backed away slowly, energy spent, as the doctor's hand remained on my shoulder. Though I averted my eyes while I reached back into my cell, I was aware of the agents drugging them and carrying them out.

When the final agent left and the Manipulator drew away, the door slammed behind them.

The quiet resumed once more.

The dead silence of the large warehouse was confined to the cell I was in, pushing against my ears, flaunting that I was alone. I turned slowly and rubbed my hands on my face. I tried to wake myself up or at least feel alive.

Though I had no difficulties removing others' memories, my own were a different story. It was as if they'd glued themselves to the walls of my brain, never releasing me for a moment.

I lowered myself to the ground and leaned my back against the cold wall, curling my knees up to my chin and burying my face in between my legs and torso. I sighed deeply and waited for sleep to come and bring me peace.

But peace never came. I doubted that it ever would.

52

CHANGES

{ Lavinia }

The cell door rattled open, and quiet footsteps pulled me from sleep.

I mumbled in confusion before opening my eyes. A familiar pair of green eyes stared back.

"Get up, Lavinia."

I complied and shook my head awake with a yawn, though I swatted away Anastasia's helping hand of assistance and stood by myself. Once I was upright, unsteady on my feet, she supported me with an arm around my shoulder and led us out of the cell.

I couldn't seem to remember much of anything other than my current state, let alone be concerned about anything other than sleeping in a bed, drinking real water, and eating. I didn't want to ask her questions for fear of the answers.

"I'm going to get you cleaned up with a shower and new clothes and have you brush your teeth a few times. Then I'm taking you to see Persephone and Parker."

For one last time? My thoughts echoed what she knew not to say.

I kept my lips pressed together in a thin line and leaned farther into her support.

I squinted in the glaringly bright hallways, but my eyes soon adjusted. My mind faded back into a comfortable silence and into the darkness behind my eyelids, momentarily rising to drag my feet. I was startled fully conscious when Anastasia closed a door behind us.

Glancing around, I saw we were in our shared room. It was almost dusty and forgotten, apart from Anastasia's bed—neatly made. Pieces of my stuff lay scattered around the room. I angrily swallowed down the happy memories that pushed into my mind.

That life seems so far away. Yet it had only been two months since I met him.

Anastasia pulled me out of my trance when she threw a large suitcase onto the bed, mere inches away from me.

"Shower and pack; don't take more than an hour."

"Pack?" I inquired, turning to her.

Anya kept walking to the door and turned her face just before she left. "All that you can," she stated, her voice softening. "I'll be back in an hour." She shut the door and left me to myself in the empty room.

"Well…" I said to myself, looking around. I knew I needed to ask her about what the Assassin had done to her, why she couldn't stop him. But it would have to wait.

I strode across the room, which was welcomingly warm in comparison to my cell, to tune the radio in to an upbeat station. *Anything for a distraction.* I decided to pack first.

I opened the suitcase and tightly rolled what clothes I wanted, leaving my tactical boots behind—I'd just be given new ones. I momentarily lost motivation and plopped down on the bed. A few minutes passed by while I let my mind rest before I got back up and gathered my computer and cord. I picked up my phone charger and dug the burner phone out from underneath the mattress.

I opened my makeup bag and grabbed a few items, tossed them in the suitcase, and moved on to find my hairbrush and other products. I packed a few pairs of pajamas and grabbed a few books, stuffing them in. I had a bit more room. I wondered what else I was missing.

Shower stuff!

I found what I needed, grabbed a towel, and then left the room to take a shower.

It was shorter than usual; I knew I wouldn't want to get out or even see anyone else ever again if I stayed under the scalding water long enough.

I returned, packed the things (minus the towel), and got dressed in some of what I hadn't packed: a black t-shirt and a flannel with warm jeans and sneakers.

I dried and fixed my hair the best I could and realized I still had plenty of time before Anastasia returned. Immediately deciding on a good nap, I zipped up the suitcase and gave the room a once-over before turning off the radio and slipping off my sneakers.

I placed them next to the suitcase near the door and fell back on the bed to get comfortable, not bothering to get under the blankets. I promptly fell asleep.

◆ ◆ ◆

"Time to go, Nia." I was being shaken awake.

I groaned, but I still creeped open my weighted eyelids. "I'm coming!"

I got up and put my shoes back on, hurriedly following Anastasia out the door. She had grabbed my suitcase. I caught up to her, silently studying her movements.

"If you want to ask something, ask it," she stated with her eyes averted.

"What are we doing?"

"I told you, talking to Parker and Persephone."

"And after that?" I continued.

Anastasia cast her eyes on me, expression unreadable, and didn't answer. I bit my lip and looked away, deciding to ignore her presence until we appeared outside the twins' door. I stared at it for a moment until Anya gestured to it in impatience. I grimaced, reached out, and opened the door slowly.

Parker and Persephone waited inside and rushed toward me the moment I stepped through the doorway. I closed my eyes in momentary happiness while we hugged.

We separated, and I spoke a greeting quietly. Their voices grew over each other, pestering me with questions. I realized they had been in their room, comfortably sleeping through their grief with each other as solace while I was stuck in that freezing cell.

Punishment, I suppose. For passing out and not fighting the Assassin like they wanted me to do. I don't regret that.

I shushed them, and they grew silent. Parker focused on my arms, taking one of them in a gentle hand. His lips parted in surprise, but I drew my arm back and rubbed them together, trying to fade the pain of the rough and torn skin. The handcuffs I'd shed had left raised and marred burn scars around my wrists in even circles.

"What did they do to you?" he whispered.

I stared at his shoes for a moment, then rose my head to meet his prying blue eyes. His sharp face was creased in worry. It didn't suit him.

"It was so cold down there that…my arms, well…"

Persephone reached out a small hand to take both of my arms out of my grasp and hover them over the crackling, pale skin. I studied her face full of concern and then watched when she flicked her palm over my arm to repair the skin with her powers. She left the scars around my wrist, knowing that if I chose, I could remove them myself.

I never would.

The soft glow interweaving with and repairing my skin amazed me. I wished I could have healed it myself. But after…*that*, I didn't have enough energy to read a mind, let alone heal my aches and the cracked skin.

After she was satisfied, she withdrew and let my arms drop.

"Perse…" I started, "I had to remove their memories. Liam, he…"

Parker reached a hand to rest on her back as her face fell and twisted to one of pain. I didn't want to have to tell her this, so I looked to Anastasia for help. But she was at the open door, facing away from us.

"I let them both keep memories of what we were to them, but they don't know who we are. They never will."

I smiled faintly, but it didn't help soothe Persephone's pained creases of her forehead and Parker's face cast downward. I couldn't protect them from everything, and the evidence of their growing maturity—though it was forced—showed the torture they had endured.

If only they could've been real kids.

"I'll let you talk to Parker first," Persephone muttered as she walked out of the room. Upon being noticed by Anastasia, they both stepped outside the doorway and closed the door.

I turned back to Parker, who was now looking at me. "Hey."

"Hey…" he said softly.

I studied the lines of his face. *He looks so tired.* I had almost forgotten how hard of a time he would have with this, too. Persephone and I were different, but he was still…

I worried for him.

I reached forward and hugged him tightly while wrapping my arms around his shoulders. He buried his face in the embrace.

"It's all right, I'm right here…" I whispered.

His arms tightened around my shoulders. I sniffed softly and squeezed my eyes closed. We held each other close for just a piece of comfort, hoping happiness would somehow spawn the longer we held onto the other.

"You won't be here for long, Lavinia."

"I know, Parker. I know. And"—I took a deep breath—"I wish I could change it. I wish I could stay here with you and Persephone and Anya, but I can't."

Parker pulled apart from our hug and gawked at me. His blond eyebrows were drawn close together, and his cheekbones protruded sharply from his face, making him look…almost mad.

"Listen," I pined, "we have to deal with this. Some things in life you can't change, and we have to accept this. Okay?"

"Why are you giving up?" he forced, his eyes narrowing.

Because it's not worth it anymore. Not without him.

"The Lavinia I know wouldn't just—"

"I'm not giving up," I snapped. "And she's gone now. Life isn't the same, and neither am I."

Parker simply stared before slowly softening his features. "Okay, fine. But it doesn't mean any of us have to like it."

"I don't think we ever will."

"Anything else? Maybe a parting gift?" he joked—his greatest strength, according to him. It was dangerous, though, to constantly maintain the confidence and humor that he did. Not that I was one to talk, of course.

I rolled my eyes. "Not really, just…just a goodbye, I guess."

He grimaced. "I don't like it when you say goodbye, Lavinia. We'll see each other again, as long as we work for Ivankov."

"About that."

Parker looked at me, his clear eyes wide. "What?"

I lowered my voice. "At first chance, I'm getting out. None of this is worth it."

He lightly sighed, but then he hardened his gaze. "As long as you promise to come back for us."

"You know how much I hate to promise things I can't keep." I bit my lip and looked away.

Parker paused for a moment before taking a breath. He looked at me and tightened his grip on my arms. "Promise me, Lavinia."

"I promise," I whispered.

A thud and several grunts shocked us both from outside the door. I ran to it and flung it open while Parker sped past me. Anastasia and Persephone were slumped down against the wall, knocked out.

Parker stood over a body that he'd knocked down, clearly having acted before thinking. As my heart threatened to push its way out of my chest, I rushed to Parker and pulled him back to stare at the face covered in blood.

"Sarvesh?" I stared in horror and glanced back to Parker's shocked face.

"No…no, no, *no*…" he whispered, tears clouding his eyes.

I swallowed down the anger bubbling within me and turned Parker away from Sarvesh. I gently took his jaw in my hand to force him to look at me.

"Hey, hey, hey, Parker, *Parker*! It's okay, it's okay…"

He gave me a small shake of his head. "What happened, Nia?"

"I…I don't know. I don't know," I whispered.

Parker stepped closer to me and squeezed his eyes shut, leaning down to wrap me in a hug and to hide himself from the bodies on the ground. I embraced him tightly, ignoring the faint pain in my shoulder and arms.

A grunt drew us apart; we jumped in surprise to see Anastasia trying to get up. I rushed to her and twisted my arm around her back to prop her up against the wall.

She tried to speak, but I shushed her. "Anya, be quiet, you'll hurt yourself."

She groaned and clutched her side as a response. I glanced down and winced at the sight of her surface wound. Parker kneeled down beside me in my peripheral vision.

"Anya, what happened?" he asked softly.

She coughed and clung to my arm. "I don't know, Parker. He just came out of nowhere and suddenly, I was…"

"It's okay, Anya, we can figure this out later." I glanced at Parker.

THIS IS IT

{ *Lavinia* }

"I can't believe I did that...

"The last thing I remember is sitting down on my bed, but before that, I had just finished…" Sarvesh whispered, but he trailed off, and his calm face grew tense in panic.

"What was it?" I asked quietly from my comfortable spot on Parker's bed.

Sarvesh was quiet for a moment; he closed his eyes in frustration before he raised his eyes to look directly at me.

"There's new experiments Ivankov is developing for our team." He paused with a nervous glance to Parker. "And I was the first subject. The trials went smoothly, so I came back to my room, but it must have…"

"New?" I raised an eyebrow.

Sarvesh let out a complying sigh. "I think it's M3."

"Again?" My arms twitched, and I wasn't sure I wanted to know if it was out of fear or cold.

"It was fine until just now…It must have done something to me."

"Something like induce psychosis?"

He nodded, but his eyes turned downward and he muttered protests under his breath while Parker pressed the damp cloth closer to his face. While I didn't hear what he said, my brother clearly did, as they were mere inches from each other on the couch.

Parker put a hand up to stop him. "Sarvesh, really—"

"No, don't, Parker," he responded, his voice growing louder.

I intently watched my brother's face and tried to read it, but his face was clouded from my view. Parker withdrew from Sarvesh and let him take hold of the cloth. Parker turned to face forward and placed his head into his hands, revealing a single ring on his pinkie finger. Sarvesh remained silent until he abruptly got up and crossed the room to the window.

I glanced at Parker before clearing my throat. "Sarvesh, none of it really matters. Anya and Persephone are going to be just fine, and…" I trailed off.

Not turning around, he finished my sentence. "You and Anastasia will be leaving anyway. I know. But I'll have to tell the lab about this."

I bit my lip and stayed still. I knew nothing I said would justify leaving, let alone leaving them like this.

Long moments passed before I got up, tilting my head to the door to signal Parker. We both stepped outside, and until Parker turned the doorknob closed, I stayed quiet.

"I don't know what I can say, Parker…"

"It's okay," he whispered, refusing to look at me.

I sighed in exasperation. "No, it's…it's not—"

"Yes, it will be." He looked at me. "You've taught Persephone and I to do what we can and make the best of things, and that's what we're going to do. Both of us, and Sarvesh…"

I tried to read his expression, but he dropped his eyes quickly. I was sure he could read everything from me, and I was too tired to try to hide it.

I was hurting. With every cell in my body, whatever energy I had was stretched thin. My powers had begun to thrive again, just barely, but it still wasn't enough. Exhaustion weighed my feet to the floor like concrete.

As I waited for him to say something, anything at all, I studied his body language. His back was tense, and he hadn't shifted his feet. He slowly raised his head to glance at the wall behind me and around the corner, where Anya and Persephone still sat.

"Parker, I have to hope we'll see each other again," I said softly.

"I'll hope even if you can't." His expression became readable when he made eye contact with me. I could see the hurt and pain, and I understood it.

Unspoken words—things we wanted to do but never did—passed between us seamlessly. I reached out to put my arms around him. Since his height advantage over me was quite a few inches, he wrapped his arms around my back and pulled me closer.

I breathed slowly and deeply in this one small moment of comfort before our world would tip on its edge one final time. I pulled back and, with a fleeting smile, tore my gaze away from his tired eyes. I slowly walked away from him.

I didn't know if I really would see him again. And I didn't know if hope for him was worth the pain its disappointment would bring.

When I turned the corner, Anastasia was standing with her arm around Persephone's shoulders in assistance. Both stood upright as I approached.

"This is it, Perse."

She looked up at me with her blue eyes wide, tears brimming the edges. I swallowed down the tightness of my throat, fighting the urge to tear up, and breathed deeply instead when she reached out to hug me. I returned the embrace and, a few moments later, backed away enough so she could see my face.

"I can't wait until we see each other again…I'll remember all of this forever."

She sniffled before nodding. It was almost a reassurance to herself and not to me that everything would be okay. That she could see me again.

But I twisted my heart at her hope. I would never get mine back.

"I will too, Nia…I'll miss you."

"I'll miss you too, Perse." I exhaled heavily before I nodded and walked to Anastasia.

She picked up the handle of my suitcase and walked astride me to the elevator. We ignored each other as the doors closed behind us.

When it came to the parking garage levels, Anastasia stepped out first and led me out to her car. The only sound that passed between the vast space was the wheels and the clicking of both our shoes. She shoved the suitcase in the backseat while I got in the front. Anya climbed in the car, pulled out, and exited the garage.

I folded my legs together, comfortably reclining in the seat, and glanced at Anya before I turned the other way. I decided to ask, to just get it over with.

"How far away is it? And where?"

"About two hours, but I can't tell you what direction. If you want to know, pay attention. You'll figure it out." Her voice wasn't curt but not gentle, either. It was pained but almost undetectable.

I hummed a response and let myself fall asleep.

NEW FRIENDS, NEW GUNS

{ *Lavinia* }

A door slammed me out of a deep slumber.

With a blink, I remembered where I was: in the car—but we were stopped now. Anastasia opened the side door and pulled out my suitcase before shutting it again. She opened my door and stuck her head down where I could see her.

"Have a nice nap?" she quipped.

I grumbled a response and stumbled out of the car to stretch my legs. I shook sleep out of my foggy mind and yawned. Anastasia shut my door and slid up the handle on my suitcase, which allowed me to take it from her. I gestured for her to lead the way.

She chuckled, reasons unbeknownst to me, before walking to the exit of the parking garage. I took in the sights of the new facility while she led me through. It wasn't unlike the last one, but it was smaller.

The vast, metal walls scaled high, and the windows seemed to collectively have a mind of their own. Some spaces were fully windowed, from floor to ceiling, but a few spaces were dark. Nothing. No peek into the outside world.

Or, I wondered, *is it so no one can see in?*

The numbers on the elevator slowly rose, and from what I saw through the glass walls, the communal areas were all on the lowest floors. Anastasia told me that above those were the training compounds. The living quarters were on the highest levels because they took up the least number of floors in the building.

The elevator finally dinged, and I turned to Anastasia. "For such great headquarters, they sure have slow elevators," I mumbled.

Anya gave me a look to silence me before rolling her eyes. She led me out of the elevator toward what I presumed to be our rooms. She opened the door, and I followed her as she put the suitcase down in front of one of the beds.

I glanced around the spacious room, nodding a few times. It was bigger than the one I had just been napping in, but many features remained the same; although, here, I noted that each room had its own bathroom.

Unlike our last base, this institute had a small communal area in the center of the floor. Our entire team had rooms that connected via hallways, and those hallways ran perpendicular to the living area. Anya told me that, along with a few couches, there was a fridge and some cabinets and a counter—with a small stovetop and microwave.

It sounded like a luxury compared to our previous rooms, where we would have been caught dead with anything outside the kitchens. Maybe this wouldn't be so bad after all.

"I could get used to this…" I laughed. "Who's the other bed for?"

Anastasia gave me a small smile with a disdainful shake of her head. "You'll find out later. Come on, ditch the jeans and put on a tank top, I'll be outside."

She strode out the door and closed it, which left me to open my suitcase and follow her instruction. After I finished, I opened the door and raised my eyebrows.

Anya answered quickly. "You've got to come down and join the class, or at least see everyone and join the class after dinner. They won't like it if you get a break."

When we exited the elevator onto floor seven, I memorized the path that she led me on and where the specific training areas were. She reached a door, stopped to open it quickly, then walked in.

Her hands were crossed in front of her, and once I closed the door, I mimicked her movements to follow her to the front of the room. Anya greeted a muscular and stone-faced man, and he nodded in response before holding up a hand to stop his students. I followed both of their gazes to the room full of agents my age, many of whom I knew.

Viktoriya's face was concrete as she stared back with her shaped, bleach blonde eyebrow raised. Alek shook his wavy hair out of his eyes, and we made eye contact for a moment before my gaze continued to find an Asian girl named Hannah Fallat and a boy named James Dalmatov, both of whom were on our team back home. She gave me a small nod of acknowledgment while trying to catch her breath after the sparring, and James blinked, bored.

It's not home anymore.

The trainer spoke firmly. "Everyone, this is Agent Lavinia Markov. She was on the same team with Agent Moren, Everton, Dalmatov, and Fallat, but has arrived late due to a mission and injury recovery. Treat her with respect, or you will hear from the Assassin himself."

Though it was a bold statement to make, the group only murmured, but a few of them recoiled. I kept my face even and eyes trained on the agent.

Does he know what I'm capable of?

He turned to me and introduced himself as Agent Kesar Packan, my group's trainer. I noticed his accent was not entirely American nor Russian, but a mix of Russian and something else.

Some Ukrainian maybe?

I nodded once and made eye contact. "Agent Packan. Should I join the group immediately?"

"Yes. You'll find wraps and equipment through that door." He gestured toward the back of the room. His slick, black hair didn't move an inch when he turned.

After I acknowledged him, he addressed the rest of the group. "Switch partners and resume. Fallat, take Markov. Everton,"—he glanced at his watch before looking back to Alek with sharp, brown eyes—"dismiss everyone at quarter till."

While I walked toward the equipment room door, I heard two pairs of footsteps—one pair was following me. I glanced back to see Hannah behind me as Anya closed the training room door behind her and Packan.

So much for sticking together.

I glimpsed Hannah while changing shoes. "So, Agent Fallat, you were at the old facility, right?"

She nodded. "Feel free to call me Hannah if Packan isn't around. I don't mind. And yes, but I don't think we ever talked."

I began to wrap my hands. "Yeah, I don't think so…" I trailed off.

People you spend your whole life with can go unnoticed. Funny how that is.

I stood up straight with wrapped hands and motioned to the open door.

"After you."

Hannah thanked me and walked out, leading me to her former spot. The two of us continued small talk while we sparred, her black hair swinging with her evasive maneuvers, until Alek shouted out that we were dismissed.

Hannah glanced at me. "You should probably say hi to them."

I rolled my eyes. "Let's get it over with."

That earned a slight chuckle from her. We walked over to Alek, whose partner that round was Viktoriya.

How convenient.

"Alek, Viktoriya, you remember Lavinia?" Hannah asked.

"Of course. It's only been a few weeks," was Viktoriya's curt response, accent prominent.

Unlike the rest of us, she had spent her childhood training in Russia instead of New York. She and Anastasia had bonded the quickest when we were younger—they had both been through the Black Box program, though Viktoriya never completed it. She had moved to New York instead.

Alek's gaze shifted from me, only to return to Hannah. "I could never forget a face like hers."

I held back an insult and smirked pettily instead. "I'm going to take that as a compliment."

"I must have said it wrong," he quipped, but before I could react, he winked at me.

Oh, I wish I could—

"I'm going to show her our floor," Hannah interrupted. "We'll talk at dinner."

I took that as my cue and gladly went into the equipment room to put my shoes back on and unwrap my hands. A few moments later, Hannah walked back in.

"I'd apologize for him, but I don't care." She laughed.

I gave her the best fake smile I could summon and stood up. "That, we can agree on."

♦ ♦ ♦

"You'll remember where everything is?" she asked, turning around the hallway corner.

"Sure, and if I don't, I'll ask," I replied.

Hannah nodded before she unlocked and opened a door. "And this is your room, which you—" She stopped to look at me. "Is this your stuff?"

I chuckled. "Yeah, Anastasia showed me here earlier. Although, she didn't know who my roommate was. What were you going to say?"

"I was going to say you'll be sharing it with me." She chuckled.

"Oh!"

I started to unpack, and Hannah went to shower before dinner. The minutes brisked by, and I had just shut a drawer when I heard a knock. I walked to the door and slowly opened it. Upon seeing Anastasia, I opened it wide and let her step in.

"Who's your roommate? She should be in your training group."

"It's Hannah Fallat, the one Packan paired me with to spar."

Anya nodded, sitting on the corner of my bed. "Yeah. She's one of the few good ones left." She paused and pressed her lips together. "At least it wasn't Viktoriya…"

I laughed. "She wouldn't last a week alive!"

She chuckled in agreement. I hesitated to speak but took a deep breath and started anyway.

"Do you remember putting your hand on the Assassin's arm?"

Anastasia stared at me, taken aback. "No," she answered simply.

"So, you…you remember when you took your hand off? When he looked at you?"

"Yes. I felt cold almost. But he didn't do anything."

"I know, I felt the same thing," I muttered. "And I couldn't move. Or use my powers."

Her eyes went wide. "That's why you walked back instead of fighting him?"

"Whatever he did…" I blinked slowly, "I couldn't fight it. Not until I was able to control you. I thought that maybe it would…”

“You did that? Moved me, all by yourself, with—?”

“Yeah. But it’s not like it did anything.”

I turned back around to open the next drawer, deciding to break the tension. “What did you come in here for? I thought they would have sent you somewhere else by now.”

“I hate to give you more bad news, but…” she started.

I turned back around to face her, confused. “What do you mean, more bad news?”

Like anything could be worse than—

No. *Stop it.*

“I…I can’t tell you. Just know I won’t be around for long,” she said, her eyes flickering across my face.

I narrowed my eyes, knowing she would tell me the truth…in normal circumstances.

“What is it, Anastasia?” I insisted. “I know you’re not staying at this facility. But you’ll be in New York, at least, so—”

“I can’t tell you.” She swallowed and shook her head. Then she stood from the bed and took a step toward me.

“If anyone can, it’s you. You’ve never lied to me in your life,” I said.

At that, I swore I didn’t mistake the wince she gave while backing away. She turned around quickly, took a few steps, and opened the door before she stopped. She looked at me from over her shoulder.

“This isn’t goodbye. Just…see you soon.”

I stared at her back, dumbfounded, until she closed the door. A tear found its way out of my eye, and I angrily swatted it away, swallowing down my tumbling gut.

I solemnly walked to the door and put my hand on the doorknob, letting my forehead rest on the wood as I sighed.

“See you soon…”

55

I REGRET EVERYTHING

{ *Anastasia* }

*T*his *isn't goodbye. Just…see you soon.*

I wished I had been able to say more than that to Lavinia. And when Lavinia told me I had never lied to her in my life…The lie stung, even now.

I sat in the airplane on my way to Moscow and contemplated the things I wished I had never been forced to do:

I had my childhood and parents taken away before I was trained and pushed to the point of breaking, only for the Black Operatives to push me more. I had to defeat other girls my age to stay alive, to pass tests at all ages, and to pull a trigger at ten years old.

I had to take other girls away from their families just like I was taken from mine and watch them go through the same things I did…

Firsthand—and feel guilty about it every moment of my life. I've seen young girls be grateful for being defeated because their life was worse than dying. I was that girl.

Only, I tried to be beaten. Instead of letting it go, the Operatives knew. The

Operatives knew I wanted to die, and because of that, they made sure I won every single time. The Operatives knew that if it weren't for them, I would have failed.

I know that they made all the difference, but even after this many years, I can't decide if I'm grateful or not. I know they trained me to be the strongest spy our branch had ever known—and I know that I still hold that title.

I couldn't help wondering what would have happened to all those families whose lives I'd ruined. Would they have lived normal lives, or would someone else have uprooted them? At least with the Markovs, I could protect them.

Until now.

I knew when I made the promise to myself years ago, when Lavinia was only six, that I would watch out for her. And when I became the Markov's in-team four years later, I had jumped at the opportunity. Lavinia's disastrous beginning was my fault—the reason she was in Ivankov.

And I had failed her again, despite all the rules I'd bent and lies I'd told.

I had been trained to lie and weasel my way into wherever the Operatives or Ivankov wanted me to be—I was a spy, after all. But this lie hadn't become any easier to live for the past six years, dancing around the truth of all the pain Lavinia had endured.

Parker and Persephone would never realize, but Lavinia…I worried that it would only be one slipup before she recognized who was really at fault. It wasn't Ivankov, it wasn't her dead and tortured parents, it was me.

And it was my fault again for Jesse's death.

I chuckled to myself and, for a moment, wondered what my life would have been like had someone not stolen me. I shook my head, refusing to entertain that notion.

The hours waned quickly, and soon, I stepped out of the airport and recognized the car that would take me back to the Black Box. I handed my luggage to the chauffeur and got into the back by myself.

From what I remember, it will take less than 20 minutes.

The city was unchanged, skyscrapers flying past in my vision. The world outside the window was foreign but too familiar at the same time.

We soon reached the Black Box, or, I should say, the crumbling picture of a romanticized time period that took its form as a mansion. The Moscow base's cover was a boarding school—which was indeed what this estate looked and functioned like. It was owned by a countess whose heirs had either died in the Great War or, if they escaped with their lives, were shot in the Revolution. It was left abandoned until the rise of Ivankov in Russia, who previously only had power in smaller European countries.

It was Ivankov's success in Russia that allowed its power to spread farther into larger, more corrupt countries such as America, Canada, and Mexico. America's branch, though only in the Northeast, was quickly growing with the prosperity they saw through the Markovs.

And they won't stop until they get what they want: total control.

I almost marveled at the beauty this place still held after a hundred years but stopped when I realized the amount of pain instilled in it. The pain I had been through. After the chauffeur stopped the car in the front, I exited and waited for him to come around the back of it.

He appeared with my luggage in hand. "If you'll follow me, Agent Rabinova."

I nodded and followed him into the large entryway, where we were met with two other agents, both in suits. The chauffeur handed my luggage to one of them, who promptly turned around to walk into the old servants' staircases.

The chauffeur turned around to leave, and I focused my attention on the agent in front of me. He seemed to be around ten or fifteen years older than I was, with bright green eyes that contrasted with his black skin—height formidable and build strong. He was familiar, but I couldn't place it. He nodded gracefully to me.

"Agent Rabinova. It is good to have you back," he said with a deep voice and thick accent.

I was almost startled when suddenly it clicked. "Taras? Nurse Taras Vackorev?"

Taras smiled and extended a hand for me to shake. "In the flesh. It is Agent Vackorev now, or should I say—Headmaster?"

"Yes, Headmaster." I returned the smile and chuckled, still shaking his hand. "How long after I left did you get promoted?"

"Only four years ago, shortly after you turned twenty-two."

I replied calmly and pushed down the surprise. "You know my birthday?"

"I'm the only one that knows your birthday."

"How?"

"When you first came to us, I was the nurse to settle you in. You were still very distressed, understandably, but when I asked you questions, the only ones you could answer were your age, name, and birthday."

"Oh," I said, for lack of a more intelligent sentence.

He nodded once before gesturing to the main staircase. "Shall I show you where you'll be staying?"

"Of course."

"You'll remember where everything is, of course," he began as we ascended the stairs, "so I need not explain. Nothing has moved, with the exception of rooms. Girls now share individual rooms, as opposed to the previous arrangements. Agents' suites are on the floors above the girls."

"Why did they change it?"

"When they did, I was not in a position to ask. I have not asked since. They have not brought any new girls in for the past two years, and I am told it will stay this way until all of them graduate. The youngest girls will be moved to Canada or America, where you were working. When that happens, this base will be shut down."

"Do you happen to know why that is?"

He stopped before turning the corner of the hallway and looking me in the eye.

"You know that I am not supposed to ask questions. I do not know and I will not ask." He paused, about to turn another corner. "Nor should you."

Message received, ray of sunshine.

"So, why exactly was I assigned here? To speed up the process?"

"Yes. In addition, Operative Bateau will be retiring."

I stopped in my tracks as if I'd just hit a boulder. "She's retiring? What did she do, break her back? Have a heart attack?"

Taras slowed his pace to walk alongside me, chuckling. "No, but she will if she keeps working. You forget that she is almost ninety."

Ninety? Geez...

After a walk down the last hallway, Taras stopped in front of a plain door with lights mounted on either side at my eye level. "And you will be staying here, on the fourth floor. The second and third house the girls, the fourth houses the agents most involved with the girls on a day-to-day basis, and above are the administrators.

"You will be needed for the 7:00 ballet class, where Operative Bateau will inform you of what standards she will accept. While you will be teaching and training them, she will still be their direct supervisor. Every Monday and Friday, she will expect an updated report on each of your students. If even one of them is not up to her standards, she will sit in your class until they have reached the mark."

"Sounds like her."

"Indeed. You will find the meal and cleaning schedule along with the network information on your dressing table, although I do not recommend contacting anyone. Even to other branches, this is the most protected"—his tone lowered—"and classified."

I nodded slowly. I understood perfectly what that meant:

Don't talk to anyone. Especially not Lavinia.

Not that I really wanted to, anyway. Just thinking about her sent waves of guilt through me.

"I'll be sure to keep that in mind." I paused, looking up to meet his eyes. "Do you attend the general meals?"

"Yes, indeed. You will be seated next to me."

He handed me a key and informed me that he possessed a duplicate. I nodded in satisfaction, and he turned to leave. I unlocked my door to step inside.

Well, the inside is certainly more ornate than the outside.

It was everything I expected from a massive house like this: detailed wallpaper, paneling and wainscoting, heavy curtains, ornate frames, intricate details, and grand furniture. I walked over to the dressing table and memorized the schedules he'd mentioned.

Over the next few weeks, I trained and instructed the girls. I had the most success with the older ones, but I expected that. Many kept up with my and the Operative's standards, and those that did not…They suffered.

It was painful to watch them grow, only to be defeated, but there was nothing I could do to change it. I was stuck watching their lives unfold and knowing exactly where it would lead.

To me and the life I led. Hopeless.

The only reason a smile was brought to my face, the sun shone through the curtains in the early hours, and my lungs kept drawing air was the promise of seeing her face again: Lavinia's glowing face, happy as she had been with Jesse.

That's what kept me alive.

EPILOGUE

Why is he always smiling?

Alek stared down through the binoculars and frowned at the sight. Lavinia and Jesse—at least, that's what Alek was told his name was—were on the front lawn of the Price house, throwing leaves at each other. He had never seen Lavinia laugh so loudly.

And Agent Everton had never seen anyone smile as much as Jesse.

He heaved an irritated sigh and put down the binoculars. Then, with his knees bent, he sat back on his heels to peer at their distant figures. Thankfully, the roof of a neighboring house was flat enough for him to be here safely on his own; if Ernest or Agent Price had any clue he might fall off, they would have sent the doctor, Zhanna, with him. But Alek didn't want a stranger—a Master—spying on Lavinia.

I'm *spying on Lavinia*, he thought with a chuckle.

But it was different. He'd known her since she came to Ivankov, when she was the biggest troublemaker Ivankov had ever seen. Not much had changed, apparently.

He wondered if Ivankov knew that they'd never successfully turn her to their side when they first sent Anastasia after her and her family.

Would they have done it if they knew she would never want to be their pawn?

She certainly looked free from Ivankov as she took Jesse's arm in her hand, stopping the subsequent bombardment of leaves from landing in her face. Alek watched while Jesse's grin grew amusingly wide. The entertainment soon turned to disgust in Alek when Lavinia's and Jesse's lips met.

Everton had seen enough.

The kissing pair soon went inside, hands tightly interlocked, and Alek holstered the pistol he had previously held. The roof made his descent slightly tricky since the residents of the house did not know he was there, but it wasn't impossible.

It was apparent whom Lavinia's loyalties lay with, and it was time for the Labzinas and Agent Tom Price to know.

INFORMATION KEY

Please refer to this key throughout Ivankov's manual to understand terminology discussed in our organization and its proceedings.

Signed,

    General Alexei Gorky.

BLACK BOX — a classified training program used to create new Assassins. Famous Black Box graduates include Anastasia Rabinova and undergraduate Viktoriya Moren.

DESTINED ORDER — the Order in which a Master is destined to fulfill. This order is determined by the classification of a Master's gifts and is decided by a Master once they have received their Master mentor at the age of eighteen. Strength levels of a Master's gifts indicate the level at which they can operate within their Order.

EMPATHOR — an Order in which its possessor can locate an individual(s) based on their current emotion or state of emotional well-being. Empathors are hyper sensitive to emotional states of minds, including their own. Masters with neurological or sensitivity disorders are most commonly found to be Empathors.

HANDLERS — an agent or agent couple that are responsible for coordinating missions and day-to-day activities for their agents, usually in a group of five or six. Undergraduate agents are commonly placed with Handler couples, while standard age agents are placed with a single Handler who is responsible for their group of agents.

IN-TEAM SUPERVISOR — a higher ranking agent who lives with and is responsible for a team of undergraduate agents, including Masters on the team. This agent has the highest amount of authority over a team, with Handlers having the second ranking of authority, and Trainers with the least.

MANIPULATOR — an Order in which its possessor can manipulate different elements such as thoughts, memories, matter, etc. The more elements a Manipulator can control, the higher level at which they can operate. Manipulators of the Highest Order are least likely to find. Matter Manipulators are the most common type and their powers extend to only manipulating matter, not thoughts or memories.

MASTERS — an individual which possesses a gift to control different elements of the world around them. Origins of gifts vary by each individual and are most commonly discovered at a young age.

MASTER AGENT — Masters who are operating under Ivankov's jurisdiction and protection and have full Agent status and privileges as a Routine Agent.

MASTER MENTOR — a Master Agent who is responsible for the further training of a new Master Agent of the same Order as them.

ORDERS — the classification in which a Master's gifts fall under. This can be the correct or incorrect Order for any given Master, as it can be given by an undergraduate Master or an Unknown Master. Strength levels of a Master's gifts indicate the level at which they can operate within their Order.

ROUTINES — agents who do not possess a Master's gift(s).

RECONDITIONING CENTER — a classified program used to re-evaluate and re-condition an Agent who has rejected or not maintained Ivankov's standards. Upon completion, the Reconditioned Agent returns to their full status. If incomplete, the Agent is executed to the fullest extent of their shortcomings.

REJUVENATOR — an Order in which its possessor can give new life to other Masters by using the energy and life of other Masters. Rejuvenators can channel and control the areas of which they give life into any given Master, including focus onto their tactical skills and a decrease of functions in their frontal lobe, which effectively gives the Rejuvenator the effects of mind control. Any other Order of Master can be controlled by a Rejuvenator, though if it is known a Master is a Rejuvenator, they will be ostracized.

TRACKER — an Order in which its possessor is able to channel incoming mental information to track either a Routine or Master. Based on the information a Tracker is channeling, they are able to locate any given mind that is thinking about the information. Trackers are the second most rare Order and are always accompanied by a Master Handler who can control the inflow of information a Tracker will receive. Trackers cannot handle vast amounts of information and each location, therefore, many decrease other sensory functions like sight or hearing.

UNKNOWN MASTER — an unapproved, undocumented, or anonymous Master operating under their own jurisdiction outside of Ivankov's protection. An Unknown Rank is a Master whose Order or Rank is unknown.

AUTHOR'S NOTE

I would like to thank you, sincerely, for reading this novel. I started writing this in the winter of 2018—what a long way since then! It had been my dream to create something as complex as a novel, and I have finally accomplished that. Along the way, I have discovered a genuine love and passion for writing and I hope you have discovered or re-discovered a love for reading through this novel.

I identify a passion or love as something or someone that you care for so deeply that you lose track of time while doing or being around and could talk for hours about. Writing is that passion for me. I am filled with joy and satisfaction while creating a world for others. It all creates a space that allows you, my faithful reader, to escape from the world.

I believe that is the true purpose of writing—a successful story creates a world inside their reader's mind. It creates a world they can believe in, laugh in, cry in that causes them to forget their own troubles and the real world. A world they can remain in long after closing the book. I do not mean successful as copies sold, but rather, something well-written, meaningful, and motivated—something the author themself enjoys reading (on the rare occasion they're not hating their work).

My inspiration for this novel was not only seeing my ideas come to life, but that someone, if only one person, would gain just as much joy out of it as I did. I knew someone would need to hear my story for a reason, and if I never wrote it, their life would go on to be the same. I hope that someone knows that I wrote this for them.

Forever yours,

Larissa Gault.

ACKNOWLEDGMENTS

I'd like to thank everyone involved in the publication of this novel, and I don't have room to even attempt to fit all of your names. But as Joseph Ellis himself suggested, I'll like to give you all a quote from yours truly:

"I AM SMARTNESS." Further context would point to a worrying amount of spelling mistakes, so we won't go there. But first—

To my mother and father, who did me the great favor of creating me so I could write, pet cats, drink coffee, listen to Christmas music, and dye my hair: thank you. Thank you for supporting me and loving me through my darkest moments. I love you both dearly. Thank you to both my sisters, Sarah and Katilynn, who dealt with the strangest ramblings about plot holes and character deaths and for bringing me snacks when I didn't want to get up. You're the best.

To my oldest friends in the entire universe: Shoshanna, Rebecca, and Hailey. I'm so thankful to each of you for always being by my side, because without you, I probably wouldn't have made it off Wattpad. Or finished the first draft. You've endured me from the very grumpy beginnings, and you're still here. Props to you. I love you all mostest.

To my first author friends on Instagram—Lonnie (@lj_writess), MC (@mcpending), and Ariana (@thearia-natosado): you three are a constant inspiration. I wouldn't have dreamed of publishing my book without you all, let alone actually done it. Lonnie, I doubt I will ever find someone who loves Lavinia and Jesse as much as I do, and for that, I am extremely grateful (and return the favor for Savi). I love you more than Clint Barton, coffee, and waffles, and you better not have stayed up to 3 a.m. reading this…

MC, I want you to know that every time I see a flip flop or green eyes, I think of you. You're amazing. Everyone, go thank her for saving yet another character from death in book two (subject to change…) and creating you-know-who. And Ariana—my faithful editor—where would I be without you? This book was a bit of a mess before your magic touch. Thanks to you and Knifey for getting me through it.

For my brilliant team that helped me publish, including Ariana: you're all the best. My book baby would never have gotten into the world without your skill and teaching. Paige, every time I see my cover, it stuns me. Thank you for all the hard work. Beck, thank you for bringing this design to life and to its full potential. Lauren D. Fulter deserves a mention for always answering my frantic DMs about everything to do with formatting and IngramSpark. Much love and many lemons to you.

And to Liliane for always giving me the hard truth, to Paris for making me laugh, to McKenna Grace for all the hyper fixations and infodumps, to Liah for talks about cats and God, to Elyse for knowing far more about my deepest secrets than I do, to Joelle for faithfully attending my livestreams and giving advice, and every one of my Instagram followers that have supported me—I love you all, and I regret nothing about Chapter 50. Nothing. Sorry not sorry.

And finally, the first and the last, thank you to my Creator and Savior, Jesus Christ. I would never have gotten this far in life without your blessings on my life and the people you've placed near me to help me grow closer to you.

This book would not be what it is today without all of you, and neither would I, so I say thank you. I love you from the bottom of my heart.

About the Author

Larissa Gault published her first novel, *Breaking Free*, at eighteen. She grew up in Northeastern America surrounded by dear friends and family, who all put up with her weeks of relapsed contact in the name of being a hermit. Tigger—her beloved feline and the namesake of Sarvesh's pet—is a faithful napping partner whilst she gleans new ideas from every new interest. She hopes to attend university to pursue a career in creative writing, as there is no greater joy for her future than being left to her books and a never-ending cup of coffee. You can find Larissa on Instagram at @larissagault.author to keep up with her latest chaotic operations.